The Book of Lost Souls

Michelle Muto

First Edition 2011

For my husband, who always believed in magic.

Also by Michelle Muto

Don't Fear the Reaper

Chapter 1

"I don't know, Ivy. This borders on black magic," Shayde said. "You are so dead when your mom finds out."

For as long as Ivy could remember, Shayde had been the cautious one. The problem was, Raven's take was different. From the intense expression of interest on her face, Raven thought the whole thing was a rush. Ivy should have counted on the obvious—as usual, her two best friends had conflicting viewpoints.

Great, just freaking great.

Ivy tried to relax, to not let them sense how nervous she was. This wasn't black magic. Not really. Just sort of...well, gray. Gray wasn't so bad. Was it?

She tapped the glass in front of the Horned-Toad lizard named Spike. "Who says she'll find out?"

Shayde gave Ivy an incredulous look. "You're a witch. Your mom's a witch. We live in a small town where everyone knows practically everyone else and you think people *won't* figure it out?"

"Lighten up! It'll be *fun*," Raven said as she adjusted her fake jewel-encrusted crown. Each girl had dressed in a different costume for the annual Northwick High Halloween party—Shayde was a pirate lass who would have turned any real pirate's head, Raven as an elaborate, medieval version of the Red Queen, and Ivy in a simple renaissance-style Juliet costume.

This year, Raven's parents had agreed to host the event the week before Halloween. The location made for a very happy student body since Raven's parents also owned the ideal place for such a party—the newly renovated Forever View Funeral Home and Mortuary.

Ivy wiped her perspiring palms against her dress, trying to ignore the growing tension between her friends. She stared into the terrarium. "I guess if I'm going to do this, I'd better get busy."

Spike, who belonged to Raven's younger brother, tilted his head at them as though wondering which girl held his dinner of crickets or meal worms. If Spike had known what Ivy had in mind, he might have considered retreating behind the rocks at the far edge of his sunlamp-heated enclosure. But Spike was a lizard and therefore, blissfully ignorant.

Spike's terrarium sat on top of a bookcase next to a cherry wood study desk. A wrought-iron day bed was opposite the desk, covered with a gold and black coverlet and a single red pillow. A guy's renaissance costume in dark velvet lay on top of the coverlet.

Ivy reached inside the terrarium and scooped up Spike, who at the last minute tried to scramble to the safety of his river rock hideaway.

"You *do* know what happens when Horned-Toad lizards feel threatened, right?" Raven chided.

"Yeah, I know. But everything will be fine," Ivy said, more to reassure herself than her friends. She placed Spike on top of the costume and tried not to think about him freaking out enough that he'd actually squirt blood from his eyes. The chance of anything like that happening seemed minuscule at best. In her experience, Spike was a very calm lizard.

"He'll be the perfect Romeo," Ivy said, confident she

had also managed a decent Juliet. It hadn't come without some effort, though. The only Juliet outfit at the costume shop had been two sizes too large and a much brighter green than she liked. It took a couple spells—one to trim the dress down so she didn't look like she was wearing a tent, and a second spell to change the color to sage instead of a Christmassy green. With her auburn hair, she'd end up resembling a life-sized holiday ornament, which was definitely not the look she was going for.

On the bed, her soon-to-be Romeo took a step forward and cocked his head, first to one side, then the other, eyes scanning the coverlet for insects.

"You think we should have fed him first?" Shayde asked.

If Shayde still thought this was a bad idea, then maybe it was. Maybe she should return Spike to his tank and forget the whole idea. Then she thought about Dean Matthews, one of the coolest, most gorgeous guys at Northwick High. After tonight, maybe he wouldn't act like she was so invisible.

"Oh, this is going to be too cool!" Raven exclaimed.

Instead of encouraging her, Raven's enthusiasm gave Ivy another moment of concern. Raven enjoyed living life on the edge. Shayde might be a little too much on the common sense and caution stuff, but Raven was the exact opposite. She was a vampire and vampires were almost immortal. Which made a lot of them avid risk-takers. At least the ones Ivy had met.

Ivy took *Spectacular Spells Explained*, the spell book she'd borrowed from her mother's reading shelf, flipped it open to a bookmarked section and scanned the page. From her pocket she retrieved a folded page torn from a magazine and drew a deep breath. Altering clothing by magic had been easy, but the Changing spell wasn't something she'd done on a live creature before.

"Isn't there a guideline that says witches aren't supposed to change one living thing into another without a really good reason and Council approval?" the ever cautious Shayde asked. "Won't it seem, you know, like something your dad would've done?"

"Shut *up*, Shayde!" Raven hissed. "X-nay, on the evil wizard-a."

Ivy unfolded the paper in an attempt to ignore Shayde's all too true comment about her father—a wizard who once had been associated with a very evil spell caster before leaving town—and studied the ad. In it, a sandy-haired model leaned against a brick wall. He was bare chested and barefoot, wearing only faded jeans and a seductive gaze.

"Yum!" Raven said, earning her a frown of disapproval from Shayde. "Not like that! I just meant he's pretty hot for one of *them*."

"You mean a Regular," Shayde corrected.

"Right. My bad." Raven rolled her eyes. "Humans. Regulars. What*ever* you call them, they're not *Kindreds*. There's nothing about them that's supernatural."

"Half the town are Regulars," Shayde reminded her.

Shayde and Raven's friendly sparring was nothing new. But right now, it was a distraction Ivy didn't need. "Cool it, guys, okay?"

Shayde and Raven exchanged looks and a shrug.

"I think he's a little old for you," Shayde said. "He's definitely frat material. Your mom is gonna freak when she hears about this."

"I'll be seventeen soon."

"Next spring," Raven said, fidgeting with a lock of her black hair. "Besides, he's not that old. What? Twenty, maybe? He's *supposed* to look like he's in college." Raven smirked. "You'll definitely get everyone's attention with him."

"He also looks kinda like an older version of Dean," Shayde pointed out. "Come on, Ivy!" She folded her arms across her chest, looking more pouty than angry. "How much more obvious can you get?"

Ivy shut out her friends commentary, narrowed her eyes at Spike and extended her hand, fingers spread wide as she concentrated on her spell. Spike jumped like he'd been prodded, and then ever so slowly the Horned-Toad's shape began to grow and twist. Small wisps of smoke that smelled faintly of old grease rose into the air and Ivy wrinkled her nose.

Transformations didn't impress Shayde—she was a werewolf, after all. On the other hand, Raven took a keen interest. "Wow. This is kinda gross," she said. "I *love* it."

Ivy agreed with the gross part. She found it repulsive as the lizard started to take more human form—a grotesque combination of scales and ever-shifting rubbery skin that reminded her of the piglets in formaldehyde she had dissected in biology last spring. As she continued focusing on the spell, Ivy felt an odd, sugary-like high race through her and she concentrated even harder. Spike's form slid, almost fluidly, into the surrounding clothing, sparing the girls from further having to watch much more of the half-lizard, half-human transformation. The lizard's scaly head and reptilian claws shifted into human hands and feet. A wide mouth became the soft, sensuous lips of the model. When Ivy finally completed the spell, Spike really did look human. He lay there for a minute, blinking his dark brown eyes.

Then he scanned his costume for bugs.

"I *really* think we should have fed him first," Shayde repeated. "And what's with his hair?"

Despite the spell's success, Ivy had to agree that Spike's blond hair resembled his name. It stuck out from his head at every imaginable angle.

Raven scrunched up her face. "He looks like Billy Idol."

Ivy and Shayde looked at Raven, confused.

"A contestant on American Idol?" Shayde guessed.

"*Nooo,*" Raven said. "*Billy* Idol. He was a punk-rocker back in the eighties."

"Oh," Ivy replied. Raven would know about that era. Vampires didn't age like the rest of the Kindreds. At least *most* Kindreds. Raven and her brother had been turned into vampires when they were teens back in the early eighties and would still look and, for the most part, act like high school students when Ivy and Shayde were graduating college. It had to be weird to stay young for so long, to always *feel* pretty much the same. In some ways, it'd be great to never grow old. But, to stay a *teen* practically forever? The thought was unbearable. Ivy shivered almost imperceptibly.

"Ivy," Shayde said, concern sweeping across her face. "I think you forgot to make him *think* human. And he can't go like that. I mean, really, just look at his *hair*. He looks like a porcupine with an excess of hair gel."

Spike jerked his head around in short, quick movements—eyeing the girls, the bed, the room. The spell hadn't worked quite as Ivy planned. She took another glance at the bare-chested model in the ad. His blond hair was wavy, but at least under control. The model looked smug. Spike looked, well, *mental*.

"Hmmm. He loses something from the guy wearing the jeans to the guy in leotards, but not bad," Raven said. "Shayde's right, though. You need to make him more human. And we really do need to fix his hair. Sure you don't want to make him a brunette?"

"Whatever you're gonna do with him, you'd better hurry. The party starts at seven and it's already six-thirty," Shayde said, exasperated. "I still don't know *why* you didn't go with Nick. It would have been easier."

"Ivy doesn't want who she *could* have," Raven said. "She wants who she *can't* have."

"What? Nick Marcelli too much of a heartbreaker for you, Ivy?" Shayde taunted. "Afraid you might really like him? Or, maybe it's the bad boy reputation?"

"The rep's sort of undeserved, don't you think?" Raven

said. "Kid stuff. Setting off fire extinguishers during exams, shrinking the girls' gym uniforms—"

"Putting glamours on the freshman lockers to resemble the black pits of hell, hacking into the school computers. Should I continue?" Ivy replied.

"That was over a year ago," Raven countered. "He's grown past that."

"Nick dated Phoebe. I heard she's into black magic," Ivy said. "Really dark stuff." Besides, Mr. Marcelli had been a friend of her dad's, not that Ivy would ever mention that as a reason, even if it was partially true.

Raven groaned. "Ugh! Phoebe! That was *her* story, not his. Anyway, Nick's just...mischievous. You could do with a little adventure."

"Uh huh." Ivy motioned to Spike. "Isn't this adventurous enough?" She shook her head. "Forget I asked."

"Besides, Nick is hot," Shayde added. "Don't tell me you haven't noticed."

Ivy considered Nick. Sicilian complexion, dark, short hair. When he smiled, his coal-colored eyes had a way of smiling too. And he was tall, just over six feet.

"Ever notice," Shayde said, interrupting Ivy's visual, "Nick has a way of entering a room with all eyes on him and a way of leaving without being noticed when he wants? Nick is like smoke."

Yeah, Ivy thought. She'd noticed. Nick was trouble in more ways than one. Her father had been like Nick, full of mystery with a past full of rumors. She disliked anything or anyone who reminded her of her father. And that meant that every demon and bad-boy wizard in Northwick was on her do-not-trust list, which meant they'd never make it to her must-date list. No matter how hot they were. "Nick isn't my type."

Raven sighed. "Well, I can't say you don't set high goals, Ivy. You're not the only one who lies awake at night thinking about Dean."

Raven was right about Dean being a hot commodity. Without a doubt, Dean was red carpet, paparazzi material all the way: perfect smile, lean and muscular, thick blond hair, and eyes so blue the whites looked glacial. To top it off, he was captain of the football team and a fairly talented wizard. No black magic practitioners in his family. No mysterious rumors. No glamours on lockers.

Unfortunately, Dean wasn't going to the party alone. It took both beauty and popularity to gain Dean's attention. Ivy figured that if she showed up with an eye-catching, college-aged date, she just might stand half a chance against Dean's on-again, off-again girlfriend, Tara.

Yeah, right.

It took twenty minutes for Ivy to find a makeshift intelligence charm from the advanced section of *Spectacular Spells Explained* to make Spike act more human. She skimmed through the spell, frowning at the warning written above the incantation:

Important Note: The Intelligence spell accelerates over time. Please use caution. We suggest using a Hesitation spell, (pg. 73), and a Reducing spell, (pg. 119). Best practice is to remove this spell after a few hours. May cause headaches or nose bleeds with prolonged use. In some rare cases, severe depression and paranoia have been reported.

"Two *more* spells?" Ivy glanced at the small clock sitting on the desk. "I don't have time for two more spells."

"*Ivy,*" Shayde grumbled in cautious protest.

Ivy waved her off. "It'll be fine, Shayde. Really. It's not like Spike is going to be human more than a few hours. And this way, he'll at least *have* an IQ. He's not hanging around long enough that he'll need to be Einstein."

Shayde shook her head and went back to work on Spike's hair.

Ivy felt a little better about ignoring the warning when the Intelligence spell didn't start off so well. Spike's conversational skills weren't the best—he mostly just parroted what everyone said around him. She glanced at the clock.

"Okay, I've got time for one more incantation," she said. "Feel better?"

Shayde didn't comment.

"Well, hurry up!" Raven said. "Or we're going to be the last ones there."

Ivy flipped through the spell book and found a temporary charm to make Spike appear a bit more formal and reserved. "This should work."

While Ivy worked on the last spell, Raven and Shayde finished up with Spike's hair. They'd done a good job. He now looked just like the magazine photo. Sort of. From a distance. Maybe.

Spike had a strange look in his eyes Ivy couldn't quite figure out.

Chapter 2

The bedroom door creaked open and the girls all turned their heads at once toward the sound. "It's just me," called a male voice. "Did it work?"

Gareth stepped inside. Unlike most vampire families, Raven and Gareth shared more than the same black hair, haunting eyes, and lithe bodies. They really were brother and sister. In spite of the decades they'd both been vampires, Gareth somehow managed to appear more thoughtful, more innocent than his sister—if a vampire could ever be considered totally innocent.

At least he had looked that way until tonight. Now, Ivy thought he looked...*creepy*. He wore a black suit and white shirt. He'd slicked back his jet-black hair and his lips were painted a dull red. The Phantom of the Opera mask complemented Gareth's sharp features, making him look older than his mere fourteen years. Well, if he were still human. All said, Gareth actually looked menacing and Ivy had to remind herself that the Gray family never drank blood from the living—only the dead.

Raven swore under her breath. "You ever think of knocking, Gareth?"

"Why? It's my room."

"Freaky costume," Ivy said.

"Really?" Gareth asked, apparently pleased. Then, his eyes cut to the daybed and to Spike. He grinned broadly. "Whoa! Is that him? Dude, you are awesome." His grin faltered, ever so slightly. "You'll be able to change him back when you're done, right Ivy?"

Ivy nodded. Gareth trusted her with Spike, because he trusted her ability to master advanced spells. Otherwise, he never would have let her experiment with his prized pet.

"Sure. Simple," she assured him. At least she thought it should be pretty easy.

"Let's go before someone comes looking for us," Gareth said.

Everyone filed out of the room and moved briskly down the hall. Although Ivy worried that Spike might not communicate as well as she'd like, he walked just fine. Gareth unlocked the door separating the living quarters from the main building of Forever View. The doors always remained locked whenever guests were present or during a viewing.

Bane, Shayde's twin brother, waited for them outside viewing room one. The werewolf twins both had thick sable brown hair, eyes the color of deep liquid amber, and skin that appeared lightly tanned year round. Ivy took in Bane's costume—a black bandana tied around his head with holes cut out for the eyes, a black poncho, matching boots, and hat. His partially unbuttoned black shirt fit snug against his chest.

Raven grinned at the sight of him—a long, appreciative, and very hungry grin. "Well, hello Zorro!"

Bane's grin was just as primal. "So glad you approve, your Majesty." He removed his hat and bowed low.

Shayde playfully shoved her brother as she strode past, knocking him off balance. "Please. I'd say get a room, you two, but we're late."

Ivy guided Spike past Bane and Raven. Gareth followed her. "Don't lose sight of him," Gareth instructed.

"I won't," she replied. "Spike won't leave my side."

"Good luck, Ives." Bane caught up to them and started to ruffle her hair, but after noticing her head dress he winked instead. You're too good for him, you know."

Ivy liked to say her infatuation with Dean was Bane's fault since he was also on the football team and sometimes hung out with him. Occasionally, Bane teased her about her crush on Dean, but he never did it to be mean. They'd grown up together and Ivy thought of Bane as a big brother. And in moments like this, he could be incredibly sweet and just like a *real* big brother by thinking that Dean wasn't good enough.

Ivy beamed. "Thanks, Bane. You really think so?"

"Yeah. I do. Who'd want their sister dating a lizard?" He smiled and ducked, avoiding Ivy's good-natured swat before disappearing into the viewing room and slipping his arm around Raven.

"Jerk," Ivy called after him, and laughed in spite of herself.

Shayde whispered to Ivy as she entered the room behind her brother and Raven. "Hope it works, Ivy. You're starting to scare me as much as Raven."

Gareth hurried into the room next, leaving Ivy alone in the foyer with Spike. Maybe this *was* a bad idea. If her mom found out about the Changing spell, she'd be totally furious. Oh, well. No time like the present. It wasn't like she could go back now.

"It's show time, Spike." Ivy sighed deeply, then took Spike's arm in hers and followed her friends into viewing room one.

When the Grays remodeled the funeral home, they'd installed full-length moveable partitions to separate the viewing areas. Tonight, every partition had been pushed back making it one huge room. Music boomed from the ceiling-mounted speakers which usually played soothing music meant to calm the grieving. Gourds and carved pumpkins rested on haystacks in the nearby corner. Black and orange streamers twirled from the ceiling, an obvious contrast to the room's bland beige and soothing blue-green.

A cauldron sat on the center of the refreshment table, tendrils of fog from dry ice cascading down the sides. Sparkling purple and orange confetti littered the black paper tablecloth. Teachers and chaperones were busy serving punch and soda in black plastic cups.

Cookies, cake, and fake Jack o' Lanterns topped to the brim with chips filled another table, replacing the casket that would normally have been in viewing room two. Tonight, the only coffin in sight was a black, varnished casket to the right of the doorway. Fake spider webs stretched out from the casket's handles and plastic spiders had been woven in along the thicker strands of webbing.

Spike stared a bit too long at them.

"Come on, Spike," Ivy said, urging him on.

Shayde and Bane were standing near the refreshment table, and she made her way toward them, squeezing in between the crowd chatting at the entrance. A few of them gave Spike a once-over and Ivy smiled as she passed them. Spike was definitely drawing attention.

She expected Dean to be with his usual group and he surprised her when he emerged from the crowd alone, nearly running into her. He had dressed as Robin Hood complete with green tunic and matching tights, which she tried *not* to stare at. Ivy bet Robin Hood never looked so good. In fact, Dean could make Adonis jealous. The image of the naked Greek statue crossed her mind and she felt her face flush almost painfully. She averted her eyes to his hands, which held two sodas. Tara had to be close by.

"Sorry, MacTavish. Didn't see you." Even his voice was gorgeous—smooth and masculine. He surveyed Spike, then her. "Nice costumes. They're, um, sweet."

Ivy patted Spike's arm, and Spike smiled serenely. "Thanks," she said, unable to do anything except stare at his ice-blue eyes and his to-die-for flawless face. For a moment, she thought she'd quit breathing.

"Well, see you later," Dean said with a smile before

walking away.

He smiled at me! For a second or two, Ivy thought the room spun. She couldn't contain her own grin as she met up with Shayde and the gang who were talking to Nick and a couple of his friends. Nick had dressed in all black from his shoes and greatcoat, to the tall, rimmed hat on his head. He held a beaker filled with a bubbling, greenish concoction. Apparently, he was Dr. Jekyll. It was the perfect costume for a demon.

Nick surveyed Spike. "Hey, Ivy."

"Hi," she replied nervously. It felt awkward standing here with Spike. Nick had asked her out twice now. Last week, and once over the summer. Both times she'd said no. Sure, he was a demon, and sure, he had a reputation, much of which *was* probably overly exaggerated. So why did he make her so nervous?

Because he reeks of trouble, she thought. Definitely not trustworthy.

Raven handed Ivy and Spike their drinks and whispered, "Nick still has a thing for you. His heart rate goes up when you're around."

Ivy tried to ignore Raven's comment, including her weird ability to hear someone's heartbeat, and took a swallow of her soda. Nick followed suit and took a drink of his own, never taking his eyes off her. Ivy felt a hint of remorse. If he'd been anyone other than a demon she could see herself saying yes to his advances. He was off her list as dating material. He'd actually never really even been on it due to their fathers' friendship, but maybe he wasn't quite the bad boy she'd convinced herself he was. Maybe she could be at least a little more social to him.

Nick leaned over and whispered in her ear, "Want a sip? It's got some rum in it. I enchanted the beaker to smell like soda. No one will ever know."

Ivy looked at the fizzing liquid, which now matched something else tingly deep inside her and shook her head.

Spike had downed his drink and was busily licking the inside of the cup. Ivy snatched it from him and handed it to Raven.

Nick gave Spike a long, curious glance.

"Not a good idea on the sugary stuff," Shayde said.

Ivy couldn't have agreed more. The Coke had definitely wired Spike, and she didn't think she could pass off licking the inside of a plastic cup as a college thing. His head jerked left and right, eyes intently scanning the room. She murmured a Quieting spell, hoping no one would notice and that it would make Spike appear more normal.

Unfortunately, Nick was still watching Spike pretty closely. While demons didn't always use the same spells as witches and wizards, he'd be one of the first to figure out what she'd done. On the other hand, changing Spike to human might be dark magic for witches, but probably not for demons. Would he tell anyone?

Nick slid a suspicious glance her way.

What a stupid idea this had been.

"Don't look at me like that," she warned him.

Nick grinned. "Like what? Care to talk about it on the dance floor?" He leaned forward and whispered in her ear again. "Are you always this full of surprises? I like it."

Any retort she had stuck in her throat. She fumbled for some way to excuse herself.

"*Ivy!*" a soft, lilting voice said behind her. How Ivy *hated* that voice. "Dean told me you were here with someone older. I just *had* to come see for myself."

Things were going from bad to worse. Ivy clenched her teeth, but managed a tight smile as she turned to face Tara. She wore a stunning, wispy violet dress that swirled around her hips. Thin straps gave way to a plunging neckline that created a sickening perfect meeting of Wonderbra and cleavage. The shade of violet somehow made her hair blonder, shinier. And of course, she wore colored contacts to make her eyes slightly violet, as well. Pink lip gloss glistened on her pouty lips. Pale lavender wings made of delicate silk fluttered softly behind her.

How nice, Ivy thought. *Tinkerbell goes Playmate.*

Tara sauntered forward, parting Nick's group like a sea. Everyone stared, transfixed. Even Ivy couldn't help it. She glanced at Nick, who diverted his attention away from Tara quicker than the rest of his group, his eyes meeting Ivy's. He smiled uncomfortably and coughed. The only one not staring at Tara was Spike. This obviously irritated Tara, who could never stand to be anything other than the center of attention.

She inched closer to Spike who didn't appear to notice. "And just who is *this*, Ivy? Friend of the family? A chaperone perhaps?"

It would have been clear to a *human* male that Tara was flirting—hard. Her proximity to Spike and the way she was almost thrusting her chest at him. Ivy wanted to rip Tara's hair out. Or at the very least, deflate her breasts like helium balloons and have her go flying off as far away as possible. Like out a window.

She forced a smile. "He's my date. He's a friend of the Grays." It wasn't a lie, exactly.

"I'm Tara Prescott." She extended her hand to Spike. At first, Spike did nothing, then he took Tara's hand and shook it gently.

Ivy and Shayde exchanged glances, and Ivy knew they were thinking the same thing—the spell was accelerating. Spike was becoming more human than they had expected.

"Name! *Name!*" Raven whispered in Ivy's ear.

Until now, Ivy hadn't thought about a name and she said the first thing that came to mind. "William Idolson. Friends call him Spike."

"I bet you could fly pretty far with those." Spike glanced at Tara's chest, then pointed at her wings. "The wings. They're nice."

Oh, this is so not going well, Ivy thought with a groan.

"Cleavage. Sucks the brain cells out of guys every time," Raven whispered.

Ivy had to bite her lip to keep from laughing.

Tara smiled, feigning modesty. "I'm glad you like them."

Ivy stole a glance at Shayde who looked as though she were going to puke. Ivy ran a hand down the sleeve of Spike's costume and leaned into him, willing Spike to focus on her instead of Tara, which he did. Good. The situation was back under control. She let out a sigh of relief. Still, she couldn't help but notice that both Nick and Tara were sporting scowls.

Chapter 3

"Hey!" a voice yelled from across the room. "Who let him in here?"

Everyone's attention turned toward the commotion. An old, haggard-looking wolf ambled to the middle of the room and flopped onto the floor, a long and whitish-grey object hanging from his mouth. What was it? Ivy couldn't tell with people moving in and out of the way.

Tara flung her hair over her shoulder, exposing two embroidered dragonflies attached to her dress. Spike leaned toward Tara and Ivy took a tighter hold of his hand.

"What's that old wolf got in his mouth?" a voice inquired through the rising murmur of the crowd.

"Oh my God, it's a bone! A *human* bone!" someone else yelled.

"*Uncle Lucas?*" Shayde said quietly.

Oh, no, Ivy thought. Not Shayde and Bane's crazy geriatric werewolf uncle. Not now! And he'd obviously been to the old section of the cemetery. Again.

Someone screamed.

"There go the Regulars," Raven complained.

Shayde and Bane rushed forward, bending down as they spoke to Uncle Lucas. Shayde tried to pry the bone from his mouth, but Uncle Lucas was having none of it. He grumbled and held the bone tightly between his teeth. He growled, although it came out more like a wheeze. At least to Ivy's ears. From the look of the crowd, some people weren't so sure the growl was harmless.

"What the hell?" One of the teachers asked, his voice high and panicked. "Did he eat someone?"

Someone else chimed in. "Did he dig up someone's *grave?*"

Raven shrugged. "Yeah. He does that."

The Connor pack had done a great job of keeping Uncle Lucas's senility low-key. Until tonight. Uncle Lucas loved to dig things up in the graveyard. He'd been doing it off and on for years. And tomorrow, everyone would be talking about it.

A small group of people headed for the exit.

Spike shifted back and forth on his feet.

"What's with you?" Ivy asked, not really expecting an answer. His eyes had that weird, crazy look again. In fact, his eyes were enormous and he was staring at the embroidered dragonflies pinned below Tara's right shoulder. Tara of course, would think he was staring elsewhere. That was so like her.

Ivy whispered, "They're not real, Spike. Can't you tell the difference between real and fake?"

Spike's tongue unfurled from his mouth and he snatched at one of the dragonflies.

Apparently not.

Tara squealed in surprise and threw a hard punch, hitting Spike squarely in the chest. "Pervert!" she shouted.

Spike simply grabbed her by both arms and made another attempt at catching the dragonfly with his tongue.

People were starting to shove in their attempt to distance themselves from Uncle Lucas. Some probably thought he'd gnaw on them next. Regulars began to run for the exit. Folding chairs clattered to the floor. Spike remained oblivious, intent on the elusive dragonfly attached to Tara.

"Maybe we *should* have fed him first," Raven said almost casually.

Tara wasn't taking it as well as Raven. She continued to curse and beat on Spike. Ivy cringed as Spike took a direct punch to the head.

"Take that, you sick son-of-a-bitch!" Tara yelled.

Raven smoothed her red corset as she watched Tara and Spike. "Hmmm. You'd think with her prestigious witch and wizard bloodlines, she could manage a simple Repelling spell. Still, not a bad left hook to the jaw, wouldn't you say?"

Tara took another slug at Spike, but he caught her fist and held it. "Let go of me!" she shrieked.

With all the commotion, Ivy didn't know where to look first. Shayde was still tugging at the femur bone in her uncle's mouth. The remaining Regulars continued to scream and race around in circles. Every Kindred capable of magic was busy hurling Calming spells, Cloaking spells, Memory Spells—anything to regain control of the situation. Tables and chairs were sent flying, sending drinks and snacks everywhere.

Raven's observation that the Regulars had lost it was an understatement.

Most of the Regulars who lived in Northwick for any length of time were used to a lot of strange things. Usually, they chose to ignore it, or maybe they didn't see it, no one knew for certain. Regulars had a way of seeing only what they wanted. At least that's what many of the Kindreds thought. Even Ivy had to admit tonight's events would be hard to ignore. The thought of becoming dinner tended to freak them out.

"Stay calm!" Mr. Evans ordered. Mr. Evans, one of Northwick's science teachers, was an older wizard with thick black glasses and a balding head that he tried to make less noticeable by combing hair from one side over to the other. He'd worn a kilt as his costume, which was bad enough, but his bony knees and hairy legs were enough to make a troll blanch. And besides, how convincing could anyone be when a wolf crashes a party and decides to chew on a human leg bone while another partygoer tries to devour a student?

Okay, so Spike might not *actually* be trying to eat Tara. Although the thought was a pleasant one, Ivy realized she had to call off her date.

"*No! No!*" Ivy shouted at Spike. "*Stop it!*" She tugged at Spike's arm, trying to pry him free of Tara. But Spike seemed determined to get the dragonfly. Ivy stepped back, prepared to cast a Repelling spell of her own when she caught a flash of olive green from the corner of her eye. Dean barreled toward them, ready to tackle Spike.

In the same instant, a long, thin object spun mid-air, changed directions, and hit Dean squarely on the head.

Oh crap! The bone!

Dean started to go down, precisely as the refreshment table toppled over in his path and he met it head-on with a loud *thunk*.

"Whoa," Nick said, the only one standing near the overturned table. "Sorry about that, Peter Pan, that's *got* to hurt!" Nick didn't make any effort to help Dean from the floor, nor did he seem surprised at the bone's sudden change in direction. Nick grinned, then leaned against the back wall where he watched the mayhem as though it were a weekend tennis match.

"Robin Hood," Ivy corrected. "Not Peter Pan. And that wasn't very nice."

"Whatever," Nick replied, still watching the chaos.

Dean struggled to his feet in time to see Tara take another swing at Spike. Spike finally let go and tried to retreat, but Tara flung herself at him. "Come back here, you freakin' pervert!" she demanded.

As Tara grabbed him by the hair, Spike did the unthinkable. He'd finally had enough. Before Ivy could blink, Spike ejected blood from the corners of his eyes directly at his attacker, just like Raven had warned.

Droplets of blood sprayed Tara's hair, dress, and face.

She opened her mouth to scream and instead let out a shrill "*EEeep!*" before passing out in a rumpled heap on a bowl of tortilla chips.

Raven lifted the hem of her dress and prodded Tara with her shoe. "I think the fairy outfit was a bad choice. She makes a better Carrie look-alike."

Spike wheeled around and darted for the exit along with a few more screaming and panicked Regulars. Bane and Gareth chased after him.

Less than a dozen or so people remained in the room. Even Mr. Evans had managed to shove his way out the door with the last of the Regulars.

Raven grimaced at the sight. "I'll never fantasize about what men wear under kilts again."

"Uh, oh." Shayde motioned toward the teachers and the Grays heading their way. "We are all so dead. This is way worse than I expected." She picked at a clump of orange icing hanging from her hair. "Spike's gone, and I think your mom is the least of your worries, Ivy."

Chapter 4

Ivy thought it was a good thing they had wooden floors throughout the house or her mother would have worn a path in the living room by now. Her mother paced around the antique cherry coffee table, past the sofa and the love seat by the window, pausing only to cast another spell into the kitchen. There was an audible click as the dishwasher closed and turned on.

Ivy sat on the sofa, unsure of what to expect. Her mother seemed more worried than upset. Her lips were pressed tight, and she nibbled absently on a fingernail. Whenever her mother became worried, her eyes changed to a cloudy shade of moss green instead of the usual brilliant emerald that Ivy wished she'd inherited instead of her father's steely grey ones. She'd always loved her mother's eyes. And while Ivy hadn't been happy to share her mother's hair color as a child—a deep shade of auburn the color of a worn penny—she loved it now. It meant that at first glance, she resembled her mother more than her father with his dark wavy hair. Thankfully, her eyes and a propensity to be tall and lean were the only other physical characteristics she inherited from him. While everyone said she had his mannerisms and personality, her father was the *last* person on earth she wanted to be like.

Ivy moved her gaze from her mother and stared out the window into the flower bed. The front porch lights of their old Victorian house lit part of the garden that her mother devoted so much time to on weekends. The first frost would come soon and the flowers would lose their already fading splendor. Her mother loved flowers. Whenever she felt depressed or had a bad day working at the library, Ivy would snip a small bouquet for her. Ivy didn't think there were enough flowers left to make a decent bouquet, especially one suitable enough to brighten her mother's present mood.

"What were you *thinking*, Ivy? That was a very dark spell. You don't ever change one living thing into another! Why did you do it?"

Ivy shrugged. What could she say? It would sound desperate if she said she'd turned a lizard into a date because she wanted Dean to notice her. And she hadn't thought the spell was all *that* dark. She hadn't used Spike to do anything wrong.

"I didn't mean to hurt anyone," she said finally. "And Spike found out Tara wasn't really a dung beetle, so no harm done, right?"

"Don't make light of this!" her mother snapped. But the sparkle had returned to her green eyes, belying her serious tone. "I'm serious, Ivy. I'm really disappointed."

Ivy drew into herself, trying to appear sorry. Sorry didn't begin to cover it, especially since she'd lost Gareth's pet, but imagining Tara in a dung beetle costume was pretty funny and Ivy had to fight the grin tugging at the corners of her mouth.

The same grin played on her mother's lips, and she folded her arms, trying to appear angry. Finally, she dropped her hands to her side. It seemed that her mother was also mentally picturing Tara dressed as a dung beetle. "I'm sure he thought she was a ladybug or something, Ivy. Be nice!"

"Fine. She was a fairy, okay? A fairy princess with an apparently edible dragonfly tacked to her dress. But, she would have made a better dung beetle. Suits her personality."

"Ivy," her mother said soothingly as she took a seat next to her. "You're a beautiful young girl. You're top of your class and can perform some very advanced spells for a witch your age. Sometimes that intimidates boys. I'm sure that's why no one asked you to the party and that's okay—"

"*Mom!*" Ivy interjected. This was embarrassing. She hated it when her mother decided they were going through some pivotal mother-daughter moment. Ever since *he* left them, her mother went overboard during times like this, trying to compensate for two parents instead of one.

"When I was your age, I didn't have a boyfriend, either. It'll come, sweetheart. Maybe if you were a little more sociable. Not that I'd ever complain about your grades, however your people skills could use a little work."

Ivy avoided looking at her mother, trying not to show her growing annoyance. She didn't want to hear this. Instead, she petted her dog, a rare Kindred breed known as a Beezlepup. Some people mistook them for a fox-dog hybrid or even part coyote, but every Kindred knew that Beezlepups were pure mischief, which apparently was the perfect breed for Ivy lately. Devlin lifted his head and looked at her with his beady, slanted eyes.

"Someone did ask me, Mom. I just didn't want to go with him. Can we drop this?"

Her mother clasped her hands together and her face brightened. "Who?"

Ivy patted Devlin's side and he rolled over, eager for a belly rub. Ivy obliged. "Nick."

"Nick *Marcelli?*" her mother asked. "Ah! I understand why you didn't want to go with him."

"Huh?"

"Well, he's a *demon*, Ivy," she said in the same tone she'd used when they had their mother-daughter talk when Ivy turned twelve. "They're a little intense. You're not ready to date a demon."

Ivy frowned. She was more than ready. If she wanted to date Nick, she could. Nick clearly liked her. And she'd have no problem handling a demon. She wasn't a child, after all. She was one of the most responsible and intelligent girls in her entire class.

"Mom—"

"Now, Ivy, it's okay. You really haven't dated much, so I understand he might be a bit much for a first boyfriend."

"I said I didn't *want* to go with Nick. Not that I couldn't," Ivy nearly shouted. Raven was right, it was safer to want what she couldn't have. Besides, if she went out with Nick, how long before he grew tired of her? Look where love had gotten her mother—broken hearted. A mischievous dog was all Ivy cared to deal with. A troublesome boyfriend? No thanks.

"I'm not interested in Nick," Ivy reiterated.

"Oh?" Her mother looked puzzled. "Then why do this, Ivy?"

"Dean Matthews," Ivy replied in as small a voice as possible and still be heard. She didn't want to have to explain it further than that.

"OH!" her mother said, eyebrows raised. She leaned forward and smiled wickedly. "So...you used Spike to try and make Dean jealous? Isn't he dating the dung beetle princess?"

Ivy managed a laugh. "Yeah, Tara Prescott, the dung beetle princess."

"Well, he *is* handsome. Your fath..." She absently smoothed her skirt.

Ivy placed her hand over her mother's. *He'd* left them over nine years ago and her mother understood Ivy's reluctance to refer to him as her father. It was as though by not saying it Ivy could forget him, like he'd forgotten her. Sometimes, the memories still found a way to make the pain fresh again, especially for her mother. Mentioning him upset her. Ivy wondered what color her own eyes turned when she was worried. How hard was it for her mother to look into her daughter's grey eyes and not see *him*?

"I'm sorry Mom," Ivy said. "I guess it was a pretty stupid thing to do. Did anyone find Spike, yet?"

Her mother shook her head. "No."

Ivy swallowed. This wasn't good.

"I'd take away your car keys, but you'll need them."

Ivy hadn't expected this. She'd been sure that the first freedom she'd lose would be the keys to her used VW bug. It'd been her great aunt's car and had been well cared for. When Ivy finished tenth grade with honors, her mother surprised her with it. It was old, a '73, but it ran great and had a fairly new green paint job, compliments of a spell her mother had cast. It was good on gas, especially after her mother charmed it, making the bug sort of a Kindred hybrid running half-fuel half-magic. It had to use *some* ordinary fuel or the Regulars would be too envious. Frequent use of supernatural powers or magic upset the Regulars. To keep the peace, Kindred tried to curb PDMA —Public Display of Magical Ability.

"You'll need your car to find Spike, so you can change him back," her mother continued. "And you'll need to be able to get to the Grays, because you, Shayde, Bane, Raven, and Gareth will be cleaning up the old section of the cemetery. The Grays have been meaning to do it, but the weeds and vines have completely gotten out of control, and you know how allergic to poison oak Mrs. Gray is."

"But the weeds will die off soon. It's almost Halloween. First frost is—"

"That's not the point, Ivy."

Ivy stifled a groan and thought for a moment. How bad could it be if she'd be with her friends? And it'd be easy enough to clear out the weeds and vines with a spell or two. Besides, she didn't lose the use of her car, and it wasn't like her mother had grounded her. All things considered, she'd gotten off easily.

"Okay, when do I start?"

"Tomorrow morning at eight."

"Eight in the *morning*? On a Saturday? *Mom,*" Ivy protested. It'd be cold. Even with their Indian summer weather, Ivy figured it'd be around forty-five degrees then.

Her mother raised her hand, palm outward. "I don't want to hear it, Ivy. You should have thought about your actions to start with, young lady."

Ivy sighed.

"And *no* magic!"

"*What?* You mean we have to work at this? It'll take at *least* a month of weekends, maybe more! That's... silly."

"I mean it, Ivy. You have no idea how much trouble this has created. Spike is out there in human form, dressed as Romeo, nonetheless. What must the Regulars think? What if he makes his way down to Burlington? We've got anyone who can cast a decent spell out searching for him, and we'll have to wipe the memory of any non-resident Regular who sees anything weird. The Council has asked if you've inherited..." She wrung her hands.

Ivy knew what she'd been about to say. Her father's dark magic.

"Pure craziness," her mother went on. "Anyway, I just hope they don't have to resort to erasing memories. It makes people drool for weeks."

There were times when Regulars from out of town witnessed things they couldn't explain, or for that matter, *could* explain. When that happened, it was in the best interest of the town and those who lived here that the outsiders' memories were wiped of the event.

"But he wouldn't have escaped if Uncle Lucas hadn't made everyone panic and run for the door. Mr. Evans left, too, and he's a teacher *and* a wizard. This isn't entirely my fault!"

"You're the one who had to have a conjured-up date for the party, Ivy. If you'd just gone with your friends and not worried about competing with Tara, you wouldn't be in this mess." Her mother stood, signaling the end of the conversation. There was nothing left for Ivy to do except take her punishment.

"So, Dean Matthews? This is a special occasion! My little girl's first real crush."

"Mom, it's not my first crush."

"Orlando Bloom and Harry Potter don't count, sweetie. I know! We'll make brownies and we'll talk. What do you say?"

Ivy wanted to say that she'd just as soon get started on clearing out the cemetery. Or crawl under a rock. And, she wanted to remind her mother that she wasn't a little kid anymore. She was sixteen now, soon to be seventeen. Well, next March.

Chapter 5

Ivy was the last to arrive at Forever View. As Ivy saw it, it wasn't because she didn't do mornings well, it was just that everyone else did them better. On weekends, while she was just getting rolling around eight or nine, maybe making some breakfast, Shayde and Bane would already be finishing up an hour-long wolf run. And Raven and Gareth generally slept no more than four hours, anyway. They never needed exercise to get moving. They never needed caffeine.

On cool days like these she preferred to still be sleeping, all warm and contentedly dreaming in bed. She wished she were more like her friends. It'd make waking up a bit easier. She opened the front door to the funeral home and stepped into the parlor where everyone else had already gathered.

"Morning, sleepyhead," Bane said, his tone far too hearty and his expression much too alert.

Ivy grumbled and tried to feign consciousness. Morning people were so irritating.

Raven handed Ivy a mug. "Mocha Latte, made from the good stuff—syrup, not powder."

Gareth walked by, drinking something steamy and foul smelling from an aluminum cup. He didn't share in his sister's all-consuming love of chocolate.

"That's not coffee, is it?" Ivy asked, wrinkling her nose.

"Nope." Gareth grinned. "But I did warm it up. Want some?"

"That is so gross," Ivy said, wincing. She'd never get used to her friends drinking blood, even if she never had to see the cup's contents.

Raven caught Ivy's expression. "At least we don't have to go hunting for it. It all comes to us. Doesn't freak out the Regulars as much when they're not on the menu."

"Yeah," Gareth said. "Home delivery. While fresh tastes better, this is easier. It's fast food for vamps."

Ivy forced herself to drink her latte and not think about the Grays' habit of drinking blood from corpses. It wasn't true that vampires couldn't eat or drink anything besides blood. They occasionally ate fruit and they often drank wine. Vampires were also the only Kindreds Ivy knew to be fond of blood pudding. Ivy didn't need to worry about calories yet. She was still slender. But Raven would *never* need to worry that what she ate would add even a single inch to her waistline.

"Good job of cleaning up," Shayde said. "You'd never know anything happened last night. Not a single sign there was a party here."

Gareth took another swallow of his breakfast. "Yeah, Mom and Dad put everything back before they went to sleep."

Guilt nagged at Ivy. "Look, guys. I'm really sorry. I didn't mean for us to get into trouble like this. I never would have done it if I'd known you'd get punished, too. And the worst part is that I can't use any magic to help us out. Mom's rules."

Bane groaned, and Shayde nudged him hard. "Don't worry about it," she said. "We'll get through it. Today's going to be sunny, so it'll be a good day to be outside anyway."

Of course, for werewolves, *any* day spent outside was a good day. Snow or cold or rain didn't bother them. The only season the twins spent more time inside than out was summer. Werewolves weren't keen on too much heat.

Bane slid off the casket he'd been sitting on. "Okay, then. Let's get moving. I have football practice later. Some of the guys are picking me up after lunch."

Ivy's heart thudded. She didn't dare mention Dean's name. She wanted to smooth her hair, or at least be sure that the ponytail she'd absently swept it into this morning wasn't a total mess. If she'd known Dean might be here, she would have dressed in something other than her well-worn jeans which had an unidentifiable stain on one leg and were frayed at the hem, a faded and dirt-stained jacket, and beat-up hiking boots. And, okay, she'd also have put on a little mascara and blush. Right now, she was just happy she'd brushed her teeth. Of course, after a day pulling weeds, her appearance was likely to only get worse.

"Don't worry, Ives," Bane said. "He probably won't even notice you're wearing mismatched socks."

Ivy lifted her pant leg. She'd worn one light blue sock and one dark one. "Great," she said as she followed the others outside.

By the time they'd made it to the maintenance shed and loaded a small golf cart trailer with shears, rakes, shovels, and an entire unopened box of super-sized lawn bags, it was nine o'clock. Once they hooked the trailer to the six-seater golf cart, they piled in and set off.

Raven navigated the golf cart through the gently rising slopes winding through the cemetery. Despite the sun, the wind was still pretty chilly and Ivy felt the bite of cold across her cheeks. As they made their way past the old and noisy iron gates whose shrill squeak was enough to alert the dead they had company, Ivy wished they'd brought a thermos of hot cider or coffee with them.

Gareth hopped out of the cart and closed the gates behind them. "Raven and I spent some time here when we first moved in. She wanted to see who could find the oldest headstone."

"This section is pretty ancient," Shayde said. "Some of

our ancestors are buried here."

"You think that's why Uncle Lucas comes here? To dig up old family members?" Ivy asked.

"No, he doesn't dig up anyone we know," Bane said.

"So, what's the oldest grave up here?" Shayde wanted to know.

"Eighteen twenty-one. A guy named John Baker." Raven pointed toward a row at the far side of the cemetery. "Dad told us this section used to be called Church Cemetery, but the church burned down during the nineteen twenties. Not a lot of people come up here anymore. Mostly, it's just some of the Regular kids on a dare from their friends on Devil's night. Gareth and I think it'd be fun to let the young kids see something *real* scary, you know?"

"I think I'm in enough trouble already, thanks," Ivy said.

Raven gave her a *suit yourself* shrug. "Anyway, there's still a few Kindred who come around to visit. Usually, it's the Harrisons visiting a great-grandparent or something like that. Otherwise, it stays quiet," Raven said, stopping the cart and scanning the graveyard. "And really overgrown. You can't read names or dates on some of the headstones because they're made of sandstone. Since sandstone is so much softer than marble or granite, they just sort of crumble after so many years."

Vines crept up old headstones, sections of them barely visible over tall weeds. The cemetery had both a serene and an eerie feel to it. Death coexisting with nature. Both had been forgotten here. Both free to do as they wished. Ivy found it sad that barely anyone came to visit, or that no one was left alive to remember those buried among the old oaks and maples.

They unloaded the cart's trailer, put on thick work gloves Gareth had found back at the maintenance shed, and after grabbing rakes or sheers they set to their tasks. Who were the adults kidding? Ivy thought that the cleanup job looked more like a lifetime occupation than a weekend's work.

The girls stuck close enough to talk while they labored away. Ivy noticed that one grave in particular had been kept meticulously maintained. Weird. Not one weed could be found growing on it, and not one vine had sought out the headstone. Apparently, this grave still got an occasional visitor.

"It's strange," Raven said. "Some of these are old enough to have been my grandparents."

"Do you miss being a Regular?" Ivy asked. Raven and Gareth were the only Kindred friends of hers who had started out as Regulars.

Raven paused for a moment. "Sometimes," she finally said. "It gets better over time. Sooner or later, everyone you know dies, unless you turn them."

"Dad turned us," Gareth said, his voice sounding both full of admiration and deep sorrow.

"Why did he do that?" Ivy asked, snipping a vine. "I thought most vampires didn't want to live forever, much less do that to someone they love."

"When he was turned, he couldn't stand the thought of living without us," Raven explained. "We started to grow older and he knew that one day, we'd die. When he turned us, it didn't hurt—much. It sounds awful, I know, but he really does love us."

Ivy didn't know what to say. Sorry seemed such a weak word. Mr. Gray loved his family and he doted on them every chance he got. How much of that was sorrow for what he'd done and how much was the way he felt, Ivy didn't know. At least their father loved them enough that he never wanted to be without them. She couldn't say the same.

"It's okay," Gareth said, apparently noticing the gloomy faces of his friends. "Really. We'll never die and leave family behind, will we?"

Ivy caught the question in Shayde's worried glance. *Are you all right?* her eyes seemed to ask. Ivy wanted to tell her she was fine. She'd done okay without a father in her life. In fact, maybe because it had only been her and her mother, she'd grown up to be stronger. At least she liked to think others saw her that way. But Bane and Shayde knew it was her weakness, too. They were there when *he* left.

The Connors had become Ivy's second family—the brother and sister she never had. It had been an easy thing to do since she'd known Shayde and Bane all her life. Their mothers had been neighbors and had given birth within weeks of each other. Ivy and Shayde figured their mothers had eaten far too many pickles and ice cream when they were pregnant, since Ivy, Bane, and Shayde had all been named after plant life. Shayde had been named after Nightshade. Bane had been named after Wolfsbane.

Ivy moved to another gravesite. The soil here had been pawed at. "I think I found where Uncle Lucas was digging last night."

Bane and Shayde stopped weeding and walked over to examine the ground. "Uncle Lucas might have started to dig here, but this wasn't the grave he took the bone from."

"There!" Gareth said. "I think he got it from there." He pointed to a pile of dirt next to a crumbling tombstone. The small marker was overshadowed by a dilapidated outbuilding overgrown with vines.

The five of them strode over to get a better look.

"Did anyone ever come out here to see which grave the bone came from?" Ivy asked.

Raven shrugged. "I don't think so. At least not yet."

"Maybe they figured we'd find out soon enough," Bane said. "But this is definitely where Uncle Lucas found the bone."

The wooden casket in the grave had deteriorated. The top had caved in some time ago, allowing dirt inside. The skeleton inside was void of hair and only scraps of tattered grey clothing clung to the remains. He or she was also missing a leg bone.

"Well, on the bright side, it has been almost a month since Uncle Lucas dug up the last one," Bane said.

"He's just getting older," Ivy said, kneeling next to the grave. "We should go back and get the bone. Re-bury it with..." The headstone was so timeworn that she could barely read the name. "Henry Laughton, born eighteen-thirteen, died eighteen-sixty-six."

Ivy snipped a vine that had wrapped around the base of the headstone. "Well, Mr. Laughton, we'll have you back together and resting peacefully for eternity in no time." She took some lawn bags from the trailer and positioned them across the bones and placed a few small rocks on the corners to hold it down.

"Why'd you do that?" Gareth asked.

Ivy shrugged. "I can't just leave him there like that."

Gareth guffawed. "It's not like he's cold or anything."

Ivy stared at the bags covering the remains of Henry Laughton. "It's not that. I—"

"Ivy," Raven interrupted. "Hey, it's Spike!"

A flash of movement along the stone wall near the back of the cemetery caught their attention. It could only have been Spike. He still wore the velveteen cape and dark tights, and he was darting around the field that separated the old section of the cemetery from the Wallace farm.

Ivy smiled. With any luck, they'd be off cemetery duty in no time.

Chapter 6

They all took off in a run toward Spike, who kept darting about the field, tongue flicking into the air.

"What is he doing?" Shayde asked.

"I think he's catching bees," Gareth replied. "Mr. Wallace has a bunch of bee hives. Sells the honey at the produce stand on weekends."

"Won't he get stung?" Ivy asked, a little out of breath. Witches didn't have the speed or endurance of werewolves or vampires, and she'd started to lag behind.

"Hard to say since he's only part lizard," Gareth answered.

Spike took notice of the five of them running toward him. He stopped snatching bees from the air and fled.

"Come on, Ivy!" Shayde shouted. "Hit him with a spell!"

Ivy stopped to catch her breath. Bane and Shayde tried to herd Spike toward Gareth and Raven, but he easily outmaneuvered them, and Ivy couldn't get a focus on Spike long enough to do any good. She might hit one of her friends instead.

Just when she thought she might have a clear shot, Spike sidestepped Bane, darted left and disappeared into a ditch.

"Damn!" Bane said. "If I'd just been in wolf form, I would've snagged him!"

"Great!" Gareth said. "We lost him again. I'll never get Spike back to normal at this rate! And when I do, he won't like eating his mealworms. He'll be spoiled eating insects he's caught in the wild."

They stood at the base of the ditch where Spike had vanished into a rusty drainage pipe leading to a small retaining pond.

Bane knelt down to look inside. "I don't know. He can't go anywhere. He's trapped in there. All Ivy has to do is go in after him."

Ivy wrinkled her nose in disgust. "Are you insane? I'm not going in there!"

"She doesn't have to," Raven said. "If he can't go anywhere, why can't Ivy just aim a spell inside the pipe?"

Shayde nodded. "Good idea. Think you can do it, Ivy?"

Ivy considered the plan. "I don't know. I've never aimed a spell at something I can't see before."

"Oh, come on, Ivy! Get him back," Gareth pleaded. "Who knows when we'll come across him again?"

Ivy sighed. Spike *was* Gareth's pet. At least he used to be. And he'd trusted her. What if someone had lost Devlin? Gareth had done her a favor by letting her use Spike in the first place, which was more than she'd have done. She'd never have let anyone do anything to Devlin. She *had* to get Spike back.

"Fine," she said, drawing closer to the pipe. Her friends hunkered down next to her, all eager to see what spell she'd choose to bring Spike out.

Ivy focused into the darkness and cast a simple Retrieval spell. There was a rustling sound, followed by the echoes of heavy thuds and thumps. Ivy distinctly heard feet shuffling against the pipe.

Gareth rubbed his hand together in anticipation. "Here he comes."

The five of them flew backwards into the soggy ditch, avoiding the family of rats that flew out of the end of the pipe. The rats sailed overhead, screeching and wriggling furiously. One by one, they fell to the ground, each with a little sickening thud before scurrying off in different directions, still shrieking with indignation.

Bane swore under his breath. Ivy disentangled herself from Raven.

"Uck!" Gareth said, wiping slimy green algae from his hands onto his pants.

"Well, *that* didn't work," Ivy said. "Sorry, guys. Really, I'm so sorry." Ivy had never thought of herself as lucky or unlucky, at least not until the past twenty-four hours. Now, nothing she did worked out right.

Bane shook excess water from his shoes. "It's okay. We told you to do it. It's sorta our fault. It seemed like a good idea."

"At the time," Shayde finished.

Gareth tentatively peeked into the pipe. "Where'd he go? Should we try it again?"

"No way." Ivy took a step back. "There's no telling what else is in there."

"Maybe alligators," Gareth said. "Like the ones they say are in the sewers in New York."

Raven shot her brother an exasperated glance. "You and your reptile fetish."

"Kidding! Just kidding," Gareth said. "Although it would be cool if there *were* giant alligators in the sewers."

"It would *not* be cool. And, I agree with Ivy," Shayde said. "Let's go back. We're all wet and soggy. We can finish up tomorrow."

They headed back to the graveyard to collect their things and return to the funeral home. As they loaded the last of the tools and bags, Ivy caught a glimpse of someone in a black coat disappearing behind a tree. She waited to see who it was, but no one ever came out from the other side. Which was impossible because the tree wasn't wide enough to hide behind.

She stared for a moment longer, thinking she'd imagined seeing anyone at all. Then, something red fluttered on the ground by the tree. Had that been there even a few minutes ago? She didn't think so. They'd passed that tree on the way to Mr. Wallace's farm. But then, they *had* been in a hurry to get Spike, so maybe she just didn't see it.

Frowning, she left the others and went to investigate. She glanced back toward the noisy gate, which was still closed. They'd have heard if someone opened it. Still, she'd seen *someone*. It had been a man—well, *probably* a man. The figure was too tall and broad for a woman. But, she'd only caught a glimpse, just a second's worth of coat and pant leg before the figure vanished.

Vanished. It was like the guy just disappeared into thin air.

Ivy turned her attention to the tree. Two books sat at the base, neatly stacked on top of a dirt encrusted burlap sack. Tucked under the books, a red ribbon fluttered in the breeze, the ends crinkled as though they had once been tied.

The books and the empty sack had not been there before. She was almost positive. She knelt down next to retrieve the books, noticing the dust jacket on the top book was torn. The first cover read: *1001 Quick Recipes.* The title of the second book read: *A Botany of Spells—Magic for the Garden.*

What a weird place to be reading. And what was with the ribbon and the burlap sack? Someone had to have placed these here within the past several minutes. Had someone set the books here while they'd been chasing Spike? She scanned the cemetery. Whoever she'd seen wasn't here now.

But people didn't just vanish. There wasn't any such spell.

"Ivy," Shayde called out. "Are you coming?"

"Yeah, sure. In a minute," Ivy told them.

"What are you doing?" Raven yelled from the golf cart. "Come on!"

She inspected the second book and the ribbon underneath it. Then, she set the first book back on top, held the ends of the ribbon together, and twisted them in a makeshift loop where the creases were. There was a four inch or so gap between the top of the books and where Ivy had loosely tied the ends. A book was missing. Frowning once more, she slid the ribbon off the books and looked around, puzzled. Other than the burlap bag the books had probably come from, she didn't see anything else of interest. Ivy opened the dirt-encrusted bag and found another torn piece of cover jacket. She checked out both of the other two jackets. Although dirty and tattered, they weren't missing a corner.

Why would anyone leave cooking and gardening books in a cemetery? Suspecting that the ill-fitting jacket on the first book wasn't what the cover suggested, Ivy slipped it off. Sure enough, the book inside was titled, *The Rise of the Dark Curse.* Ivy carefully opened the book.

Black tendrils of smoke billowed from the yellowed pages. Indiscernible whispers echoed from within the book. A long wisp of smoke touched her arm and an odd and unpleasant tingling sensation traveled over her arm and began to bury itself into her skin. Ivy gasped and dropped the book.

"What is it?" Bane asked. "Ivy, are you okay?"

She hadn't noticed the others had left the golf cart and gathered around her.

"Yeah." She stood and rubbed her arm as though trying to remove a spider web. "I think so."

Raven went to open the book. "Don't touch it!" Ivy shouted, grabbing Raven and pulling her back. "There's something not right about it."

"It really is a strange place to be reading books," Shayde said.

"Especially black magic cookbook," Gareth added.

Shayde's face took on the worried appearance Ivy knew so well. "I'm afraid to ask what someone would be doing with such a book." She exchanged nervous glances with the rest of the group.

"Unless Gareth is right and we've got a cannibal zombie, maybe they're practicing black magic?" Bane asked.

Ivy nodded. "Yeah, this is pretty heavy black magic stuff. So, yeah, I think someone could be practicing up here. And there's something else. Something much worse."

"What?" Shayde asked, her brow deeply furrowed.

Ivy gave the ribbon another pensive glance, then turned to face her friends. "There's a third book, and it's missing."

Chapter 7

"There's a *third* book?" Shayde asked, accepting a cup of hot chocolate from Raven. "Is it another one on black magic?"

"I think so," Ivy sighed.

Bane scratched his head. "How do you know there's a missing book and that it's worse than that one?" He nodded toward the books Ivy had brought back from the cemetery.

Each of them stared at the books sitting on the coffee table as though they were a pile of rattlesnakes. Ivy supposed that in a way, one of them was about as dangerous. Bane had asked that she put them in the trailer instead of carrying them on her lap during their return trip from the cemetery, a request she had been happy to oblige.

"I think these were deliberately left behind," Ivy said. "I know it sounds weird, but someone buried the books in Mr. Laughton's grave."

Gareth frowned. "Someone hid them in a grave? From who?"

"Good question," Bane said. "They even went to the trouble of putting a different book jacket on one of them in the hopes of disguising it in case someone found them."

"That's lame," Raven said.

"Not if they left them there in a hurry," Shayde said, taking a seat. The color in her face drained. "Ivy, you don't think...that book couldn't possibly..."

Ivy ran a hand over the book on magical gardening.

Touching the other one gave her the creeps. "I don't know. He left without a word."

"Your *dad*?" Raven said, clearly surprised. "You think your dad buried them?"

Bane shrugged. "He was the last person to see Helen Skinner alive before her house burned down. Well, every part of it except the library."

"Helen Skinner?" Gareth asked.

"A black magic practitioner who lived here years ago," Shayde replied.

Bane nodded. "It wasn't exactly a secret that Skinner had written a couple of the darkest books ever known to our world. She made no bones about it that she had them in her house, protected by spells. After the fire, the Council searched, but no one has ever found them. Ivy's dad disappeared right when the books did. The book Ivy found today is probably one of Skinner's lost books."

Ivy stared at the books, suddenly feeling all the pain, all the embarrassment surrounding her father's disappearance come rushing back. The Council had questioned Ivy and her mother about her father's behavior, his whereabouts, and possible involvement surrounding Skinner's death.

Eventually, the questions stopped. For a while afterward, everyone watched Ivy and her mom more closely.

"Someone buried the books, then dug them up," Ivy said. "They went to a lot of trouble to hide them, which makes me think the person who buried them wasn't the one who dug them up. Question is, who left them behind the tree for us to find?"

"You're over thinking this," Bane said. "We probably just didn't see them when we went after Spike."

"Give the books to your mom," Shayde said softly. "See what she says."

Ivy considered it, and maybe she *would* ask her mother later. "I thought about that. It's just that once I give Mom the books, she'll have to give them to the Council. And then the Council will start to wonder if I've used any of the spells in it since I've already broken some rules in changing Spike. Everyone will start talking, saying that I'm turning into a dark witch and that I'm just like him."

Ivy looked away from her friends, not wanting to catch their eyes or see the sympathy in them.

Gareth ran a hand along the edge of the table, careful not to touch the books. "But, he's been gone for so long. No one has been able to find him, not even a trace. If he was using the books—"

"*Gareth!*" Raven hissed in warning.

"I'm just saying that maybe everyone's got it wrong. Maybe Ivy's dad is part of some secret Kindred organization."

"You watch too many spy movies, Gareth," Raven said, slugging her brother in the chest. "Her dad is long gone, he's rogue. There isn't some stupid secret organization. Someone *here*, in Northwick, is behind this. So just shut the hell up, okay?"

"But, who? It isn't like there's a bunch of secrets in this town," Gareth protested. "Well, aside from Uncle Lucas's bone fetish. And even then, I bet a lot of people knew about that and just never said anything. I mean, the whole town's population is barely a few thousand."

"Maybe it's a Regular," Bane said.

Shayde looked puzzled. "Why would a Regular bury spell books?"

"They might if they were afraid," Ivy said. "If they didn't trust—"

"The Moray effect," Raven cut in. "So, it *could* have been a Regular."

Gareth slid off the coffin, fidgeting with his iPod. "*Amore defect?* I don't get it."

"Pay attention! It's *Moray*, moron!" Raven rolled her eyes. "As in how lobsters hang out with Moray eels, which keep other predators away. Don't you ever listen to Mom and Dad's conversations when they think we're not listening?"

Gareth seemed more puzzled than ever.

Shayde seemed complacent enough to explain. "The Regulars think Northwick has stayed a small town and has had virtually no crime because of the high number of Kindreds living here. So, they ignore that we're Kindred, and we don't eat them or use them in place of eye of newt."

Bane clapped a hand on Gareth's shoulder. "We're the Moray and they're the lobsters. Hence, the Moray effect."

"Why does everyone else know this stuff?" Gareth asked.

"Don't you ever wonder why there are so many graves in the old section? Haven't you ever read the dates on some of them? I swear, don't you ever notice these things?" Raven asked her brother sarcastically.

Gareth simply shook his head. "Uh, *nooo*. They're dead."

"Northwick had its own version of the Civil War," Bane explained. "The Regulars hunted down Kindreds in an attempt to exterminate anyone supernatural. We fought back. Long story short, there was a treaty. We protect them, they keep us a secret."

"We're all a secret as long as they feel safe. As long as they feel safe from us. But, if one of them knew where the books were, they'd go to any lengths to keep them away from all Kindreds," Ivy said. She thought Bane did a pretty good job of summing things up. There was a lot more to it. For starters, how the townsfolk didn't care much for strangers, and somehow, the synergy between Regulars and Kindreds in Northwick kept the majority of strangers away. It was why a small New England town was the perfect place for anyone supernatural to live completely undetected from the outside world.

"Cool," Gareth said. "Is that why we don't drink from the living?" he asked Raven. "A treaty?"

Raven put her mug aside, and strode over to where Ivy sat and picked up the book on magic gardening. "You're fourteen, Gareth. Sort of. So, technically, you aren't old enough to drink from the living, even if there weren't such a treaty."

"Oh, yeah. I forgot. No underage drinking before I turn two hundred or something equally moronic," Gareth said.

Raven ignored her brother as she paged through the book. "I don't see what's so evil about gardening. Why was this book with the others?"

Ivy frowned. She'd wondered the same thing. "No idea."

Bane shrugged. "Anyone new in town? Anyone acting weird?"

"Like out of character weird?" Gareth snickered. "*Besides* Ivy? Oh, Spike? Where for art thou, Spike?"

"That's almost funny, coming from a vampire who drinks blood from cadavers," Ivy retorted. "I think you forgot to check for formaldehyde."

Gareth gave her a halfhearted glare. He started to say something, but a horn honked outside.

"Play nice, kiddies," Bane said. "Gotta go, my ride's here." He snagged his duffle bag from the parlor floor. "Sure you don't want to step outside, Ives? Dean's here."

She glowered at him, trying to appear hateful. But inside, she felt panicked. She tossed her jacket onto the table to conceal the books.

The door to the parlor opened and Dean, Tara, and a couple of the football players walked in. Tara, naturally, entered first. Some of the guys hung back, closer to the door. The funeral home probably gave the little creeps the creeps, Ivy thought.

"Hi Shayde, Raven... Ivy." Tara strutted in, wearing tight-fitting pants and a cashmere sweater.

Of course, her hair and makeup were perfect as always. It was sickening, really.

"Returning to the scene, Ivy? Looking for another

suitable date? Dig anything up?"

"Just your gravesite, Tara. Nice and shallow, just like you," Ivy retaliated.

Ivy caught the slightest glimpse of a smile from Dean.

Tara glared at her, then spun on her boot heel. "Lizard breath," she murmured.

Ivy stepped forward, ready to turn Tara into a slug, and Shayde grabbed her arm. "So not worth it, Ivy. You're in enough trouble."

"Are you guys coming?" Tara huffed at the team members. "By the way, Ivy, your socks don't match." She stormed out the door and suddenly tripped over the threshold. She stumbled for a brief second, then regained her composure.

Shayde looked at Ivy questioningly.

"What?" Ivy whispered. She hadn't done anything.

Dean glanced over his shoulder and winked as he and the others left. Ivy watched him leave, her heart pounding happily.

"*Ivy!*" Shayde accused.

"*What?*" she repeated, suddenly feeling like she'd been reeled in from fantasyland.

"Did you make her trip?" Raven asked. "Pretty slick."

Ivy shook her head. "I didn't, I swear."

"Did I miss something?" Nick Marcelli asked with a glint in his eye. Ivy never saw him come in, but figured he'd been part of the group hanging back at the door. He looked good in his black hiking boots and black jacket. Nick glanced at Ivy's mug sitting on an end table. "Mmm. Hot chocolate." He took a sip and winked at Ivy. "Delicious. Worth the trip over here for that alone."

Everyone eyed Nick suspiciously.

"Did you see Tara's ballerina act?" Ivy asked.

Nick shrugged. "Yeah, I saw her. She just left with her poser of a boyfriend. What about her and a ballerina act?"

"She lost her balance," Ivy said. "You didn't see that?"

"Hmmm. No. What happened? Someone deflate her boobs, or her ego?" He tapped his forehead. "I forgot. They're one and the same."

Shayde, Raven, and Gareth burst into laughter.

Ivy wanted to smile and the corners of her mouth broke into a grin before she tamped it down. "How long have you been here, Nick?"

"Not long."

"*Why* are you here?" Ivy pushed her mug away. She remembered the way he'd stared at her last night. He probably wanted to know why she'd thought so badly of him, turning him down only to create her own date. She couldn't blame him. Well, except for one thing—why was he talking to her at all?

"I left something here last night. Came back to get it, that's all." He wandered over to the coat rack and removed the hat he'd worn from one of the hooks. He bumped the table and Ivy's jacket as he walked past, revealing the edge of one of the books.

"I was just going," Ivy said, rushing forward to scoop up the books and her jacket.

Nick was faster. He blocked Ivy's path. She tried to reach around him, but he lifted her jacket and stared at the books. *The Rise of the Dark Curse* sat on top. Nick's jaw hung slightly ajar. He reached for it, then quickly withdrew his hand. He frowned and spun around to face her.

She could have been mistaken, but for a second, recognition flashed in Nick's eyes.

He knows about the book!

Ivy arched an eyebrow at him.

Nick mustered an uneasy smile, and Nick was *never* nervous. "Hey, did you ever find Spike or is he still terrorizing the insect population?"

Gareth sighed. "No. He's out there, lost, homeless. We should go find him. What if he eats a poisoned bug? I'm really worried."

"He's still missing, and he's still dressed like Romeo," Ivy said. "And how did you know?"

"*Everyone* knows. You're not..." he looked at the books.

"No!" Ivy snapped. This is where everything got worse. Nick would tell someone he saw her with the books. "Those aren't mine. I found them. Today."

Nick's lip twitched, turning into a smile. "I meant, you're really not a lizard lover like everyone says, are you?"

"Go to hell, Marcelli."

"I'm not that kind of demon." He nodded toward the books again. "We're cool, okay?"

Ivy glanced between him and the books. She didn't believe him. "Then what kind of demon are you? Seems you happen to be wherever things go wrong."

"*You* made Tara trip," Shayde said, grinning. "Way to go, Nick!"

Nick feigned an expression of hurt and surprise, but the dark glitter in his eyes didn't fool Ivy. "Moi?"

Shayde leaned closer to Raven and whispered in her ear. Raven laughed softly, and the girls hurried from the room, dragging an unsuspecting Gareth with them. "Hey!" he protested to no avail. Their laughter faded, and Ivy heard the click of a door closing.

"What kind of demon am I?" Nick drew his eyes away from the stack of books to meet Ivy's stare. "I'm the kind of demon who is going to help you get rid of your scaly reputation. You keep turning me down. Come on, Ivy. How about going for some pizza at Saludo's? What do you say? Think you're up to a real date?"

"What do you know about the books?" Ivy asked.

Nick picked them both up, studied them briefly and set them back down. "I don't know a thing about the gardening book. But *this* one." He tapped *The Rise of the Dark Curse*. "I know more than you, lizard lover. If you can handle it, maybe I'll tell you."

Nick's playful expression changed to something more

serious. "Now about that pizza. After a hard day working in the cemetery, a girl's gotta eat. We'll talk about your favorite subject. Books."

Ivy sighed. Maybe Nick could prove helpful yet. "Fine. Pizza's good. And yeah, I can *more* than handle it."

Nick grinned. "I bet you can. I'll pick you up at six." He gave Ivy a half-smile and motioned to the books. "You didn't by chance find another book, did you?"

Oh, yeah. He knew all right.

"No, it seems to be missing. What do you know about it?"

Nick shook his head and sighed as though this bit of information wasn't what he'd hoped to hear. "Leave the gardening book at home. Bring the other one. And whatever you do, tell the rest of the group to keep quiet. Tell *no one* else."

Ivy nodded. How much did Nick know? Did any of it have to do with her father? Her dad and Mr. Marcelli knew each other very well. They had been friends, actually. She hated that Nick was so hard to read. She hated all the mystery and rumors surrounding him. It was nearly impossible to know where she stood with people like that. People like her dad.

Asking her to bring the book on a date seemed like an odd request. Had she been wrong in her belief it had been discarded? Maybe Nick had gone to take the books himself and startled someone else. If Nick had any part in the missing book, then she needed to stay clear of him. If he knew how to use any of the spells in *The Rise of the Dark Curse* he was probably the most dangerous person she knew. But, despite her mistrust of him, she didn't really want to believe Nick would be part of something so dark. Maybe this was another case of wrong place, wrong time. Sure, maybe he startled the person in the cemetery. Or, maybe he knew about all this some other way. Just what was his part in all this? She supposed she could wait to hear what Nick had to say before turning the books over to her mother.

She watched Nick as he drove away in his black Mustang GT.

"So," Shayde said, entering the parlor. "You finally listened to me. You've got a date with Nick."

"Eavesdropping again, Shayde?" Ivy asked without turning around. Nick made a left onto the main road. The Mustang's tires chirped against the asphalt and within a few seconds, he was gone.

Shayde tried her best to appear innocent. "I*vy*, I was with Raven and Gareth. We went into the last viewing room. You can't hear anything from there."

"Right," Ivy said. "I know you."

"Okay, I might have overheard *some* things," Shayde said. "Nick could help undo the damage you caused to your reputation by dating Spike. He likes you, Ivy. You'd have to be blind not to notice."

"Uh, huh. Well, he knows about the books. You did hear that part, right?"

Shayde frowned. "Yeah, I heard. But seriously, how much could he really know? That happened a long time ago. He was just as young as the rest of us. And, honestly, I couldn't hear *everything*. Gareth kept asking too many questions about the Moray thing."

Ivy shook her head. "It was the way he looked at the books. Other than a witch or wizard studying black magic, who else would know about *The Rise of the Dark Curse* besides a demon?"

"Think he'll say anything about you having them?"

"That's what I intend to find out," Ivy said.

Chapter 8

Before they'd taken a single step into Saludo's, Ivy knew it was a bad idea. Saludo's was the local pizza hangout between Maple Avenue and Hill Street and like every Saturday night, it was pretty busy. After last night's fiasco, the place was crammed with students sharing their version of what had happened.

Saludo's decor hadn't strayed much from the forty-year-old photos that hung in black frames on the walls: brown brick front, vinyl flooring, paneled walls, Formica tables with plastic checkered tablecloths, and large picture windows across the front and side facing the corner sidewalk.

Four tables opened at once and were promptly cleared, so the wait didn't turn out to be as nearly as long as she thought. Ivy heard the occasional whispering and laughing as their waitress seated them at a booth near the front window. A few students nudged their friends. Nick hadn't been kidding about everyone knowing she'd turned Gareth's pet lizard into a date for the Halloween party. If they only knew that she was carrying one of Skinner's books, they'd all look at her differently. She'd taken care to put the mismatched dust jacket back on it and had carefully tucked it into her book bag. Ivy shifted the book bag to her other hand, carrying it low, and hopefully not in the line of everyone's sight.

Just act casual.

Ivy pulled her book bag up against her and tried not to pay attention to the sixty or so of eyes staring at her.

"Don't worry about it," Nick said, plucking a couple of laminated menus from between the napkin holder and glass shakers of seasoning and parmesan cheese. "I've got a plan."

Nick gave her his most wicked smile. Ivy thought she'd had enough of schemes and excitement over the past twenty-four hours, but the constant stares and giggles were enough to make her game to at least hearing Nick out.

"First, what do you want on your pizza?" Nick asked.

Ivy shrugged. "Pepperoni's good."

"Perfect." Nick ordered a medium pepperoni pizza with extra cheese and two drinks. The waitress finished scribbling down their order and hurried off, promising to come right back with their sodas.

"Is it in there?" Nick asked, nodding toward the book bag at her side.

"I brought both books, yeah."

"I'm only interested in the one. *The Rise of the Dark Curse.* I have no idea why the other one was with it. It means nothing." Nick studied her with those dark, mysterious eyes of his.

Ivy forced herself to stop fidgeting. Other than Nick, no one here knew she had the book. What if he stood up and said something right here, right now? "Since you know so much, then what's the deal with the *The Rise of the Dark Curse?*"

Nick gave her a long, curious look. "You don't know, do you? You mean to tell me you never knew about the books? Your dad never told you why he and my father wanted them? What they did and all?"

Ivy said nothing. Her father had left without a goodbye, much less an explanation. She only knew that Helen Skinner, a half-witch, half-demon, was undeniably the darkest Kindred ever to set foot in Northwick. She knew

Skinner had written a few books containing black magic. After the fire and her dad's disappearance, the Council had questioned both her and her mother extensively. But no one ever told her anything. Not what the books were called and not what they did. Until now, she'd been just fine with that.

"You really don't know. Interesting." Nick surveyed her a second longer, then sighed. "Okay, well, it's like you suspected. The books are pure black magic. No surprise there. If you haven't already looked, it's supposedly filled with a lot of really nasty spells and curses. Anything from causing various forms of insanity to flesh rot. There's a chapter on turning people into major-league plague-carriers, a curse that puts someone in a near death state, and I think there's another one that makes the victim have an insatiable craving for toxic substances. You know, like antifreeze and triple A batteries. Mmm. Tasty."

Ivy *had* paged through the book. She hadn't gone through the whole thing, because the book freaked her out and she kept dropping it every time one of those tendrils of smoke drifted out. She didn't know anything about curses containing flesh rot, although she had seen the one with the rats and another that Nick hadn't mentioned—a curse designed to make the intended victim pull out their teeth and fingernails. After reading that one, she'd set the book aside and took a shower to scrub her skin from the cold, tingling sensation it'd left on her. She had vowed to never open that horrible book again. Not that she didn't want to. She did. It had been hard not to go through it again before tucking it into the book bag. It had been as though the book had called to her. Beckoned her. Had it called to her father, too?

Ivy suppressed the urge to shudder. "So how do *you* know about this book? Why was it in the cemetery?"

The waitress brought them their drinks and Nick unwrapped his straw. "The book was small press. Maybe less than four hundred in print. The missing book, Skinner's second work of dark art and considered the most dangerous of all is *The Book of Lost Souls.* There's only one."

Nick paused and rubbed his chin. "As for who wants it, well, there are certain witch and demon families. My Dad, for one. Others might want it for how much they could sell it for. To some, it'd be a collector's item. But, I'd bet that every dark spell caster in existence would probably kill to get their hands on it."

Spell casters were those capable of, well, casting spells. Witches, demons, wizards, fairies. That meant half the Kindred in Northwick could use the book if they got hold of it. And then, there were the Regulars who'd want to hide them the best they could.

"My dad tried to swindle Skinner out of it about eleven or twelve years ago. But, he wasn't the only one." Nick's eyes locked on to hers as he paused, waiting for her reaction.

Ivy blinked. She remembered her parents arguing over something to do with Skinner and some books, but it had meant nothing to her then. Except that her parents were fighting and they *never* fought.

She leaned forward. So, he did know about her dad. His father clearly told him more about the books than her own father told her. Ivy was shaking inside, both scared and angry. Scared that Nick knew so much. Angry that Mr. Marcelli and Nick had known what her dad had been up to while she and her mother didn't matter enough for her dad to explain a single thing.

"What do you want, Nick?"

The corner of Nick's mouth eased into a grin that made Ivy's insides somersault unexpectedly. "You," he said without breaking eye contact.

Ivy's heart raced, then tumbled somewhere into her midsection, leaving any response she'd been planning frozen in place.

The waitress returned with their pizza and two plates. "Get anything else for you two?" she asked.

Ivy shook her head, still unable to speak or look at Nick directly. His gaze was far too intense and flirtatious for comfort.

"No, thanks, Angie," Nick said with a casual and charming smile, and Angie tucked her pad and pen into her apron and left to attend another table.

"Well, and I also want the books, of course," Nick added. "Want to know what *The Book of Lost Souls* does?"

She did.

"It's a list of some of history's most notorious dead and damned: Jack the Ripper, Lizzy Borden, Al Capone, just to name a few. The book details how to resurrect their souls from hell," Nick said, offering her a plate with a slice of hot, gooey pizza.

"Thanks," Ivy said, taking the plate. The pizza smelled good, and she hadn't eaten any lunch. She chose to ignore Nick's first answer. "So, this book you want raises the dead?"

Nick shook parmesan cheese on his slice of pizza. "It's not what you think, Ivy. There are three kinds of Kindred that want it. Anyone who practices black magic wants it. Then, there are the collectors who want it because it's one of a kind. It represents power."

"And the third?" Ivy took a bite of pizza. There couldn't be any such spell. Once you were dead, you were dead. Well, unless you were a zombie or a vampire.

"The third believe the books shouldn't fall into the hands of either. Those books need to be put away. Someplace safe and out of reach."

She swallowed. "And which type do you fit into?"

As if she didn't know.

Nick raised an eyebrow. "The third type."

"You're kidding, right?"

"What have you got against me, Ivy? You seem to think

I'm this terrible person because I've had a few scrapes. I've made some poor choices. I've had some bad timing. Guilt by association, too. In your situation, you should understand. If the word gets out about the books, about how you found them, everyone will think your father gave them to you. Especially after last night. I know that's not the case. I trust *you*."

True. They'd all imagine the worst, which was exactly what scared her the most. It's why she wasn't sure she could tell her mother about the books. Her mother would think that going straight to the Council would clear her daughter's name. But, Ivy didn't believe that for a second.

"What do you want," she repeated. Lower this time.

Nick looked up from his food. "You're no pushover, are you? I want to help you find the other book. And, to show I'm trustworthy, I'll also help you clear your reputation. It isn't good for a girl to create her own dates."

She just bet he wanted to help find the books. This had nothing to do with her *reputation*. "What will it cost me?"

"Another date. Maybe more. Trust me. Like I said, I have a plan." His eyes met hers again, and she swore she could see a smile behind them.

Ivy laughed. Nick was nothing if not opportunistic. "You never date anyone more than twice."

"What? You think I can erase the damage Spike caused in one date?" He nodded slowly. "So, you *do* think a lot of me."

Ivy narrowed her eyes. If he thought he could sway her, win her over with that come-hither charm of his, then, well, Nick Marcelli had another thing coming. She wouldn't be swayed. Not by that smile. Not by those smoldering eyes or his dark hair or—"

"*Nick!*" a voice called out. "Oh, hello, Ivy." The voice belonged to no other than Phoebe. Phoebe's gaze fell on Ivy's book bag and without another word, she slid into the booth against Nick.

"You're so bookish, Ivy. Helping Nick with one of his classes?"

"We weren't studying," Ivy said firmly.

She had no idea why she felt the need to be so defensive. Her tone caught Nick's attention, and he raised an eyebrow in question. It didn't escape her that he hadn't moved over to offer Phoebe more room. Was he trying to see what her reaction would be? From the subtle disapproving look he'd given Phoebe, Ivy decided Nick wasn't thrilled about the intrusion, either.

And what did she care, anyway?

"Actually," Nick said. "We're on a date."

Phoebe looked at Ivy. "Really? Weren't you dating a lizard?"

"Ivy and I had a little spat, that's all," Nick lied.

Ivy and Phoebe both stared at him in disbelief. What was he doing? What a ridiculous story! *This* was his great plan?

"But we patched things up," he said quickly.

"Oh," Phoebe said, sounding disappointed. Yet, she didn't miss a beat. "So how *is* Spike, Ivy?"

"Still missing," Ivy grumbled.

"Well, better luck with your next creation." Phoebe turned and smiled devilishly at Nick. "Made up dates are so much easier to handle than demons like Nick here." She patted Nick's leg.

Ivy took a deep breath. "Hate to be rude Phoebe, but our food is getting cold."

Phoebe slid out of the booth. "When you get smart, call me, okay, Nick?"

Ivy glared after Phoebe. She pointed a finger at her and cast a spell that made the back of Phoebe's hair frizz. Nothing permanent, it'd last a half-hour, tops. It made her stop and consider why she'd done it, but she couldn't come up with a reason except that Phoebe had pissed her off—just like Tara had yesterday. Still, she should be careful.

Throwing hexes around after last night, even small ones, would only bring unwanted attention. And, it'd be worse if word of the book ever got out.

She took a deep breath. It was okay, she was just on edge. That's all. Perfectly understandable. She caught Nick snickering and leaned toward him, "Please don't tell me that was your plan to rescue my reputation as a lizard lover."

Nick looked at her sheepishly. "Well, yeah. It sorta was."

Ivy leaned back and took a sip of her soda. That was the best Nick Marcelli, Master of Mystery and Chaos, could do?

"So, are you jealous?" Nick asked.

"What?" Ivy said, nearly choking.

"Are you jealous? Even a little? I mean, some of the guys think Phoebe is pretty hot. At least before you made her look like a Chia Pet. Nice. I like a girl who isn't afraid of a little mischief."

All laughter vanished. *Was* she jealous? No, she couldn't be. She liked Dean, and Nick was nothing like Dean. Dean was predictable, outgoing, and far from mysterious. And Phoebe? Well, Phoebe was just being bitchy and had irked her at a bad time. "No," she said. "Not at all."

Nick smiled and leaned forward. He gently grasped one of her hands. When their eyes locked, Ivy didn't pull away. Why didn't she pull away? Why couldn't she *look* away?

"Oh, come on Ivy. We both know you only *think* you want Dean. Now, I may not be anything like him, but I'm not like anyone else you'll ever meet, either."

Two women raced past them outside the window. One screamed for help. But what the other cried out caught her attention the most.

"Right here in Northwick. In daylight! He's been murdered!"

Chapter 9

Ivy and Nick dashed out the door along with everyone else. Really? A murder in Northwick? Ivy couldn't believe it.

A crowd had gathered around two older, heavyset women who were screaming and crying hysterically. The younger of the two women, Vivian, was Mr. Nash's wife. She was a large, beefy woman with a double chin and small, watery eyes. The Nashes were long-time Northwick residents and while neither of them could be considered very nice, Mr. Nash was downright hateful. Even his looks weren't nice. If Ivy didn't know better, Mr. Nash resembled an ogre who'd caught a whiff of something nasty. But, despite his appearance, Mr. Nash was a Regular and the only powers he had were of the bullying kind.

Ivy recognized the other sobbing woman as Vivian's sister, Gloria Albert. Both women wore a heavy coating of makeup, including purple eyeshadow the color of a nasty bruise. They were the town gossips, and on more than one occasion they'd talked about Ivy's father and how they thought his daughter would turn out just like him. It wasn't a nice thought, but Ivy couldn't stop thinking that Gloria Albert resembled a rather ugly man in drag. The woman's complexion was unnaturally pink, and she sported jowls like a mastiff.

"He's dead!" Vivian continued to wail. "Please, someone... he's back there. He... he... these *awful* people came out of nowhere!" She pointed to the rear parking lot.

"The man, this *lunatic*, he charged my husband. And, this *horrible* woman, stopped us from helping Robert. She had a knife. Oh! My poor, brave Robert." Then, she collapsed onto the crowd. Bystanders groaned as they fought to keep Vivian upright. Someone, Ivy couldn't tell who, was trying to comfort the distraught woman as they led her toward Saludo's.

Ivy started to follow them back inside.

Nick held her arm. "Wait."

"Some freak in a costume killed my brother-in-law," shrieked Gloria as she followed her sister's entourage. Another bystander patted her shoulders consolingly.

But who'd do such an awful thing? Mr. Nash might not have had many friends—okay, *any* friends but Ivy couldn't believe that someone living in Northwick would resort to killing him.

"It's starting. This way," Nick said, pulling Ivy in the direction of the parking lot. A few others were headed that way, too. Maybe they thought Mr. Nash was still alive. Maybe they just wanted to see the body.

Ivy hurried after Nick as he sprinted down the sidewalk and disappeared around the corner of the building. Ivy rounded the same corner a few seconds later. No one seemed to notice or mind as she and Nick pushed their way through the crowd. They were all in shock. When they reached the front, Ivy understood their reaction. She froze, too stunned, too horrified to take another step. Mr. Nash's attacker had impaled him against the iron fence dividing the alley from a storage warehouse. Mr. Nash hung limply, his blood trickling down the wrought iron into a glistening pool at the fence's base.

Mr. Nash wasn't a small person. Whoever did this was either incredibly strong or wasn't a Regular. Maybe both.

Three or four people gathered around the body. Someone wretched and vomited, and although Ivy stood too far away for the smell to reach her, she covered her nose and mouth fighting off her own gag reflex. A bystander was on his cell phone, calling the police. How different Mr. Nash looked from the people Raven's mother dressed and made up to appear peaceful and serene. Ivy had never seen a dead body outside of Forever View. This looked anything but peaceful.

"Come on," Nick said, returning to her side. He slipped an arm around her and gently escorted her back to Saludo's.

"Who'd do such a thing?" Ivy asked, not bothering to care that Nick had wrapped his arms around her as he guided her back around the building. She was cold, and the warmth and comfort of Nick's arms felt good.

"It's the book," he said in a weak voice. "We've got our answer. Someone's using the book, and it's not a Regular."

They walked back to the crowd, some still gathered outside the restaurant.

"Nick, the books!" Ivy said, suddenly aware she'd run outside and forgotten her book bag. "We've got to get back inside!"

Nick took her hand, and he pulled her along through the crowd. When they reached the door, his Uncle stood, blocking the entrance. Inside, Vivian and her sister were seated in a booth. Three police officers and a waitress stood near them.

"Ivy forgot her book bag," Nick explained. "I just need to get it for her."

No way was she allowing Nick to get the books. "I can—"

"*I'll* get it," his uncle said. "Stay here and don't let anyone in." He turned and headed toward the table she and Nick had been sitting at.

Ivy gave Nick an uncertain glance. Nick on the other hand, remained ca20lm.

"*Nick!*" Ivy whispered in protest.

"Shh!" he whispered back. "Listen."

Gloria was giving a full description to the police. It was

somewhat hard to hear everything over Vivian's wails, but it was still enough.

"Tall, mustache. Black cape or some sort of cloak. Boots, weird little hat with a band of beads and something like a star on the front," Gloria said.

Vivian let out another loud sob.

"What? How should I know?" Gloria went on. "It's nearly Halloween. It was some freak in a costume. And that woman he was with! *Gaudy* attire if you ask me." She snapped her fingers as though trying to jog her memory. "Some Shakespearian dress. Looked like someone shot the drapes, if you know what I mean. Dark hair. He called her Elizabeth. She called him Vlad. Their accents were fake—horrible renditions of something Hungarian or maybe Romanian. Once, I heard them call each other Count and Countess. Surely, some concocted hoodlum names."

"Barbarians!" Vivian wailed, then blew her nose loudly into a napkin. "They were barbarians!"

Nick and Ivy exchanged glances, neither of them daring to say a word. Nick's uncle returned with the book bag and Ivy hurriedly took it.

"Thanks," she said, holding it tightly against her side. For a moment, Ivy thought she heard someone call her name. She glanced behind her, then dismissed it.

"You okay?" Nick asked.

"Huh?" Then she nodded. "Yeah. Just a little freaked out."

"Pizza's on me," Uncle Joe said. "Take Ivy home. She must be pretty shaken." He shooed them outside, then locked the door behind them.

When they returned to the parking lot, the police were busy ushering onlookers away. Ivy counted four squad cars. Yellow tape sectioned off the parking lot.

"We've got to find out who's doing this," Nick said. "I have no idea who the book brought back, but it's not good. Of course, no one in that book could ever be good."

Ivy stopped and Nick turned to her.

"What?" he asked.

"I know who's been brought back," Ivy said. It was hard to rid herself of the image of Mr. Nash hanging from the wrought iron fence, a spike protruding from his back. She thought of how terrible his death must have been and how dangerous and ruthless his killer was. "History, last year. Fifteenth century. Vlad the Impaler. I'm just not sure who the woman is. Not yet. This has gone too far! We've got to tell someone who's doing this!"

Nick grabbed her arms, snapping her to full attention. "Tell them what? That someone used *The Book of Lost Souls* to bring back Vlad the Impaler? Who's holding the *other* book, Ivy? They'll find it. The Council will think you've done this."

"But—"

"We say *nothing*," Nick replied firmly.

Chapter 10

The coroner pulled alongside one of the squad cars in a black hearse. It looked nearly identical to the one at Forever View and Ivy wondered if Raven and Gareth would enjoy drinking Mr. Nash's blood—what was left, anyway. The thought made her stomach queasy. On more than one occasion Raven had said she'd like to drain him dry if she could. Of course, Raven hadn't really meant it. Lots of people had said things about Mr. Nash. But no one had ever harmed a hair on his head.

A group of about twenty or so still loitered in the parking lot, including Dean and Tara.

"I can't believe someone in Northwick would bring back Vlad the Impaler," she said to Nick in a low voice as she scanned the rest of the crowd. "He was horrible! A cold-hearted mass murderer. This whole bringing back the dead thing—it's not right. It's not *normal*."

"There's no part about this that's normal," Nick retorted. "Worse, whoever is doing this is going to keep using *The Book of Lost Souls*."

Not one of the stunned faces in the group looked like someone who'd do such a thing. She'd grown up in Northwick. She'd known most of these people all her life. "Maybe they will stop. Maybe they only wanted Mr. Nash."

Maybe all *of this will stop.*

Nick shook his head. "I doubt that. We haven't seen the last of this yet. All this is going to draw a lot of attention to

Northwick. We'll be lucky if this doesn't bring in outsiders."

"I was just thinking the same thing," Ivy said. Outsider attention wasn't a good thing for Kindreds. Too much PDMA made the Regulars nervous. When the Council found out who was behind this, she bet there would be a *whole lot* of memory wiping going on.

"Outsiders will definitely mean too many questions," Nick said.

She couldn't stop thinking how brutal the attack had been. Had the Nashes been on their way into the pizzeria? She shuddered. Whoever it was, they wanted Mr. Nash and they knew where to find the books. "This isn't the work of a visiting Kindred, Nick. Someone was searching for that book. It's someone we know. Maybe even someone we trust."

She drew her arms more tightly against herself, trying to escape the cold seeping into her bones.

Nick gently pulled her into his arms. "We'll find who did this, Ivy. We will."

Ivy let herself lean into him. Right now, she could use a little comforting.

Nick stroked her hair, and Ivy felt the weight of someone staring at her. She raised her head from Nick's shoulder and her eyes met Dean's. His brow was furrowed in disapproval and his jaw was tightly clenched.

One of Dean's friends pulled him away, Tara in tow. Tara seemed too busy talking to notice Dean looking over his shoulder with a pained expression Ivy knew all too well. How many times had her heart ached at the sight of Dean holding hands with Tara, at the sight of them kissing in the halls between classes? Part of her wanted to push Nick away. Another part of her wanted to keep him close. It felt —nice. She wondered if it was because of the cold night air, the horror of what had happened, or if she just liked the idea of finally making Dean notice. Another thought crept into her mind and she tried not to dwell on it. Maybe it felt nice because *Nick* felt nice.

Ivy stared after Dean for a moment longer.

"You might want to check to see if the books are still there," Nick said. "But not here. In the car. Come on, I'll drive you home."

Although he'd whispered in her ear, Ivy jumped. Dean had stayed on her mind, and checking to see if the books were still safe hadn't occurred to her. Not to mention the sound of Nick's voice so close, so soft, so warm against her ear had lulled her into a false sense of calm.

Her hands flew to the book bag, feeling the density, the weight of the books inside. She'd check again, once they got into the car. A quick peek. The thought of actually touching *The Rise of the Dark Curse* seemed revolting at best. Still, it felt like the books were there.

"Yeah, they're still here," she answered, relieved.

Nick scanned the crowd a final time, and Ivy did the same. *Had* the Kindred behind Mr. Nash's murder been here with them? Had they passed them on their way into Saludo's? Were they sitting, waiting in a car in the parking lot?

Mr. Evans pushed his way through the crowd toward the street. He looked every bit as freaked out as everyone else. Maybe more. His face was ashen and he wiped sweat from his balding forehead. Someone bumped into him and Mr. Evans shoved the bystander back, completely unlike his normally demure personality. Then he walked away, mumbling under his breath.

The vision of Mr. Evans wearing a kilt at last night's party was still scorched onto her brain despite the fact he now wore more normal clothing. That was, if too-short, navy slacks with cuffs and black socks were normal. His thick, black-rimmed glasses made his face resemble a frightened owl's.

They followed a few other people headed toward the parking lot, neither of them saying much. Nick held the

Mustang's car door open, and Ivy tossed the book bag into the back before sliding into the passenger seat. Nick's car was much nicer and newer than her VW Bug. It was a great match for Nick—black, with charcoal grey interior and a decked-out stereo.

"I had fun tonight," Nick said, "Well, except for the whole impaling thing of course. Hard to believe, isn't it? A murder, here in Northwick. The Regulars shouldn't be the only ones freaking out about this one. Whoever has that book is a threat to the whole town."

He rubbed his eyes with his thumb and index finger. "I'm rambling. What I mean is, I enjoyed being with you."

Ivy thought about their embrace, the way Nick made her laugh, and how easy it was to be with him. Would it hurt to let him help her? Would it hurt to believe in him just a little, as if he were a friend? "It was...nice. The rest of the evening, I mean. And thanks for trying to save my reputation as a lizard lover, although I'm not so sure that worked out so well."

But hadn't it? Dean wasn't the only one to have seen her with Nick tonight. He wasn't the only one there as Nick held her close. Surely the word would be all over school come Monday.

"So, when's our next date?" Nick asked on their way back to her house. "It wasn't a proper first date with a murder and all."

He looked at her with hopeful eyes. What could she say? Murders on first dates had to be a really bad sign. Part of her wanted to say *yes*. But another part felt uncomfortable. Dean obviously knew she existed now. In fact, she thought she registered a little jealously when Nick hugged her.

"You're not part of his circle, Ivy. No matter how pretty he thinks you are, no matter how smart, he's still dating the most popular girl in school."

Ivy felt herself flush. It felt awkward discussing Dean. "I wasn't thinking about him," she lied.

"You know what happens to liars, right?" Nick said. "The car interior isn't fire-proof. Come on, Ivy. He might be dating the most popular girl in school, but in my eyes, she's nothing compared to you. What can I say? Demons are suckers for fiery redheads. Give me a chance." He brushed her hair from her cheek.

Her face felt like it was sunburned, yet she couldn't help but smile. Fortunately, she was saved from answering when Nick pulled into her driveway. The front porch and the living room lights were on and at the sound of Nick's Mustang, the shadowy figure of her mother appeared in the doorway. In a small town, news traveled fast. Her mother would already know about Mr. Nash.

"Besides, we're a team on this, right? Let me help you find the other book. And, it wouldn't hurt with the whole Spike thing," Nick said with a coy smile and a shrug.

Nick too much of a heartbreaker for you? Shayde's words echoed in Ivy's head. The last thing Ivy needed was to pine away for someone who didn't have the reputation for sticking around past a few dates. She didn't need someone like her father. She didn't need someone to say the right things to her and not mean them. Her father had done that. He might have told Ivy and her mom that he loved them, but they were just words to him. Everything had been a lie.

No way would she allow someone to do that ever again.

She wanted someone normal. Someone safe and predictable. Someone who went with the flow and didn't make waves. That person, despite his other faults—namely his attraction to Tara—was Dean.

"You've got your own reputation, Nick. You date lots of girls. That's not my type either." The last thing she was going to do was tell him that he made her tingly and nervous. That'd only stroke his ego. Worse, she hated not being able to read him as easily as she did Dean. Besides, she was in enough trouble as it was. She didn't need another complication, another reason for the Council or anyone else to think she was like her father. Nick had said it best—guilt by association.

"Well, there you go doubting yourself again," Nick said, grinning. "Or, I should say, doubting the effect you have on me."

She shot him a sarcastic grin. Oh yeah, Nick was smooth. Hard to tell when he was joking or if he could even be serious for a minute. Well, he could practice his lines on someone more gullible. She opened the door and he placed a hand gently on her arm. She turned toward him and for a moment couldn't do anything except stare into his dark, velvety eyes. "Um, thanks for the pizza," she said finally and got out of the car. She leaned in to take the book bag.

"You could leave them with me," he said, placing a firm hand on top of the book bag. "I think you've probably worried your mom enough lately. She'd only ask more questions."

"No, I found them. They're my responsibility." She snatched the bag and closed the door, then hurried around the car.

"Ivy," Nick called to her. He leaned out the window. She turned and went back to him. If she hadn't already had a crush on Dean...

If she hadn't had a crush on Dean? What the hell was she thinking?

No matter how she tried, she couldn't get the thought of what it'd be like to kiss Nick Marcelli out of her head. It was a dangerous thought. Ivy bent forward.

"Look, Ivy. I may not be who you end up with. I'm not even who you *think* you want," Nick said in a low whisper and she drew nearer to hear him better. He lightly stroked her face and an unexpected warm thrill passed through her.

"But Ives," he said softly, "We both know that right now, I'm just what you need."

Chapter 11

Her mom swept her into her arms the instant Ivy walked through the front door. "Nick's uncle called to tell me you were on your way home. Thank goodness you're okay," she said, squeezing Ivy tightly.

"I'm fine Mom," Ivy replied, trying to break free. "It was just a date."

She hoped her mother would find some humor in this. Instead, her mother continued to cling to her. She let herself be held for another minute or two, then tried again. "Mom, I'm still wearing my jacket and it's really hot. Can you let go now?"

Her mother nodded and let go, sighing heavily. "I just worry about you, Ivy. I don't know what I would have done if something had happened to you."

Her mother hadn't always been so fragile. She'd once been confident, strong-willed, and fun loving. A twinge of anger coupled with hurt rippled through Ivy's chest. This was *his* fault.

"We were at Saludo's. We'd been there for nearly an hour before we heard the screaming and saw Mrs. Nash and her sister."

"The Nashes were going to eat at Saludo's?" her mother said, perplexed. It was more of a statement than a question.

Like her mother, Ivy had been surprised that Mr. and Mrs. Nash dared to eat at an establishment owned by a Kindred. Then again, considering everything, she wasn't.

Mr. Nash probably had other motives. With the Nashes it was hard to tell. It could have simply been that, given Vivian's love of food, she just wanted a slice of pizza *before* going elsewhere for dinner.

"He wasn't there on... *business?*" her mother asked, suspicious.

Over the thirty years he'd been employed with the city, Mr. Nash had given many of the town residents a hard time when it came to repairs or additions. He liked to yell a lot and took great satisfaction whenever he made someone start a repair or project all over again. His favorite trick had been to overlook something on one inspection—wiring or some other building code infraction—only to find it during the next inspection when it became more difficult to fix. He took special pleasure when the home or business belonged to a Kindred.

When the Grays were renovating Forever View, Mr. Nash had made sure to find anything and everything he could to delay the next phase. Finally, Raven's father offered him a discount on a coffin, and it had nothing to do with money. The threat struck the right vein, so to speak, and Mr. Nash finally stopped finding excuses to impede work on the mortuary. Shayde's mother once said Mr. Nash held a grudge for a great-great grandparent who had been killed by a Kindred during the Northwick conflict. Shayde's father said it that deep down inside, Mr. Nash was jealous of the Kindreds. The only way to feel more powerful than them was to exert power at his job.

"I don't think the visit had anything to do with his work," Ivy said. "But who knows? I guess everyone will be talking about it tonight and wondering what he might have been up to."

"It is ironic," her mother said. "Seems the sisters are the ones who'll be the talk of the town now."

The sisters, also known as the Gossip Queens, thought it was their duty and their right to spread *their* version about everything that went on in Northwick. Of course, by the time they told it, it usually had little in common with the actual events. Ivy recalled the nasty rumors the Queens had circulated when her father disappeared.

"He's in another country using his powers for evil!" the sisters had told nearly everyone. "He kills any of those supernatural freaks who are sent to find him, and God help any *human* in his path."

Fortunately, most of the Regulars weren't fond of the Nashes either and never listened. They didn't think of Kindreds as freaks. For the most part, Regulars and Kindred got along nicely. Just another small town where everyone stuck together. But, Ivy couldn't help but feel a bit of justice had been served with the Nashes now on the receiving end of the talk.

"Yeah," Ivy said. "Considering how Mr. Nash was killed, it'll be years before people stop talking."

Her mother was fidgeting again and Ivy feared another hugging, are-you-all-right jag moment. Devlin barked at Ivy and wagged his tail furiously. She bent next to him and considered picking him up to prevent another lung-crushing hug.

Devlin wasn't a big dog, but forty pounds of squirming, licking Beezlepup wasn't easy to lift. Ivy loved his curled tail, squinty brown almond eyes, and feral appearance. His color was a few shades lighter auburn than her own hair, and felt softer than velvet as she stroked his back. Right now, she envied a dog's life. Devlin didn't have to worry about murders or spells gone wrong or what anyone other than his family thought of him.

Her mother had regained composure and managed a weak smile. "I'm just glad you're okay, sweetie. This is just so *horrible*. Apparently, whoever killed poor Mr. Nash did it in front of his wife and his sister-in-law. There weren't any other witnesses."

"Yeah, I heard. Did Nick's Uncle say anything else?" Ivy

asked, as she scratched under Devlin's chin. He leaned into her hand, eyes closed in delight.

Her mother sighed. "He said it might have been a Kindred dressed in costume, and that the Council is calling for a town hall meeting."

Ivy swallowed and tried to remain calm. "Well, maybe since Halloween is so close, the killer figured no one would pay too much attention if he wore a costume. There's always a lot of Halloween parties going on. So, maybe it *could* be a Regular," Ivy suggested. The longer everyone searched in the wrong direction, the better.

"You sure you're okay, sweetie? You look a bit rattled."

Ivy shrugged, prepared for another hug. "Who wouldn't be?"

"Oh, *Ivy!*" her mother said, pointing to Ivy's book bag instead. "Tell me you didn't bring your homework to Saludo's. Soon, we need to talk about dating."

Ivy stopped petting Devlin and glanced at the book bag. She didn't want her mother to look inside it. If her mother found the book, she'd freak. Maybe she'd reconsider what her daughter had inherited. The Council would surely think Ivy had become a dark witch. She'd changed Spike, and if Ivy surrendered the book now, they'd think she'd used it to kill Mr. Nash. After all, Ivy could be placed directly at the scene of two incidents, and she was carrying a book on the use of black magic.

If she turned out like... like *him*, it would destroy her mother.

"*Aaaarrrr!*" Devlin whined in his other-worldly Beezlepup voice, demanding more attention. He rolled on his back and wriggled himself along the carpet.

"Sure, Mom. Later, okay?" She kissed her on the cheek and picked up the book bag. "It's been a long, upsetting day and I'm really tired. Come on, Devlin."

Her mother nodded, and before she could say anything more, Ivy scrambled up the stairs with Devlin on her heels.

Ivy did feel tired, at least physically. Sleep eluded her though, and all she thought of that night was Vlad the Impaler, the mysterious woman with him, the books, and despite her best efforts, Nick.

Chapter 12

If Devlin hadn't been so incessant about his Sunday morning walk, Ivy would have preferred to stay in bed. It was three in the morning before she'd finally fallen asleep. Now, as she and Devlin stepped outside into the brisk sunshine, Nick and the books were back on her mind. It wouldn't be much longer before the Council figured out that someone had found Skinner's missing books. Although there was no real proof, the Council had always suspected that her dad had been the one to burn down Skinner's house and take the books. Since everyone drew so many comparisons to her and her father, they'd probably suspect he'd left them for his unusually talented daughter. Besides, she'd already proven she wasn't above using forbidden magic.

There was only one way to clear herself—find out who had *The Book of Lost Souls*. Fast. Which meant that she needed not only the help of her friends, but Nick's as well. He had the advantage of knowing more about the books and their history than anyone else at this point. At least, anyone she could ask.

Ivy and Devlin caught up with Shayde, who was waiting at the end of the sidewalk. Ivy liked that Shayde lived next door. She didn't think she could stand it if she had to drive across town to talk privately with her best friend.

"So, how was Nick?" Shayde asked, trying to engage in normal conversation as they walked past their houses.

Neighbor children who'd ventured out to play in a few leaf piles were bundled in heavy jackets. What Ivy wouldn't give to have a carefree morning like them.

"He's okay. I suppose you heard about Mr. Nash?"

Shayde shook her head. "Who hasn't? Someone in a costume. A Kindred, or so everyone thinks. Someone strong enough to lift Mr. Nash up and, well, you know—impale him like that. It's gotta be spells or superhuman strength. So, the Regulars aren't likely to be among the suspects. You seem really shook up. Did you see it happen?"

"No. No one saw the murder except the sisters," Ivy said, and before Shayde could ask, she added, "I am kinda freaked. Look, there's something else. Something I need to talk to you about. And you can't tell anyone, okay?"

Shayde's expression grew tense. "Sure. You've got my word, you know that."

"The books. Why would Nick want them?"

Shayde eyed her curiously. "The gardening book? Because... because he's into gardening for Satan?" Shayde said, in a dry attempt at humor. "What's this got to do—"

"I'm serious, here. The *other* two books. *The Rise of the Dark Curse* and the one that's missing."

They turned left at the stop sign. "Who says he wants them? Maybe he's just curious. You were. Or, maybe they startled him a little, Ivy. After you changed Spike and he saw the books on the table, he probably started to wonder if you were getting into black magic."

"But he said he *knew* about the missing book. That's what we talked about over pizza. Nick said there were some witch and demon families who want the books."

"But why would anyone want something so awful?" Shayde asked. "There has to be consequences for the spell caster who uses them, right?"

"I guess. Good question."

Shayde laughed. "What would Nick even do with those books? I really don't have him pegged as being into black magic. He's mischievous, sure. But, black magic? I don't think so."

"He said loads of Kindred families want the books for the power they represent. He said his dad wanted the books. Maybe he wants to give them to him."

"You know what bugs me? If you were into collecting rare books, why leave one and take the other?" Shayde asked.

Ivy shrugged. "I don't know. Didn't think of that."

"If Nick or his dad knew the other book was in the cemetery, why not go there instead of the funeral home?" Shayde asked. "Why even leave the first one behind to start with? I'm telling you, it's not Nick. It's not his dad, either. If it were, Nick wouldn't be talking to you about this."

Ivy thought about the shadow that vanished behind the tree, how the burlap sack was in plain view, yet it hadn't been there a few minutes before. It was as if someone put the sack there for them to find. "Did you see anyone else out there that day in the cemetery? Besides us and Spike?"

Shayde shook her head. "No. Why?"

"I thought I saw someone else out there. But, it was like they were there and then they weren't. I only caught a glimpse."

Shayde frowned. "I didn't see anyone."

"I was serious when I said more than one person is involved here. Someone buried the books, someone else found them. And, maybe there's a third, someone who wanted us to find the books left behind. The books were lying neatly on top of the burlap sack. Which meant that they were put there on purpose," Ivy said.

"But who knew we'd be there? Raven said that very few people visit that section of the cemetery. But, okay, let's go with your theory. *If* someone was there, they'd have seen us. So why not just hand the books over? Why leave them for us to find?"

Ivy shook her head. She'd asked herself the same

question.

"And what would they expect us to do with them? You're the only one who can cast spells," Shayde said. "If they wanted us to give them to someone else then why didn't they leave a note? If found please return to *whoever*."

"So it was someone who followed us there. Someone who was watching," Ivy said.

Shayde shook her head. "I don't know Ivy. Sounds weird. What does your mom say about all this?" She glanced at Ivy. "You didn't give her the books, did you? Oh, geez!"

"No. How could I? Everyone will think it's me, Shayde. It'll tear Mom apart. I've got to figure out who really has the book. Nick knows more than he's saying. He's offered to help, although I'm not sure if it's some trick to get me to give him the other book or not. But, it's all I've got. I'll have to play along."

"Okay. Your funeral." Shayde let out a long sigh. "But, *about* Nick. Does this mean you two are going out again?"

They crossed the street, Shayde grinning widely. "Everyone will forget about you and Spike in no time if you're dating Nick!"

"I'm *not* dating Nick. We went out once. I wanted information from him," Ivy said.

"I believe him. I still don't think he's after just the book. He might really be trying to help you because he likes you. Ever hear of that? You know, a *crush*?"

Devlin tugged on his leash as they entered the park. It was empty, just like most early Sunday mornings when the weather turned cold. A few Pigeon doves took flight from their spot on a nearby bench, finally settling back down atop the swing set.

"Maybe he's just *saying* he knows about the books. You turned him down. *Twice*."

"He knows I like Dean."

Shayde let out a small laugh. "A *lot* of people know you

have a thing for Dean. So, maybe Nick figures if he pretends to know about these books you're so interested in, you'll go out with him. He's probably hoping that by the time you realize he's been faking it, you'll like him instead. Nick's got that demon determination thing down cold."

"That's not it," Ivy said, bending down to unleash Devlin. "*Behave*," she warned.

Devlin took off across the park, scouting for squirrels. Ivy watched as Devlin watered several bushes and circled a tree that a squirrel scurried up. "He said that the third book brings back people, Shayde. It has curses that bring back really bad, dead people."

"Yeah, right. And Bane's entering the Westminster dog show. See? He's playing you. You can't bring back the dead. Well, there's vampires and the whole zombie thing, but you know what I mean."

Ivy ignored the comment. "The missing book is called *The Book of Lost Souls*. It brings back *famous* dead people. Like Vlad the Impaler and some woman Vlad called Elizabeth. Maybe some Countess."

Shayde stared in disbelief. "He couldn't possibly know that."

"He would if his dad told him all about it," Ivy said.

"Vlad the Impaler? Nick told you who attacked Mr. Nash? How would he know that?"

"He didn't. I'm the one who told *him* it was probably Vlad based on the description Gloria Albert gave the police."

Shayde sighed. "Wait. You're the one who identified the attacker? Wow. I see your point. If anyone knows you have that book, you're suspect number one. You knew who the conjured soul was."

"Yeah. That's why I need everyone's help," Ivy said.

Devlin barked loudly.

"Devlin!" Ivy shouted. "Leave Mrs. Quincy's cat alone!" Devlin had Midnight trapped up a small oak and clinging to a branch. The slight breeze didn't account for the violently shaking tree limb Midnight clung to. Of course, the culprit for the tree's behavior stood directly underneath, grinning, tongue hanging out between canine teeth.

"Why does he always do that? Why her cat?" Shayde asked.

"He did it once with the neighbor's Guinea pig that got loose. Swallowed the thing whole. Hacked it up on the living room carpet and totally freaked us out. It was all wet and slimy, so we didn't know what it was at first."

"Ewww," Shayde said.

"Yeah. It was really gross. It squealed and ran across the room and Mom smacked it with the broom mistaking it for some strange Beezlepup thing like a possessed hairball or something. Wasn't a pretty sight."

"Yeech!" Shayde said.

Midnight let out a high-pitched *me-owww*. The tree limb shook harder as though trying to dislodge him. Devlin stood underneath, barking excitedly.

"Devlin!" Ivy called out in warning. "Midnight is *not* a squeaky toy!" She broke out into a run across the park. "*Devlin!*"

He shot her a fleeting look. Why did anything and everyone belonging to the demon species have to be so difficult?

"Stop that right *now* Devlin!" Ivy demanded. She picked up a fallen leaf and held it in front of her. It swirled and shifted, changing into a replica of a fuzzy grey squirrel. Ivy squeezed it, and the toy squeaked. Instantly, Devlin whirled around, running at her full tilt, Midnight completely forgotten.

"Midnight makes the same noise as a squeaky toy when Devlin catches him," Ivy explained. "Ever since the Guinea pig incident he's had a thing for stuff that squeaks."

Shayde watched Midnight hurry down the tree and take refuge under a bush. "Can't say I haven't been tempted to chase Midnight a few times myself. And the squeaky toy from a leaf thing? Cute. Nice to see you're back to doing normal witchcraft. Anyway, what are you going to do? If Nick really is telling the truth..."

"The only thing I can do. Go on another date with him," Ivy said with a sigh.

Shayde raised an eyebrow. "And if Nick's on the level, why do you sound so gloomy about it? He's really hot. Sorry, bad demon pun."

"Because he's not who I want," Ivy replied, recalling Nick's words from last night. "But right now, until I get some answers, he might be exactly who I need."

The only problem was that Ivy wasn't sure which question she wanted the answer to first—who had the third book, or why it bothered her that she kept thinking about Nick, and if he *really* liked her or just wanted the book.

Chapter 13

By the time Ivy returned to Forever View, it was just after eleven and she was in a dour mood. Since Bane hadn't actually been part of the conspiracy to turn Spike into a human, he didn't have to show up for the cemetery work, and since Gareth had lost the most—his pet—he didn't have to, either. This left just the girls to work off another day of punishment.

Shayde's interest in any development in her so-called relationship with Nick had started to get on Ivy's nerves. She'd spent the last twenty minutes going on about Nick being so much better than Dean.

"If *you* have such a thing for Nick, why don't *you* go out with him?" Ivy finally asked Shayde.

"Because I *don't* have a thing for him. What I do have a thing for is seeing my best friend happy. He's smart and cute. And he has a wicked crush on you."

"Besides you, who says?" Ivy retorted. "I think Dean kinda likes me."

"I'd give a bucket of Mr. Nash's blood to see him dump Tara," Raven said with a snort. "Of course, there'd have to be more than a bucket left. He'd pretty much bled-out before the medical examiner got there. Pity. We only got a couple of glasses each."

Ivy grimaced. "I didn't need to visualize that twice, thanks. Anyway, if Nick really liked me that much *before* the books, why'd he wait until after I'd found them to be so incessant? Okay, yeah. He asked me out twice. Ever since the books came into play, he's not taking no for an answer. Usually, he'd be on to the next girl by now."

Raven grinned. "Guys. It's the testosterone. He can't stand to see you with Dean, especially if he senses he's got an edge. And that only makes it worse. Demons *love* a challenge."

"And you're certainly a challenge," Shayde mumbled.

"I heard that," Ivy said.

"Well, don't you think it's a bit unfair that you won't give him a chance because his father and yours were friends?" Shayde asked.

Ivy shot her friend a hard, *that's off limits*, glare. Shayde shrugged and went back to pulling the last of the weeds from the area she was working on. Shayde was right, of course. It probably was a bit unfair. But whenever Nick was around, Ivy felt like a tangle of nerves. It was as though she was always aware of him and his every move. But, she had to admit that she was a bit hard on him. If she was going to use his help, she needed to give him a break.

Careful, she reminded herself. *Don't start thinking you really like him.*

Ivy shook the thought from her head. After cleaning up a few last grave sites and loading up the golf cart, the girls found themselves staring at Mr. Laughton's grave.

"Dad is coming up here later with Gareth to rebury the bone and fix the grave," Raven said. "I wonder why someone picked this grave to bury the books in?"

Ivy shrugged. "Maybe they knew that no one visited this row of graves? Random choice?"

"Well, it was a good hiding place for a while," Shayde said. "I still wonder who put them there and who dug them up."

"Maybe there's a newcomer we don't know about yet," Raven countered.

Shayde shook her head. "We always know about

newcomers. If there's one around, they're on the down-low."

"We've actually got a mystery in our pretty boring little town. Exciting, isn't it?" Raven rubbed her hands together. "So! Who would you suspect? Who did Mr. Nash in?"

Ivy considered Raven's question. She'd practically thought of little else. Problem was, most of the town was less than friendly with the Nashes. "Well, it's obvious, isn't it? Mr. Nash had to have pushed the wrong Kindred too far. He's always trying to cause trouble. He was just asking for something bad to happen sooner or later. I never thought someone would kill him, though."

"I'm surprised no one has roughed him up before this," Raven said.

"That's because Mr. Nash knew that if a Kindred really did pound some sense into him, it'd upset a lot of Regulars," Shayde replied.

"Has he denied any building permits lately, failed anyone on inspection, cited anyone for code infractions?" Ivy asked.

Shayde laughed. "That would be a really long list."

Ivy agreed. But what other leads did she have? The thought haunted her all the way back to the funeral home and the entire drive home.

All Ivy wanted to do when she walked through the front door was to take a warm shower. Hopefully, her bad mood would wash down the drain along with the dirt and sweat. She'd managed to make it up the stairs and halfway down the hall when the floor creaked and her mother called to her.

Mental note to self, Ivy thought. *Remember to charm that particular floorboard.* The last charm had apparently worn off already.

Pretending she hadn't heard, Ivy headed straight for the bathroom. Her mother was just concerned, but Ivy had never felt less like talking.

Her mother tried to get her to talk about what was bothering her over dinner, and Ivy did her best to brush it off. When her mother suggested that she was probably just having boy trouble deciding between Dean and Nick, she let her mother think exactly that. With each bit of advice, Ivy nodded on cue and replied with the required *thanks, Mom*. She endured the last of the speech while they did the dishes.

"I'm going to read a little," Ivy said, hanging the dishtowel up to dry.

Her mother smiled warmly, clearly happy to have done her motherly duty by giving her daughter something to think about.

Devlin followed Ivy up the stairs and into her room. Ivy shut the door and sifted through her dresser, retrieving a lavender sleep tee. After changing and tossing her clothes in the direction of the clothes hamper, she pulled the book bag out from under her bed.

Why had someone buried all three books? Who had left the bag and the remaining books there for them to find? And what did a gardening book have to do with *The Book of Lost Souls?*

She looked at *The Rise of the Dark Curse*. Her hand hovered over it for a second or two. Giving in to her curiosity, she picked the book up and a sudden surge of energy rushed through her like an electrical current.

From his spot on the end of the bed, Devlin whined.

"It's okay, buddy," Ivy assured him. She sat on the bed and rested the book on the covers. "Just a minute or two. Maybe it'll give us a clue on who's using the other book."

Devlin whined again and lay down, paws over his snout.

Heart racing, Ivy gently flipped the book's cover open. The tendrils of black mist twirled and danced as though rejoicing.

She's back, little one is back!

Ivy paused and listened, but the voices had grown silent.

It was her imagination, nothing more. Although the tendrils of mist had died down, the immense cold that began to seep from the pages had not. Ivy flipped through a section of the book, the buzzing in her head, the adrenaline-sugary rush tingling inside her. It was both horrible and exhilarating.

The spells within the book bordered dark to down-right gruesome. She read one page after another, each spell more and more like a train wreck she couldn't look away from. Each spell filled her mind, feeling oddly like they'd settled down for a long visit.

Devlin barked. He stood inches from her, snarling, teeth bared. A sudden rage flared through her and Ivy raised a hand, preparing to repel Devlin off the bed—and maybe into the wall—for his uncommon outburst of disloyalty.

Devlin lunged. Surprised at her beloved pup's behavior, Ivy's spell missed. She jerked back, out of the way of Devlin's teeth. He clawed at the book, slamming it shut, yelping in pain as one of the tendrils of mist touched his paw. He scurried to the edge of the bed, ears and tail tucked in fear, paw still lifted in pain. But, he was still snarling at the book.

It was the book he'd been after. Not her. He'd wanted her to stop reading it.

Ivy couldn't believe that she'd almost struck Devlin. She'd *never* do such a thing. But, something had come over her while reading the book. She scooped Devlin into her arms. "I'm sorry," she repeated over and over. Devlin licked her face in accepted apology, but his eyes darted back to the book.

"Yeah. You're right." Ivy retrieved her book bag, and using the covers as a barrier, slid the book into the bag. She exchanged it for *A Botany of Spells—Magic for the Garden*. She zipped the bag shut and pushed it under the bed.

She examined Devlin's paw, which looked okay. He tentatively set it back down on the bed, applying a bit of weight to it. The book was far too dangerous. She had to get rid of it soon. Ivy glanced at the alarm clock. She'd been going through the book for over half an hour. The longer she'd spent with it, the more engrossed she'd become and more it had affected her. Devlin had seen that and tried to protect her from it. But, it had affected him, too. Beezlepups were very in tune to their owners, and Devlin was feeding off her energy.

Ivy scratched under his chin. "Thanks, buddy."

Devlin sneezed, hopefully meaning, *you're welcome*. He curled back up on the edge of the bed, seemingly at ease with her second choice in reading material. He watched her for a little bit, but soon drifted to sleep with a few short snuffling sounds.

Ivy flipped through the first few pages of the gardening book, not knowing exactly what to look for. It wasn't until chapter three that she stopped flipping through pages and started reading. The chapter's title was enough to generate interest. It read: *Chapter Three: Ivy*. A faded, penciled-in star appeared next to this. According to the book, ivy was one of the most revered plants in witchcraft. Supposedly, it offered good luck, health, and could ward off despair and disaster. Greek and Roman gods often wore wreaths of holly and ivy.

Ivy traced her fingernail across the words that had been underlined: happiness, health, good luck. She would have underlined another bit of text that exemplified her personality—that although ivy was cultivated and grown in several places in the world and sometimes used to cover buildings in disrepair, it was a plant that *thrived* in nature. Perseverance. Determination. Six spells were included in this chapter, using the plant for anything from hangovers and infertility to sunburn and depression. She read the last sentence in the chapter several times.

The powers of ivy are strongest during the Ivy Moon, which coincides at harvest's end. Harvest's end fell on Halloween this year, six days away.

She continued to browse through *A Botany of Spells*, pausing again on *Chapter eight: Wolfsbane*. Again, a penciled-in star appeared next to the chapter's title. Fully engaged now, she read on. Aside from the fact the plant was highly poisonous, it also had the qualities of strength, intelligence, and peace. A true spell caster's plant, the chapter concluded.

Bane. Wolfsbane.

Without browsing through the rest of the book, she searched the index for Nightshade. Finding it, she turned to chapter twenty and stared. There was another star here. She paged forward, but none of the other plants had a star penciled next to them. She flipped back to Nightshade. Beauty was the one word that was repeatedly used with the plant, and she read a few spells that used Nightshade. One was thought to encourage one's artistic abilities. Another was to enhance sight temporarily. Other spells revolved around Nightshade's powers to sever life.

Nightshade. Sever life?

Shayde?

That was hardly a trait she'd put with her best friend. She paged through the book again. Only three of them had stars next to their chapter headings. Three. Ivy, Wolfsbane, and Nightshade. Ivy, Bane, and Shayde. Coincidence?

No. Something said it wasn't. But why would a gardening book with her name and the names of her friends be included with books on black magic?

Either this had something to do with her father, or someone had tried to make it look that way. Which meant, either he'd buried the books, or the person who dug them up was *setting* her up. Maybe both were true. Her thoughts went back to Nick's father.

"What are you reading, sweetie?"

Ivy jumped, knocking the book from her lap. She'd been so preoccupied that she hadn't heard her mother enter the room.

"Nothing," she said. "Just a book on plants." Her mother picked it up before Ivy could snatch it from atop the covers.

Her mother's face went white, her hands trembled, and tears filled her eyes.

"Mom," Ivy said. "What's the matter? It's just a book." Even without her mother's reaction to it Ivy knew that *A Botany of Spells* was anything other than *just a book*.

Tears spilled down her mother's cheeks and she wiped at them furiously. "Where?" she asked, her voice nearly choking. "Where did you find this, Ivy?"

"It's not a bad book, Mom! It's just about some plants. What's wrong?"

"WHERE did you find this?" Her mother closed the book and held it to her chest.

"Mom, you're scaring me."

Ivy's words must have made her mother come around and she took a deep, controlled breath. "Your father gave it to me the summer I learned I was pregnant with you. I wanted to take up gardening, and he surprised me with this book. I haven't seen this book..." she paused. "I haven't seen it since your father left. Where on earth did you find it?"

Chapter 14

"One of the books was your *mother's?*" Shayde blurted out. "You're kidding."

"Shhh!" Ivy warned. She hurried to her locker and wriggled her fingers. The dial turned right and left and the locker popped open.

"Sorry," Shayde whispered. "Does she know you found it buried in the cemetery?"

"I said that I found it stuffed behind some other books on a shelf in the study. She didn't look at me like I was lying," Ivy shrugged. "But she did seem surprised to see it. Said she hadn't seen it since *he* left."

"He?" Shayde's eyes widened. "Oh, him! Your dad," she finished softly.

Ivy exchanged books and closed the locker. "I really think he buried the books. What I can't figure out is why he did that and just left, unless he'd planned to come back for them. Or, unless he was hiding them from someone. And, why didn't he tell Mom?"

On the rare occasions when the topic of her father came up, there was a small twinge inside her that Ivy always found confusing. It was anger, surely. And pain too, no matter how much she denied it. And now, Ivy felt awkward discussing with Shayde how easily she'd lied last night. But there was no way she could have asked her mother how her gardening book had ended up buried with Mr. Laughton.

"You didn't ask about the other books then, did you?" Shayde inquired.

Ivy shook her head. "No."

"Ivy," Shayde said, concern evident in her voice. "Your mom doesn't have the other book, you know that. She'd never be involved with black magic. If your dad really did bury those books, he didn't do it to prevent your mother from using them."

Ivy knew this for fact. If she'd learned anything from last night, it was that the books should never stay in anyone's possession for any length of time. It changed people. Nick had alluded to that much over pizza. Could it be that Nick was on the level about making sure the books were put away someplace safe?

"Yeah, I know. But, here's what scares me the most— both of those books were in our house—at the same time." Ivy took a deep breath. "That's not all. I found something else in the gardening book that I need to talk to you and Bane about."

Shayde started to say something more, but then grew quiet when Nick walked up.

"Hi," he said, eyeing them. "Am I interrupting?"

"Nope," Shayde said, giving Ivy a quick smile. "We'll talk later. I'm off to history class. See you at lunch, Ivy. Bye, Nick." Shayde hurried away before Ivy could think of something to say to keep her around.

She didn't feel like Nick's company at the moment. He'd ask questions she didn't want to answer.

"Something wrong?" Nick asked as he walked alongside her. They both had English during third period with Mrs. Wilkes.

"Nothing, I'm fine." She walked faster.

Nick stayed right with her. "Yeah, I can see that," he said. "Want to tell me about nothing, then?"

"No. I just didn't sleep well." She strode into the classroom, choosing a seat near the window.

"It's a bit overwhelming, isn't it? The book. The whole past resurfacing just when you thought you were putting it behind you."

She nodded. His words were soothing, comforting, and Ivy replayed the way Nick made her feel when he had held her tightly against him. Her heart skittered a few beats. Why did he make her feel this way all the time? It was downright scary. Scary, because she couldn't control her thoughts *or* her reactions.

Nick took a seat next to her. "How about another date? You know, just to take your mind off the nothing that's bothering you."

She stared straight ahead, trying to seem eager for class to start.

He smirked and looked around the classroom in exaggerated fashion. Ivy followed his gaze, wondering what he found so interesting. There wasn't much to take in. Northwick High had been built in the fifties when classrooms weren't very large.

"I know you're really smart, Ivy. Right at home with books and exams and classrooms like this. But, I was thinking of a date that doesn't revolve around sentence structure. I wasn't asking for a *preposition*. A date is more like a *proposition*."

She forced a sarcastic smile, but looking at him, a real one worked its way onto her face. "Just so you know, it's because of our deal, right? It's not a real date. I suppose you want me to bring a few books anyway?"

"Nope. Unless there's something in one of them that'll help locate Spike. Maybe we should go hunt for him."

"And you call that a date?" Ivy said, astounded.

He shrugged. "*You* said it wasn't a real date. Look, I know it's hard for you to think about anything other than a study date, so I'll go slow. How about thinking of Spike as a misplaced modifier we need to find."

She stared for a long moment, then blinked. Where did

he get his material? Tortured stand-up comics from hell?

"Come on. That was funny. Spike. Modifier. Modified? Tell me you got that? Well?"

"Yeah—"

"Excellent. It's a date, then. Sort of. See you after dinner, say six-thirty?"

"That was outright trickery," Ivy said, scowling.

"Uh, yeah," he said. "I'm a demon, remember?" He winked and quickly feigned interest in his homework, cracking open his English book and turning away from her.

Before she could protest, Mrs. Wilkes entered the room with an armload of books. She was a round witch with a round face and a button nose, and her grey hair was pulled into a severe round bun. Mrs. Wilkes set her books on her desk and gave Nick and Ivy a warm smile which made little cherry-colored orbs of her cheeks. The only thing that wasn't circular on Mrs. Wilkes were the deeply etched laugh lines behind her half-moon bifocals.

She waved a stubby finger at Ivy. "You resemble your mother more every day, Ivy dear. I always did like Claire. Kindest, most down-to-earth witch I've ever met. Honest and good as they come. How's the library treating her these days?"

Mrs. Wilkes's words about her mother's near-angelic nature stunned Ivy. She wished that her resemblance to her mother was more than just physical. Hadn't her mother mentioned that she was more and more like her father? With every passing year she wondered if her sharp-tongued wit and impatience was a trait she had inherited from *him*. Hard to say since he'd been gone for so long. She felt another sudden stab of guilt for lying about where she'd found the book.

Nick nudged her for a response.

"Everything's fine, Mrs. Wilkes," Ivy managed. "Thanks for asking. Just fine."

"Oh, how lovely, dear." Mrs. Wilkes turned back to her

desk as the classroom started to fill up with students.

Nick shot Ivy a suspicious glance, which clearly stated he didn't think things were fine at all. Great. That meant tonight he'd be sure to ask even more questions she preferred to avoid. Maybe she could call him later and tell him she felt sick and had to cancel.

They worked their way through subjunctive verbs and subordinate clauses the first half of class. Ivy couldn't have been more bored. She'd already studied this material over summer break.

"Paul," Mrs. Wilkes said, striding to the blackboard. She motioned to one of the sentences she'd written earlier. "Where's the subordinate clause in this sentence?"

Paul, a boy with mousy hair and a baby face, fidgeted as he read, *Julie walked home after her car broke down.* He scratched the back of his neck. "Julie walked home?"

"Oh, dear!" Mrs. Wilkes said, disappointed. "You've been neglecting your grammar. Nick? Can you help Paul?"

"After her car broke down," Nick said nonchalantly. He gave Ivy a smug smile.

Bored with adverb clauses, Ivy turned to stare out the window watching the clouds cross a clear, chilly sky. The Maples had all lost their leaves and offered knotted, arthritic limbs toward the sky as though pleading for warmth. Only the Pin Oaks kept their leaves, wearing them like a tattered winter coat. She started to zone, thinking about the incantations in *A Botany of Spells* and how her mother's book had ended up buried alongside Mr. Laughton.

"And now, just for fun, let's work on metaphors and similes," Mrs. Wilkes said gleefully. "Let me find my worksheets." She fumbled through her papers. "Oh, dear! I must have left them at home. We'll just improvise. Remember, similes use the verbs *like* and *as* to draw a comparison between two objects. Metaphors use *is* and *are* to show that an object is what it resembles. Paul, let's try again. Give us an example of a simile."

"Hey, it's the lizard guy!" Paul commented loudly, and pointed out the window.

"Oh dear!" Mrs. Wilkes exclaimed. "That would imply he's really a lizard. That's a better example of a metaphor and not a very good one, I'm afraid."

Most of the class had left their seats, scrambling to the window to get a better look. On the short stone wall around a bunch of trees, was Spike. He was sprawled on his back, arms stretched outward, sunning himself in true lizard fashion.

Jogging along the path that wove through the lawn was the girl's gym class. Tara and one of her cheerleading buddies were running ahead of the others and fast approaching Spike. Not only was the distance between the window and Spike farther than Ivy had ever attempted to cast a spell, she might miss and turn one of the girls into a lizard instead of Spike. On second thought, the idea didn't seem so bad. Her hand twitched at her side.

Suddenly aware that Mrs. Wilkes was standing directly behind her, all contemplation of having Tara join the ranks of sun-seeking, scaly-skinned bug eaters ended.

"Oh, dear!" Mrs. Wilkes said, squinting. "That really is him. Stand aside."

Positioning herself directly in front of the window, Mrs. Wilkes recited a spell from *Spectacular Spells Explained*, one clearly meant to return Spike to normal. Mrs. Wilkes might have seemed fairly harmless and somewhat feeble at times, but everyone knew she was a witch to be reckoned with. Once, she levitated an old oak that had fallen across the road outside the school entrance with only a whispered incantation.

Spike jumped from his spot like he'd been struck by lightning. He looked around cautiously, still in human form. Mrs. Wilkes tried again, this time managing to catch Spike's shoes on fire for a brief second. A small cloud of dark grey smoke billowed from his toes. He screamed and flung his shoes off. Tara and half the cheerleading squad stood beside him, trying to calm him down.

Great. Tara, the one person who couldn't manage to make a pencil hover without wobbling would get credit for catching Spike. Like she *needed* more popularity. Ivy could just hear the talk around school now—how Tara had managed to snag Ivy's runaway date.

"Spike's not acting entirely lizard-like," Nick said as though she hadn't noticed this tidbit of information herself. "I mean, a lizard would just run off, not think to remove his shoes. And he's talking to Tara without your help."

"It's the Intelligence spell," Ivy whispered back. "One of the side effects is that it accelerates over time. He's probably starting to think more like a person than a lizard, especially since he's in human form."

Spike dusted himself off and appeared to be easily conversing with Tara and another girl. They each took one of Spike's arms and led him away. As long as the girls were touching him, even Mrs. Wilkes didn't dare cast another spell. And what would it have mattered, anyway? Something didn't seem right. How could one of her spells be stronger than Mrs. Wilkes's?

Nick shook his head. "That's not good. The longer this goes on, the more likely it is he won't want to be a lizard again. Didn't you read the warning on that spell? Isn't there a bunch of other side effects?"

"Yeah, well, I wasn't thinking about all that at the time. But, Spike doesn't exactly give me the impression that he's depressed right now. On the bright side, he's probably already smarter than Tara."

A murmur rippled through the classroom, and Ivy heard the shuffling of feet as people backed away from the window, leaving just Mrs. Wilkes, Nick, and her standing there.

"Dark magic," someone murmured. "Anyone who'd

want to keep him in human form is definitely practicing dark magic."

Ivy heard her classmates whispered agreement. Who were they talking about? Mrs. Wilkes? Couldn't they see she had tried to turn Spike *back* into a human? Ivy turned to face them, to tell them that Mrs. Wilkes would never do dark magic and found that everyone, even Nick and Mrs. Wilkes were staring at her.

They weren't talking about Mrs. Wilkes. To Ivy's horror, they were talking about *her*. They thought she had somehow countered Mrs. Wilkes' spell to keep Spike a human.

Several students, winced as though waiting for Ivy to turn them into something hideous. Others stared at her with what Ivy interpreted as serious respect.

"Too cool. She's the most powerful witch in school!" one classmate said to another, who nodded eagerly.

"Wish I was a witch," sighed one of the Goths who frequently hung out with the other Kindred-wannabes.

"Like father like daughter is what my mom would say. I heard her father was a dark wizard," Paul said quietly. "The darkest there is."

The whole room buzzed with Paul's comment and Ivy never felt worse. She was *not* like *him*. Couldn't be. He'd been gone so long that he no longer had an influence on her. Fear crept into her. Had she inherited some special powers?

Mrs. Wilkes frowned and appeared quite worried. "Oh dear!" she said. "Oh, dear!"

Chapter 15

"Are they kidding?" Shayde asked, taking a seat next to Ivy in the lunchroom. "*You*? A dark witch?"

"Congratulations, Ives," Bane said. "I think you've gone from being nearly invisible to being voted most popular."

Ivy felt the weight of the stares around her. "It's like the entire cafeteria is staring at me."

"That's because they *are*," Raven said with a grin. "And Bane's right. I think you're rivaling Tara as Ms. Popular. You're the only witch who's tried dark magic and actually succeeded. It backfires on everyone else, or so I hear. "And," she said with a laugh, "You're dating the hottest demon in all of Northwick."

"I'm not really dating him. And why is that so funny?" Ivy glanced at the next table and found a group of freshmen gawking at her. They smiled nervously and turned away.

"It's funny because *everyone* is talking about you."

"Yeah, that's a real riot, Raven," Ivy said, picking at her food.

"No, silly. I mean *everyone*. Even Dean Matthews."

Ivy's head jerked up. "Dean?"

"I thought that'd get your attention," Raven said. "I overheard him talking in the hall. I also heard Tara is real ticked about it."

"Great. So he's attracted to dark witches now?" Shayde went beet red, realizing how her comment must have sounded and quickly backtracked. "Not that you are a dark witch. It's...your powers. They're like your brains—better than most."

"Maybe turning Spike more human is a new subconscious power or something," Bane suggested.

"I didn't do anything! I didn't!" Ivy said, feeling a flush of anger and panic. She hadn't *tried* to do dark magic. It was just that lately her spells had more punch to them. Like every other subject, Ivy took spell study and practice seriously. All this new power was probably because she'd spent too *much* time on spells. It didn't explain how she could make things happen without always casting a spell, though. There were times when all she had to do was think about something happening, concentrate a little and *poof!*

"Well, Mrs. Wilkes didn't do it, did she?" Raven teased. She obviously thought having a hint of dark power was appealing. It wasn't.

"Raven and Bane have a point, Ivy," Shayde said. "You think you could've...you *know*."

Ivy shook her head. She was not whatever her father ended up being. "No. I'm just a witch. An ordinary witch."

"Unless she's a goddess or some other super-chick from the Netherworld. I read that there's this guy who's the reigning deity of all people and things supernatural," Gareth piped up. Then, taking in the response of his friends, he said, "Total myth, of course. There's no such person."

Raven gave her brother a pained smile. "Sure. There's this deity who is Lord of all us Kindred. Right. My brother still believes in fairy tales." She gave a little laugh. "Gareth, is this like the time you were afraid of monsters and we all had to sleep with a black light on?"

"Shut *up*, Raven," Gareth pleaded. He'd turned the slightest shade of pink from his usual pale white.

Bane laughed. "What monster could a vampire possibly be afraid of?"

Gareth shot his sister a hateful look. Then, apparently decided it would sound better if he told everyone the story instead of her. "The tooth fairy, okay? Lay off me. We'd just been turned, and everything was new and scary."

Even Ivy couldn't help laughing. "The *tooth* fairy, Gareth? Even back then, weren't you a bit old to believe in that? You do know there's no such thing."

"Yeah, I know, but vampires weren't supposed to be real, either. We'd just been turned! I was *stressed*, okay? Really freaking stressed. I wasn't afraid of anything until Raven used to tell me tooth fairies really existed and that they'd steal my fangs in the middle of the night and stick pureed carrots and mashed beets under my pillow." He took in everyone's faces and appeared even more embarrassed. "Geez, guys! A vampire without their fangs is... what? I didn't *totally* believe her. Just, well, sort of. I already wondered if we'd ever have to go back to the dentist. What if they knew we were vampires? Would they pull our teeth?"

"Oh, you're cruel, Raven!" Bane said, choking and laughing.

"You see what I live with for an older sister?" Gareth had gone from light pink to almost red around his ears. "Why do I have to *have* a sister? Raven! Why can't I just say *nevermore* and watch her vanish?"

The pun on Raven's name reminded Ivy about the penciled-in stars she'd found in the gardening book. "I've got a question," Ivy said to Shayde and Bane. "Do either of you know why our moms picked our names? Besides the whole plant-life name theory, have you ever really thought about it? What your names mean and stuff?"

The twins exchanged glances. "No, why?" they asked simultaneously.

Ivy squirmed. "In that book, the *Botany of Spells*, I found our names."

"So," Bane shrugged.

"Our names had little stars penciled in next to them. No other plant, no other herb. Just ours." Ivy watched her friends as they considered what she'd said. She wondered which one would get what she was driving at first.

"You think someone your mom knew buried those books and that *none* of our names were random choices?" Shayde asked.

"And everything that's happening has something to do with the three of us? That's nuts," Bane said. "Werewolves don't have powers like a lot of other Kindreds do. We can't do spells, and we're not exactly vegetarian. Plants aren't our thing."

"I think there's more here than just a missing book that brings back the dead. I think our names might have been chosen for a reason," Ivy said.

"Sounds far-fetched," Bane said. "But, if it'll make you feel better, Shayde and I will ask about it."

They finished their lunches as the bell rang, signaling they had ten minutes before the next class started. Ivy took her tray and walked to the trash, trying not to notice that people were still staring at her. It felt uncomfortable. What if she tripped? Popularity wasn't all that it was cracked up to be. Or should she call it infamy?

Ivy stopped at her locker to switch out books for her afternoon classes, thinking about Spike and whether Tara had turned him in yet. If she had, then why hadn't the principal called her to the office?

"Hey, Ivy." Dean Matthews sidled up alongside her locker.

Her heart stopped and restarted with a hard thud. "Um, hi, Dean." She quickly looked around for Tara. The hallway was thinning out and Ivy couldn't spot Tara anywhere.

"Your hair looks nice today," Dean said in his most charming, charismatic voice.

"Um, thanks!" Was all Ivy could muster. She resisted the urge to reach for her hair. Had Tara finally managed a spell and put gum in it or something?

"You know, I was thinking maybe you'd like to swing by tonight during practice." He smiled his perfect, heart-fluttering smile. "We've got a big game this weekend."

Had Dean just asked her to come watch him practice?

"Well, I'm sort of busy—"

"Nick Marcelli I hear. It's nothing serious, I hope?" He grinned again and Ivy couldn't help but notice how truly perfect his teeth were. Was there anything *not* perfect about him?

"Not really I guess," she replied. *Not really?* Had she said that? There wasn't anything between her and Nick, at least on her end, so why had she said that? Why did it feel weird talking about him like they were an item?

"Good," Dean said. "Then I still have a chance." He pushed away from the locker, brushed her hair over her shoulder and walked away.

Ivy turned in stunned silence to watch him go.

"Catch you later, Ivy," he said, turning his head to give her one of his famous winks.

Ivy couldn't quit grinning as she shut her locker and turned to head off to class. Tara stood right in front of her and she wasn't wearing her happy face.

Ivy's grin vanished. Major oops moment. She'd almost forgotten Tara existed.

Apparently, so had Dean. Ivy hadn't done anything wrong—not exactly. It wasn't like she'd thrown herself at him. He'd been the one to approach her. And he hadn't asked her out again once he knew she had plans with Nick. He just hinted that he would.

"Stay away from my boyfriend," Tara snapped.

"Maybe you should ask him how *he* feels about that," Ivy said.

"Popularity doesn't suit you, MacTavish. You don't have what it takes."

Ivy couldn't resist. "Apparently, I do."

"Hmmmpf!" Tara scoffed. "You think you're so pretty and so smart. You think all the guys think you're hot. Well, let me tell you something! Beauty and brains aren't everything!"

"Got me there," Ivy said turning and walking away, trying not to laugh at Tara's ditzy observation. She fully expected Tara to come flying up behind her, but she didn't.

"I'll *get* you, MacTavish. You better be afraid. You stay away from Dean."

Ivy glanced back at Tara, at her bleached blonde hair, her tight sweater, and perfect lip gloss. Oh yeah, she could see how that'd be terrifying—attack of the Barbie doll.

Ivy's day didn't get any better when she got home. The news about Spike had already reached her mother. No one knew Spike's current whereabouts, including Tara, who'd said Spike ran off before she could bring him into the school. Worse, no one could explain what had gone wrong when Mrs. Wilkes tried to reverse the Changing spell. Apparently, the principal had called before Ivy got home from school, asking her mother if she knew what spells Ivy had been studying and had strongly encouraged a mother-daughter talk.

"I don't understand why a Reverse Change spell didn't work. Are you sure Mrs. Wilkes followed this spell correctly?" her mother asked during dinner. She slid a spell book across the table toward Ivy. It was the same book, *Spectacular Spells Explained*, and it contained the same spell Ivy had used to change Spike into a human. Her mother had already asked this question at least twice.

"I told you! How many ways are you going to ask me? And I don't know why Mrs. Wilkes's spells didn't work," Ivy nearly shouted. "Why do you think I do? Why is everyone treating me different and acting like I'm secretly studying dark magic? Even you."

Her mother lowered her eyes and nervously bit at her

lip. "Because you've always been special, Ivy. You've always been so smart. Things just come so easily to you—studies, spells." She shook her head. "You were twelve when you got most of your powers, a full year before most Kindred girls. But even before then, you had *some* powers. Little things. I don't think you were ever even aware. When you were three, birds you saw in the park and thought were pretty would land on your bedroom windowsill the following morning and sing. Cardinals sat next to Bluebirds. The entire windowsill would be full of singing birds. Worn, stuffed toys would mend themselves."

"Mom, that doesn't mean anything," Ivy said.

"It does!" her mother snapped back. She seemed angry now. "You *are* just like your father, Ivy. You're full of strange magic, and I don't have anyone on his side of the family to ask about it."

Hot tears welled in Ivy's eyes. She felt both angry and hurt. How could her mother compare her to *him*? "What a horrible thing to say! He *left* us. Is it because you look at me and see his eyes? I can't help that! But I'm *not* like him. I refuse to believe anything you say about that. I hate him. I'm not some black magic *freak* like everyone thinks!"

The dishes rattled on the table. The teakettle on the stove whistled, blowing its stopper and shooting it across the stove with a clank. The lights flickered. Ivy and her mother locked gazes. Ivy's eyes were too full of tears to see her mother's expression clearly, but she seemed on the verge of crying as well. She detected something else there, too. Fear? Was her mother afraid of her like some of her classmates had been? What the hell was happening?

Ivy ran from the table, Devlin hurried behind her, whining and she turned to stare at him. He wagged his tail and his bright eyes shone happily back at her. She grabbed his leash and her coat from the hook by the front door.

Ivy stormed out of the house with Devlin, trying to push back more tears. If she was such a dark witch, why did she feel like her heart was breaking? Weren't dark witches evil and heartless? If she was so powerful, why couldn't she stop the relentless flow of tears? She'd rounded the corner before she realized she might just be like her father in one respect—she'd walked out without any hesitation at all.

Chapter 16

Ivy knew she should go home and work this out with her mother. But how could she work out what she didn't understand? None of this was her fault! She hadn't done anything to stop Mrs. Wilkes from reversing her spell. How could she have?

Devlin tugged at her coat pocket. "Grrrr." His mischievous eyes beamed up at her, a Beezlepup grin forming on his cute fox-like face.

She tried to smile back at him, but let out a sob instead. Devlin's smile faded and his face wrinkled up as he whined.

"I'm okay," she tried to assure him. Devlin sat and waved, a trick she'd taught him over the summer. He followed up with a bark, then walked backwards around her, weaving around her legs before settling at her feet with an *How about that?* expression.

Ivy managed a choked laugh. "Thanks. I needed that, buddy." She reached into her pocket, conjured a squeaky toy from a piece of lint and handed it to him.

Devlin squeaked the toy furiously just as Shayde pulled up to the curb in the Suburban. Through the tinted windows, she could make out someone else sitting in the passenger seat. The window slid down and her eyes met Nick's. She'd forgotten completely about their date.

"Hey guys," Ivy said.

"Hey!" Shayde said.

"You didn't forget, did you? Didn't get a better offer?"

Nick asked.

Ivy gave him a puzzled look.

"Get in, we'll talk on the way. As for tonight, I talked to Shayde after I saw you. When it comes to Spike, I figured we could use all the reinforcements we could get." Nick smiled at Devlin. "I've always been fond of Beezlepups. He's really cute."

Devlin wagged his tail at Nick's compliment, and squeaked his toy. Glad the subject had turned to Devlin, Ivy hoisted him onto the back seat then slid in next to him.

Shayde pulled away from the curb and headed out of the development. "Did you hear about Dean and Tara?" she asked. "They broke up. She's really ticked because I guess Dean told her he needed some space again. He said he'd like to date other people."

"They broke up?" Ivy said, her voice warbling. Nick was looking at her and she couldn't meet his eyes. "Wow. Imagine that." Devlin squeaked his toy and offered it to Ivy. She ignored him.

"We need to talk," Nick told her. "When we get out of the car."

It was one of those moments that Ivy swore lasted forever. The kind of moments that made her sweat and feel like being anywhere except where she was, and yet there was no escape. How much did Nick know? Did he see her and Dean in the hallway? Did someone else see everything, including the bit with Tara? What if they had and it was on YouTube?

"I didn't do anything!" She blurted out the words, realizing she sounded like a kid who had been caught eating cookies before dinner. Why did she even feel the need to explain? This was turning out to be the most craptastic day. *Ever.*

"That's my whole point," Nick said, clearly a bit grumpy. "From what I saw, you didn't *discourage* him."

Great. Nick was acting like there really was something

between them other than this stupid deal about the book. She wanted to tell him he was taking the whole *saving her reputation* thing a little too far, but decided to keep her mouth shut.

"Before we picked you up, I heard from Raven and Gareth," Shayde said. "They know where Spike is, and you won't believe it."

"Where?" Ivy asked.

"He's at the Wok of Life Chinese buffet with Tara."

Ivy's mouth dropped. "Seriously? So Tara lied about Spike taking off?"

"And better yet, Tara took Spike shopping," Shayde replied. "Raven can't wait for us to see him."

"Shopping?" Ivy asked.

Raven didn't have to wait long. They pulled up alongside Raven's Saturn Sky roadster—her birthday present from her parents. Of course it was Raven's favorite color—red. Gareth sat next to her, looking frantic.

"What's with Gareth?" Nick asked Raven as they piled out of the Suburban.

"He's afraid Spike is too far gone to be changed back. He thinks that's why Mrs. Wilkes couldn't reverse Ivy's original spell."

"Ridiculous. I'm sure Ivy can change him back. There isn't a spell out there Ivy can't manage," Shayde said.

Except how to catch Spike and erase the whole day. For that matter, the whole week, Ivy thought.

They peered through the plate glass window of the Wok of Life. If she hadn't seen it herself, she'd never have believed it. No one would have ever known that Spike had once been a lizard. The Intelligence spell was accelerating faster all the time.

Inside, Tara laughed at something Spike said. She had indeed taken Spike shopping. He was wearing a dark blue silk sport jacket and a matching button-up shirt. From where Ivy stood, the wild, bug-searching expression was gone, replaced by a knock-out all-knowing look. He'd grown a small five o'clock shadow that made him handsomer still, and his hair was golden and wavy, and perfect.

"*That's* Spike?" Ivy heard herself mutter, feeling slightly jealous that Tara had managed to make Spike more gorgeous with the use of a credit card than Ivy had with a complex spell.

"Yeah, that's Spike. But you haven't seen the best part yet," Raven said. "Watch."

Ivy couldn't do anything *but* watch. Spike was *eating*—with chopsticks.

"He'll never eat crickets again!" Gareth complained.

"Don't be so sure. I've heard crickets are a delicacy in many countries," Nick said, trying to sound comforting.

"Great! I'll probably have to fry them in peanut oil or sauté them in lobster sauce," Gareth said, disgusted.

Devlin squeaked his toy several times in a row, trying to get someone to play with him.

"What's with the squeaking?" Nick asked Ivy.

"Oh, Devlin has a serious thing for squeaky toys. Obsession, actually," she replied

"Okay ladies," Nick said to Shayde and Ivy as everyone's attention returned to Spike. "Wipe the drool off your chins and take a last look at Prince Charming before we turn him back into a toad."

"A *lizard*," Gareth mumbled.

"We have to wait for them to come out," Ivy said. "We can't just go storming in there. What happens if I set him on fire like Mrs. Wilkes did?"

Nick sighed deeply. "Good point. The Wongs wouldn't appreciate it. Trolls have absolutely no sense of humor."

They all settled back to wait. It was true—when it came to being no-nonsense, trolls took the cake and Mr. and Mrs. Wong went to the extreme. Unlike the Adams and the Roths and several other trolls living in Northwick, the

Wongs didn't waste time with charms to hide what they were. The Wongs were short and stubby, with small slits for mouths, beetle-like eyes, and a pitted complexion that resembled the moon's landscape. They even looked alike. The only way Ivy ever knew which was which was that Mrs. Wong wore her jet-black hair in a ponytail that stood upright on her scalp.

Thirty minutes later, Tara emerged with Spike, her hand interwoven with Spike's in a way that seemed all too friendly. Spike leaned over and gave her a long, passionate kiss.

Ivy's eyes went wide. Shayde and Raven swooned beside her. Gareth whimpered, and Devlin squeaked his toy.

"You know," Raven said, impressed. "I don't think she's upset about Dean anymore."

"Something's happened to Ivy's spell. He's never going to be a lizard again!" Gareth complained.

Ivy stepped forward, prepared to take aim at Spike and reverse the spell.

Reluctantly, Tara pulled away from Spike to see what the commotion was about. "Oh, no you don't, Ivy!"

She stood protectively in front of Spike who cowered behind her, drawing his arms as close to his sides as possible and ducking his head down. Okay, so either he was a coward as a human, or at least some of his lizard instinct was still intact.

"Seriously?" Tara said, hands on hips. "What's your problem, Ivy? You want all the best-looking guys for yourself?" She motioned to Nick.

"Flattery will get you nowhere, Tara," Nick said. "Although feel free to keep trying."

"Yeah, I imagine your ego isn't doing so well, Nick. First, your girlfriend there would rather date a lizard than you, then she dumps you for Dean, and now she wants Spike back. Doesn't speak well for you, does it?"

Tara put her hands on her hips and smiled smugly.

"Don't worry, Nick. There are loads of girls waiting on the sidelines. Not that you'd have stuck around Ivy long anyway. I mean, really Nick. You can do better."

Ivy cast a sideways glance at Nick who was oddly silent. She raised an eyebrow. Why did she care?

It didn't go unnoticed. "Like I said, we need to talk," Nick said. "And it isn't what you think. But right now, you need to change Spike back. I'll distract Tara."

"I bet," Ivy said through gritted teeth, noticing the fleeting smile of satisfaction on Nick's face. *Why* did she have to like two of the hottest boys in class at once? There. She sort of admitted it. In some weird way she couldn't explain, she liked Nick. Hadn't her mother always said these would be some of the best times of her life? It must have been better when her mother was sixteen. Way better.

"Doesn't seem like you miss Dean very much," Ivy said to Tara while watching Nick out of the corner of her eye. She needed to stay focused on Spike, not Nick.

"Nick has a plan, Ivy," Shayde whispered. "He's going to try to get her to move away from Spike."

Gareth and Raven moved left. Shayde moved to Ivy's right.

"Why would I miss Dean when I've got Spike?" Tara spat. "You'll have to agree he's much more handsome."

"He's not yours, Tara. He's Gareth's pet. He needs to be turned back."

Tara laughed. "He's *my* pet now. That's so like you to come up with such a lame excuse for taking him from me. You're jealous of me Ivy, why don't you just admit it. I'm rich and I'm beautiful."

"I think you've got your nose so far in the air, you can't see past it," Ivy said, grinning. The thought had given her a wonderful, terrible idea. An Insult spell would only last a second or two, so whatever Nick and Shayde were up to had to be quick.

Nick was walking up to Tara, who took her eyes off Ivy

for a split second. That was all Ivy needed. With a flick of her wrist, Tara's nose began to grow wide and fat until it protruded upward like a giant pig snout.

Horrified, Tara screamed. Spike dragged Tara behind a car, keeping Nick on the other side. Tara steadied herself, and said what Ivy thought was, "Smard grass."

Tara's pig snout vanished and Ivy raised a hand, meaning to cast another spell, but merely blocked Tara's instead.

"Cute, Tara, you've actually mastered a simple spell." She hurled another Insult spell at Tara, who at the same time managed to fire off a spell of her own while Spike shoved a shopping cart toward Nick. The force of their simultaneous spells threw Ivy and Tara onto the pavement. Ivy picked herself up in time to see Spike dodge Raven and Gareth, do a high-flying leap past Shayde, and dart inside the door to the Wok of Life. Gareth looked as though he might go in after him but Mr. and Mrs. Wong were standing at the window, scowling and waving a finger in an *I wouldn't if I were you* gesture.

Tara had been thrown the farthest, and although she seemed a bit dazed, managed to stand. "Whoo! Whoo hoo! I foiled the mighty Ivy's plans to capture Spike. Again. Whoo!" She danced around in a sickening cheerleading routine.

"Can't you change her into something less revolting?" Raven asked.

Devlin ambled over to Tara and lifted his leg.

Tara screamed in disgust. "Nasty thing! Why, I should change *it* into something." She raised a hand, preparing to hit Devlin with a spell.

Devlin growled.

Ivy didn't really think about the spell she chose, only that a sudden rage of anger welled inside her. For some odd reason, she wished she had *The Rise of the Dark Curse* with her. She felt herself grin as she hurled the spell at Tara. A glamour. Not a real hex. Just an illusion.

Tara's voice faltered. She glanced down at her arms where open sores and rot appeared. She screamed and stepped backward, pulling clumps of hair from her head. Black mold ran along her veins.

"Go in there and get Spike!" Ivy ordered her friends. "Do it. Now."

Devlin whined and ran behind Nick. No one else moved. Everyone stared wide-eyed at Ivy.

"Ivy?" Shayde called out. "What are you doing?"

Ivy looked at Tara and the hair she held in her withered hands. What had she done? It was just a glamour. Everyone should see that. But they didn't. And, Ivy had to admit, the glamour was rather cruel.

Glamours at this level were also forbidden.

Tara stared at Ivy, "Why?" she shrieked. "Do you have to be so heartless?"

Everyone was still staring at her. Devlin absently squeaked his toy.

Ivy waved a hand, removing the glamour. "I—I didn't mean it. Look, Tara. It's just a glamour, see? You're *you* again. Not that you weren't you. But now, well you're *really* you."

Her friends stood and stared between them. It was as though no one dared to breathe. Couldn't they see it wasn't a real spell? Couldn't they see it was just a glamour?

"I don't believe you. You're *horrible!*" Tara frantically felt her hair, her face. No matter how freaked she was, Tara wouldn't turn her back on Ivy. If she had, she'd catch her normally perky, pretty reflection in the window. "I wasn't aiming spells like that at you. You don't have to be so...sadistic."

Ivy waved her hand, casting another spell. Tara screamed as she felt something land on her head.

"Is that...is that a tea cozy?" Shayde asked.

It was. A knitted tea cozy was the most harmless thing Ivy could think of. Her grandmother had them.

Tara wheeled to see her reflection. She was still for a moment, taking in her usual perfect image. Then, she snatched the tea cozy from her head and threw it at Ivy, hitting it with a second spell. The tea cozy burst into flames and landed at Ivy's feet.

"What's gotten into me?" Ivy said, putting her face in her hands. "Maybe I *am* turning into a dark witch."

Her friends gathered closer, still clearly shocked.

Nick put his arms around her shoulders. "Hey, *I* don't think the Curse of the Tea Cozy is exactly dark magic," he joked half-heartedly. "It's the book, isn't it? You went back and read more of it."

She shrugged away from him. This isn't what she wanted to hear right now. It wasn't the book. It was *her*. She glanced up at Tara, making sure she was okay.

"A little fire and smoke scare you, Ivy? I beat you at your own pathetic game and Spike's safe," Tara taunted, but her voice had an odd quiver to it.

Ivy did feel completely beaten. Not by Tara, but by the whole day. Still, she had to get Spike back.

"Send Spike out here, Tara. Don't make this harder than it needs to be. I don't want Spike because you..." She fumbled a bit. What should she say? Because Tara was dating him?

Well, just who had lizard breath now? Tara was going to need a whole tin of breath mints.

The humorous thought disguised as false bravado didn't do a lot to make her feel better. She stared at Tara, hoping she wouldn't sound as though she were pleading, though that was closer to the truth. She *hoped* that she could manage to sound tough—something she didn't feel. "I want him because turning Spike into a human in the first place was wrong. I should never have done that. Spike belongs to Gareth. Tell me you at least have common sense enough to realize that."

Tara shook her head. Slowly, and with her chin raised in

defiance, Tara eased backward into the restaurant's doorway. Like Ivy, Tara was also trying to seem tough, but the only person she'd fooled was herself. Tara's wide eyes betrayed her. Tara looked as scared as Ivy felt.

Chapter 17

Ivy waved as Shayde pulled away from the curb in front of Nick's house. She wasn't sure if she was glad Shayde had left or not. At least werewolf ears wouldn't be listening, but her best friend was her comfort zone, too.

She smiled nervously at Nick, unsure of what to say.

"Ivy…" He paused, as though speaking hurt him somehow, then rubbed a hand through his hair. "Geez, where do I begin?"

They came to rest on his front porch, each taking a seat on the top step, Devlin lying on the step below them. It was dark now, except for the sliver of light the moon provided.

Ivy sighed. This wasn't easy. How could she be certain he wasn't playing her? "What do you *really* want with me, Nick? Is it me or the books?"

"Does it matter?" he asked, his voice terse. "If I said it was you, would you believe me? Would you give up this fascination with Dean?"

Nick's response wasn't what she'd expected. *Would* she believe him? *Would* she give up the chance to date Dean after dreaming about it for so long?

"Didn't think so," Nick said somberly. He stood and fumbled with his car keys. "Come on, I'll take you home. I know you've had a really bad day. Let's not make it worse, okay?"

She wanted to say something, anything, but the lump in her throat wouldn't let her talk so she nodded. Today *had* been pretty awful, and she could see it had been bad for him, too. Maybe he was telling the truth. Could she take that chance? Maybe not just yet. She needed more time to sort everything out.

Although Nick lived just a few minutes away Ivy thought the silence between them felt like hours. Every once in a while Devlin whined or squeaked his toy, although even he seemed to understand something wasn't right and finally curled up on the back seat. Nick pulled into the driveway. The front porch light shone brightly, while the house itself remained dark. With late fall approaching and the first frost already on the ground, the only sound was the wind making the barren tree limbs creak as they rubbed against each other.

Nick left the motor running. "Ivy," he said, touching her hand as she started to get out. She slid back into the passenger seat. "I understand. I really do. It's about you. Not the books. Never has been, although I do want them, yes. I'll explain if you'll go out with me again. If you're not seeing Dean."

The lump in her throat returned and Ivy swallowed hard, forcing it back down. She nodded, not knowing exactly what she was nodding to. Yes, she'd go out with him? Yes, she believed that his interest was strictly about her? This time, he didn't stop her as she got out and pushed the seat forward to allow Devlin to jump down.

Closing the car door sounded so loud, so final. Nick put the car in reverse and backed down the driveway. She had to say something. She couldn't let him go like this. "Nick!"

He stopped, but didn't pull forward. "I can't wait for you forever, Ivy. Even if you're worth it."

She watched the Mustang's taillights until it rounded the corner and vanished from sight. Devlin whined and she bent down to stroke his fur. "I don't know what I'm going to do either, Dev. No idea at all."

She entered the house as quietly as possible, careful to

keep Devlin's leash from jangling as she returned it to the hook by the door. She fully expected her mother to be furious at her for storming out of the house.

"How was your date?" Her mother wanted to know. From the shakiness of her voice in the darkened living room, Ivy thought this question sounded like small talk in preparation for the real topic of discussion.

"It went okay," Ivy lied softly.

"Do you want to talk?" Her mother's voice still had a quiver to it, like she'd been doing some crying of her own and Ivy wasn't sure if that meant she was in deeper trouble or not.

Ivy's heart felt like dead weight falling into the pit of her stomach. She hadn't meant to hurt her mother. Not intentionally. Her mother needed her, counted on her. Ivy always felt she had to be strong for the both of them. She took a seat in the chair across from the sofa. The light from the porch gave off just enough light to outline her mother's features.

"I'm sorry Mom."

"Me too, Ivy. I shouldn't expect you to understand." The table lamp switched on with an indifferent wave of her hand. She looked at Ivy for a moment, then shut her eyes as though to recall, or possibly block out a memory.

"You were young. You didn't know him very well. To you, your father was the greatest person on Earth, full of surprises and wonderful magic. He did things no one else could do—not a witch nor wizard nor demon. He could cast complex spells in seconds, and I swear he could do them without uttering a single word or a moment's concentration. You look like me, Ivy. But your powers are more like his. You were starting to do strange things before he left. It wasn't normal for such a young witch to have the kind of magic you did. We talked about it many nights after you were asleep."

Her mother gave a small choked laugh. "Well, *I* talked

about it. He insisted he was just a pretty clever wizard and you had inherited nothing more than that."

"But his parents were a normal witch and wizard, right?" Ivy asked in earnest.

"Your dad never met your grandfather. He barely remembered his own mother. She died when he was young. He only remembered that she was a beautiful and kind witch."

Ivy let out a small sigh of relief. She hadn't wanted to hear she was related to a dark Kindred of any sort. "So it's probably some fluke, right? I'm not a dark witch or something... *freaky*, am I? I didn't inherit anything... evil?" Tears had started to spill, and Ivy wiped at them furiously and drew herself up. She wouldn't cry. Not in front of her mother who'd cried enough for both of them over the last nine years since her father had been gone.

"You're a *gift*, Ivy. Don't ever let anyone tell you otherwise. Yes, you are different, but you couldn't be a dark witch if you tried. Your heart is too good. I'm sorry for worrying so much. I probably worry more because of just how special you really are."

Ivy managed an uncomfortable smile. "Mom, why did you name me Ivy?"

Her mother sighed and turned her head with her own bittersweet smile, remembering. "Your father's idea. I wanted Rose, after your grandmother. So we compromised and named you Ivy Rose. Good thing, because your father seemed so insistent. He believed if we named you after one of the most powerful plants known to witches it would bring you luck and keep you safe as you grew older."

"In the book I found," Ivy said, "There are stars marked next to Nightshade and Wolfsbane."

Her mother nodded. "Hanna and I were pregnant at the same time. She thought Ivy was such a cute name, she borrowed *Magic for the Garden* and after your father, of all people, suggested a few names, Hanna decided on Shayde and Bane. But she never marked it with stars. I did that. Pregnancy hormones, I suppose. Hanna and I were just so excited to be sharing that part of our lives together."

A sudden horrible thought occurred to Ivy, and she wanted to be alone. Without telling her mother about the other two books, there wasn't anything else to ask, anyway. "Mom, if it's okay, I'm going to bed now."

"I think we could both use a good night's sleep." Her mother got to her feet and followed Ivy toward the stairs.

"And Mom? Thanks." Ivy hurried up the stairs.

"For what?" her mother called after her.

"For not grounding me after I stormed out of here tonight," she called back.

"If you don't catch Spike soon, I just might," her Mother said, trying to sound authoritative.

Later, as Ivy opened *The Rise of the Dark Curse*, she wondered if her mother would still have thought she wasn't a dark witch. The black tendrils of mist swirling out of the book did not deter her this time. This time, she didn't feel nearly as afraid. Ivy turned the pages, curiously noting how the drawings shifted and moved about. Spiders scurried up the margins, spinning webs around letters. Bulges appeared from behind the pages as though something, or someone was on the verge of escaping from them. People shifted and turned to stare at her. Words whispered up from the musty pages.

She knows... she sees...

Devlin let out a low grumble. She supposed he'd had enough of her magic for one evening.

"Five minutes," she promised him. "Remind me."

He lay down to watch her.

The Rise of the Dark Curse had a lot of dark secrets. But Ivy knew the answer to one of them—her father had absolutely been the one to take the books from Helen Skinner and bury them in the graveyard. Had the books affected him, too? Were they what turned him? If he was the dark wizard everyone thought, then why had he gone and left them behind?

What was stranger yet was that someone had strategically left the other two books for *her* to find.

Chapter 18

When Ivy arrived at her locker the next morning, she found Shayde waiting for her. Shayde was leaning against the locker, arms folded tightly around her books. She gave Ivy a rather lackluster smile. In all the years they'd been friends, this meant one thing—Shayde wanted to talk and was very uncomfortable about it. After dwelling over her dad's involvement half the night, this wasn't the conversation Ivy planned on having.

"Uh-oh," Ivy said. "I know that look."

Shayde hung her head. "Don't kill me for this, okay?"

Ivy opened her locker with a quick charm. "Promise. I won't even turn you into Malibu Zombie like I did Tara. Witch's honor."

The joke only got another small smile from Shayde. "And that's the other thing I want to talk about. You'd never have hexed Tara like you did if it wasn't for that book you keep carrying around. Get rid of it! This whole thing is really creeping me out."

"And have someone else find it? Or worse, know I've hidden it? No way! Someone meant for me to have this book. That guy who was there in the graveyard wanted *me* to find it."

Shayde cringed a little. "You're scaring me, you know that? Listen, I'll help you. Whatever it takes to put this whole thing behind you and get rid of that book. I'm just afraid it has to be real soon. I swear, if I see you getting any weirder, it's intervention time, 'kay?"

Ivy smiled. Shayde was a true friend. Always had been. Ivy stuffed her jacket into her locker. "Sure."

"There's more," Shayde said, sheepishly. "I want to talk about you and Nick."

Ivy shook her head. "Shayde, just drop it."

Shayde raised her eyes to Ivy's. "When are you going to stop doing this to yourself?"

"What are you talking about?"

"Pretending you don't feel anything for Nick. Pretending you're over the hurt when your dad left."

Ivy frowned. "I AM over it. And I don't think that way about Nick." She rolled her eyes and sighed. "Alright. He's cute, but that's all. Nothing else."

Shayde was determined to get the most use out of whatever soapbox she'd gotten up on today. "No. You're not over it! And how could you be? You loved your dad more than almost anyone else in this world. He felt the same about you, Ivy. At one time, he did. You don't just get over that and it's affecting the way you think about Nick."

Ivy started to walk away. She'd had enough of this. "I don't want to get into this, Shayde. We'll be late."

Shayde wasn't deterred. She blocked Ivy from leaving. "I'm your friend, and before you sabotage yourself, I'm going to tell you this and *you're* going to listen!"

Ivy sighed heavily.

"Everyone can see it except you. There's definite chemistry between you and Nick. You won't give him a chance all because of this foolishness that his dad and yours were friends—"

"That's not the whole reason," Ivy interrupted.

"And because you're afraid to *feel*, Ivy. You're afraid to fall for someone. You're afraid to take a chance."

Ivy blinked. "That's not true. I'm taking a chance on Dean. I like Dean."

Shayde tapped her foot, clearly irritated.

Good, Ivy thought. *We're bonding. A real share the experience kind of thing.*

"Are you even listening to yourself? You know perfectly well Dean will go back to Tara. You know that all you really want is a few days, maybe a kiss or two. You're just trying to see where you fit in—"

"Jeez, you sound like my mother."

"Oh! I forgot! Little Miss Stubborn. So determined to prove she can't be wrong. Well, you're wrong about Dean. You're wrong about your feelings toward Nick. Speaking of..."

If Ivy hadn't been ready to walk away before, she was now. Only one problem. Her feet wouldn't move. Sauntering down the hallway was Nick.

"I'm interrupting again, aren't I?" he asked.

Shayde shook her head. "Nope. Actually, it's *good* timing." She gave Ivy a long stare before heading off to class.

"Nick, look, I'm really late. I'd like to talk about last night, but I've gotta get going," Ivy hooked a thumb over her shoulder.

"Sure. Hey, you okay?" he asked.

Ivy nodded. "Yeah, it's Shayde. She...never mind. It's not important."

"Hey, Ivy," Dean called out behind them.

Ivy wanted to groan. This whole morning couldn't get much more awkward.

Dean gave Nick a brief, dismissive nod. The muscles in Nick's jaw tightened, but he didn't budge. Dean shrugged as if to say, *suit yourself,* and turned to Ivy. "You want to get together later?" He flashed one of his winning smiles, then stole a sideways glance at Nick. "Unless you've got other plans."

Ivy wanted to run, to leave both of them standing there. Nick and Dean stared at her, waiting for a reply. If she said she had plans, which she didn't, Dean would walk away. Again. If she said she didn't have plans it was as good as accepting a date with Dean in front of Nick.

"I..." she faltered, shifting her panicked gaze from Dean to Nick. This really was one *hell* of a morning.

"See you around, Ivy," Nick said and walked off in a huff. Several lockers rattled noisily, their dials spinning. The fluorescent lighting flickered and buzzed.

"Wow. Such a temper!" Dean said in mock distaste. He brought his flawless face closer to Ivy's, the smell of his cologne intoxicating. She backed up, bumping into the lockers.

"Guess I'd be a sore loser, too, though." Dean moved closer still. Ivy felt helpless to do anything except stare at his beautiful blue eyes. The whites really did look glacial in comparison.

Without warning, he leaned down and kissed her.

This was what she'd waited for, worked so hard for. She returned the kiss, letting her lips feel the warmth of his. It felt wonderful.

And yet inexplicably and *terribly* wrong.

Ivy pushed against him, resisting. He slipped his arms around her waist and pulled her closer.

"Don't tell me you're hung up on Marcelli," Dean murmured in her ear.

Ivy squirmed out of his grasp. She wanted to tell him she wasn't, but something stopped her. Doubt? Was Shayde right? "Are you still interested in dating Tara?"

Dean seemed to think about this. "Well, yeah. Sort of. Don't go getting all jealous on me, okay?"

Ivy glanced at the clock on the wall. They were both late for class.

She should have been jealous, but she wasn't. In fact, she wasn't sure what to think. He'd been all she'd dreamed about, and now that Dean had become a reality, it wasn't at all what she'd imagined.

So much for Adonis. Along the way, somehow, she discovered that legends—Greek, Roman, or otherwise—weren't all they were cracked up to be. It had been a really good kiss, but it had been missing something, some spark. Her thoughts went back to Nick.

Damn it, Shayde! It's your fault for putting that thought in my head and ruining what should have been a perfect kiss.

But, hadn't it been there all along?

"I'm not jealous, Dean."

Dean looked puzzled. "You're not?"

Ivy backed away, already setting off for class. She shook her head, then turned and ran down the hall, fully aware Dean was staring after her.

For once, she didn't care.

Ivy slipped into Chemistry a full five minutes late, pleased to see that Mr. Evans wasn't there. She slid in next to Raven and quickly stowed her book bag under her chair as though she'd been in class the whole time. Mr. Evans seemed oddly temperamental lately and barely tolerated breathing in his class much less being late.

Raven didn't look up from doodling in her notebook. Her sketches were always complex and completely awesome. Ivy made a note to ask if it was a natural talent developed over the years or some vampire ability.

"Matthews, or Marcelli?" Raven asked, still sketching.

Ivy frowned.

"The reason you're late. You're never late. So, which one was it?"

Ivy let out a heavy sigh. "It's just been one of those days. Nothing more."

Someone snickered in the back of the class.

"That's not what I overheard," Raven said. "You've got two of the hottest guys in school on a string. That makes *you* Ms. Popularity. It's totally pissing Tara off." With this, Raven grinned.

"Is *nothing* I do private?"

"Nope."

"Nice," Ivy said sarcastically. She turned away from Raven and thumbed through her book quickly, tearing one of the pages.

"So. Which one ticked you off?" Raven asked, setting down her pen. "With your growing reputation as a dark witch, you'd think they'd know better."

"I'm *not* a dark witch," Ivy snapped.

"Just kidding there Ivy. Yeesh. One black magic spell and you lose all sense of humor. You're getting as moody as Mr. Evans."

Ivy shot her a dark look, but considered Raven's previous comment to be spot-on about one thing—one of them really had ticked her off. Nick. If he hadn't... well, if it weren't for Nick she'd be happy with Dean. It occurred to her that Nick was the one she was angry with instead of Shayde. She was *not* falling for Nick. She wouldn't let it happen.

"At least you're not the only one late." Raven motioned to Kevin, a dark-haired Regular who strolled in and took the empty seat behind Ivy.

"I don't think Mr. Evans will be here anytime soon," Kevin said. "And neither will Kim. Looks like the Kindred are in the spotlight again. There's been another murder."

Ivy spun around in her seat.

"Yeah," Kevin said, leaning forward. A lock of hair fell over one eye. The entire class was perfectly quiet, everyone tuned in to the conversation at the back of the class. "Kim's sister, Angela, was found murdered this morning."

For a moment, Ivy couldn't breathe. It was happening. Again. Another murder. "She's dead? Are you sure?" Ivy asked, although there wasn't any need to doubt Kevin. His dad was a cop. Kevin wouldn't joke about something like this. No one would.

"Not just dead. Murdered. "In the hotel on Walnut.

They found Angela next to a tub filled with blood. *Her* blood from the sounds of it."

Raven's eyes went wide. "Blood? Someone drained her in the tub?"

Kevin brushed back the lock of hair, his eyes meeting Raven's. He spoke louder to compensate for the ongoing murmurs of their classmates. "She wasn't drained *in* the tub. Just over it, then she was dumped on the floor, hands and feet bound. But, from what I overheard my dad say, someone *bathed* in her blood. Pretty freakin' gross, huh? There was a washcloth in the tub."

"Was it the same guy that attacked Mr. Nash?" Ivy asked.

"Nope," Kevin replied. "Not a dude at all. From the bloody hand and footprints they found in the bathroom, and a single eyewitness who saw the murderer leave, it was a woman dressed in costume, just like that other guy was. Well, not like the other guy, since the woman was wearing a gown and that'd be *really* weird if they'd both dressed alike. Still, I bet they're in on it together."

"Let me get this straight," Raven said. "A woman in costume kidnapped Kim's sister, bled her out over a hotel tub, then bathed in her blood with the body growing cold on the floor next to her? Man. That's brutal."

"So. It's a vampire, right?" Kevin asked.

Raven gave Kevin a hard stare and ran her tongue over an incisor.

"Or not." Kevin nervously retrieved his things and moved to Kim's empty seat.

The class grew noisy with talk. Ivy scribbled down a name on a piece of paper and slid it over to Raven.

Countess Elizabeth Báthory

Raven frowned.

Ivy leaned closer, whispering into Raven's ear. "From *The Book of Lost Souls!* It's got to be the Blood Countess! Reportedly, she bathed in the blood of young maidens thinking it'd keep her from ever growing old."

Raven let out a sigh. "Well, that's a relief."

"*Relief?*"

"Yeah," Raven replied. "The killer isn't a vampire. Just a vampire wannabe."

Chapter 19

It was nearly an hour before Ivy could pry herself free from a small group of admirers who Shayde and Bane had started to refer to as the *Ivy league*. Life before popularity had been so much easier. Before school let out, she'd turned down an invite to go to the mall in Burlington from one of the girls on the cheerleading squad and another from a group of sophomore witches who had started their own spell casting practice club and wanted Ivy for their president.

Ivy called Nick on his cell phone once she reached the school's parking lot, which was now mostly empty. He had to know what had happened to Angela. She dismissed the idea that it would also be a good excuse to see him. After the third ring, she thought she'd have to leave a message, but then Nick answered.

"Nick, hey, it's me—"

"I'm a little busy," came his curt reply. He sounded angry, but Ivy also detected that he was hurt. She wondered if he knew Dean had kissed her, and that she'd kissed him back.

"I need to talk to you about what happened today." She considered the significance of her choice of words and added, "About the book. I know who else has been brought back from the dead."

"Oh." His voice seemed less distant now, but the anguished undertone was still detectable.

Why did he make this so hard? Why did he make *everything* so difficult? His continued silence made it all the worse.

"You still there? Can I meet you someplace?" Ivy could hear people talking in the background. No answer. "Nick, I need to see you," she pleaded. "Where are you?"

"Are you bringing Dean?"

"No." She'd answered so quickly that there had hardly been a pause after his question.

"I don't know, can we talk about it tomorrow?" he asked.

"Don't be like this. Please? Where are you?"

There was a long pause, then Nick sighed. "I'm at Saludo's."

"I'm on my way," Ivy said enthusiastically, and snapped her cell phone shut. The restaurant was just around the corner. She slid behind the VW Bug's wheel and the engine came to life. It'd been months since she'd actually turned the keys in the ignition. How had she ever managed life before mastering automation spells?

A few minutes later, Ivy walked into Saludo's. She spotted Nick and his uncle sitting with one of the waitresses—and Phoebe. No wonder Nick hadn't wanted her to stop by. Boy, was this going to be awkward.

Ivy made her way over to them just as the waitress slid out from the table and disappeared behind the kitchen doors. Nick's Uncle Joe leaned across the booth, speaking softly. Phoebe hung on his every word. As much as Ivy would have liked to find fault in Phoebe's actions, Ivy couldn't blame her. Nick and his Uncle were discussing who might have had motive to set Vlad the Impaler loose on Northwick.

Phoebe gave Ivy a *you are such a loser* look that any hope Ivy had of Nick *not* knowing about the kiss went right out the window. Demons banded together and Phoebe was far from over Nick. Ivy noticed how close Phoebe sat next to him and she fought off the urge to glare back.

It wasn't jealousy. It was the principle of the whole thing.

Sure. That was it. A glare like that deserved one in kind. Especially from Phoebe.

Nick's uncle looked up at her and brought their conversation to a quick close. "Can I get you two anything else?" he asked Nick and Phoebe. When they both shook their heads, he turned to Ivy. "How about you, Ivy?" he asked politely enough.

"Sure, a Coke, thank you," she replied, and he left the booth to get Ivy's drink. Awkwardly, Ivy slipped in across from Nick. Phoebe continued her *I know what you did* stare. "Hi Phoebe," Ivy said.

Phoebe didn't reply. Instead she slid out from behind the table and placed a hand on Nick's shoulder. "I'll be right back. You two need to have a talk." With another chilly glance in Ivy's direction, Phoebe strutted off to the ladies room.

"What's all that about?" Ivy asked, not really wanting the answer.

"I know about the second murder," Nick said. "Don't get any more involved in this. Maybe you need to let us demons handle it. I know you found the other books and all, and you're really bent on the idea someone meant for you to find them, and that's great, but let the last book be a demon matter."

"I thought you said it was both witch *and* demon. And I'm in this, Nick. Everyone thinks I'm a dark witch. I've done a couple things that have made me start to think they're right."

Aside from the glamour on Tara, she hadn't told anyone about the night she almost hurt Devlin, and couldn't bear to. She didn't want to tell anyone that the book had started to talk to her—to recognize her, or her own *need* to keep the book nearby. "I need to find out who's behind this before the book *really* starts to affect me."

Nick reached across the table, briefly touching her wrist before withdrawing his hand. Clearly, he was still upset, maybe even a little angry. He looked around the restaurant, as though the words he wanted to say could be seen somewhere. He let out a deep sigh.

"I can't be near you. I can't do this. You don't know what you do to…" He paused and took a deep breath. "I'm sorry that you've got me all wrong. The only reason I've never dated anyone for very long is that it didn't feel right. I'm not nearly the player you think I am. And the things I've done, it's like you when you changed Spike. I never meant to hurt anyone."

A group from school ushered in.

"I don't know what to do, Nick," Ivy said softly.

"About the missing book or us?"

It took a second to answer. "Either," she said honestly.

"But you do know what to do, Ivy. On both counts." His voice was gentle, yet firm. "I need to go help my uncle." And before Ivy could say another word, he slid out of the booth and walked away, shoulders slumped.

Ivy stared after him.

"I'm trying to make him forget about you," Phoebe said.

Ivy hadn't seen her approach.

"He's pretty hung up on you. He knows about you and Dean in the hallway. Guess I let it slip. He's going to need some consoling. You got what you originally wanted, Ivy. You have Dean. I want Nick. Do as he says and stay away from him. I don't need much more time to make him mine." Phoebe leaned forward and whispered, "I'm *real* close."

Phoebe's hand touched her and a hot bolt of pain shot up Ivy's arm. Ivy jerked away. Phoebe left the table and made her way to where Nick stood at the counter, busily folding silverware inside napkins. She bumped him slightly with her hips, and smiled flirtatiously.

The ache in her wrist had been nothing compared to the pain coursing through her entire body at the sight of Phoebe's open flirting with Nick. She wanted to hurt Phoebe back, wanted to... to what? She thought she could hear the book beckon to her from within her book bag. Ivy stood, feeling unsteady on her feet. She slung the book bag over her shoulder and pushed her way through a small crowd heading toward the table.

"Ivy?" Nick grabbed her wrist as she went past. His touch felt warm over the spot that had hurt just a second ago, but it didn't begin to make the ache in her chest feel better.

His eyes were softer than before, concerned. "Are you okay?"

She was definitely *not* okay.

"I've got to go," Ivy said, her feet still reluctant. Her whole body felt like it'd been stung and Ivy knew tears were only moments away. She turned and ran out of Saludo's. She heard Nick right behind her, and then Phoebe calling him back.

Ivy sat in her car for a minute or two, trying to steady her breathing. Nick didn't follow her outside. When she thought she'd collected herself enough, she drove home with the radio blaring. She had no right, no right at all to expect Nick to wait for her to make up her mind. Hadn't he said as much? He couldn't wait forever, even if she were worth it.

And what *was* she contemplating? That she preferred Nick over Dean? Did one kiss mean she and Dean were really even dating? Because in her mind, they weren't. It had been just a kiss. Why did everything she felt for Nick seem so out of control?

Ivy excused herself after dinner and went to her room, locked the door, and curled into a ball on the bed. Her phone buzzed, and Ivy checked the incoming text message.

It was from Dean.

I hear you're still trying to get together with Nick. No big deal. It was just a kiss, right? We'll keep it our secret then?

She snapped the phone shut.

Devlin licked her face and whined. "Go lay down," she said, turning her face into the pillows.

Not to be ignored, Devlin chewed at her hair and pawed at her arms. When she turned onto her side, he whimpered, blinked his almond-shaped eyes, and lay down. He scooted forward and flipped onto his back, resting his head on her pillow.

Ivy kissed his soft fur. "I hate my life, Dev."

Devlin made a half-grrr, half-yowling noise that Ivy took as agreement.

How could she understand how to conjure up some of the most complicated spells possible for a witch her age, get straight A's in every subject, and yet she couldn't understand the person capable of all this grief—herself? She could control how far or how high to levitate a book, but had no control of the tears falling onto her pillow.

She thought she'd wanted Dean. She'd thought his wavy, golden hair, chiseled face, piercing blue eyes, and brilliant smile had been enough. That riding off his popularity would help define herself somehow. How long had she dreamed about kissing him? And yet today, when his perfect lips pressed against hers, she felt... nothing. No tingle, no spark. He had been all she'd dreamed about the past few months, and now he meant almost nothing to her.

She also hated being popular. Hated having all eyes on her like some actress on center stage. It annoyed her that everyone expected her to come up with some outrageous or cool new spell. Whatever was happening *wasn't* cool. And she hated that she was supposed to behave a certain way just to give people something to talk about. Maybe that was the worst.

This wasn't what she'd planned. *Nick* wasn't what she'd

planned. She wanted to hate him along with everything else, be mad at him for Phoebe, be mad at him for interrupting her plans with Dean, but she couldn't. She wanted to let him go, let him fade from her thoughts and found she couldn't do that, either. Far from it.

You know what to do, Ivy. On both counts.

And she did. There were a lot of things Ivy needed to set right. Tonight, she'd see what she could do about two of them. As she wiped away her tears, Ivy picked up her cell phone.

Ivy waited until one in the morning, when she knew her mother would be sound asleep. Then she dressed in a pair of black sweats and a black sweatshirt that she enlarged enough to wear a long sleeve t-shirt underneath, eliminating the need for a bulky coat. She pulled her hair into a neat ponytail and levitated a white baseball cap from the top shelf in her closet.

"This won't do," she said quietly to Devlin, who sat on the edge of her bed, alert and wagging his tail. With a flick of her finger the cap changed color to black. Ivy positioned it on her head, and checked her book bag to ensure she had everything she needed: the power cord to her computer, an empty shoe box, a pair of sunglasses she'd already hexed to have night-vision, a squirrel squeaky toy (also hexed so that only Devlin would hear it), and *The Rise of the Dark Curse*.

"It's important that you stay close, okay?" she said sternly to Devlin.

He grinned and wagged his tail.

"*Devlin!* I mean it. No mischief."

He stopped grinning, then sneezed indicating he understood.

"That's better. Otherwise, you'll have to stay."

Ivy made a lifting, upward movement with her hands and her bedroom window slid open without a sound. She fetched the power cord from her book bag and zipped the bag shut. She hung the cord out the window, where it unfurled and changed into a vine, vigorously sprouting leaves and reaching the ground in seconds.

"Okay Devlin. Come here."

Devlin hopped from the bed and stood beside Ivy. The end piece of vine spread out once more, down inside the window and around Devlin's legs and under his chest and belly making a harness. The vines rose, lifting him off the floor and out the window, gently setting him on the ground below.

Ivy hoisted herself over the windowsill, took hold of the vine and repelled down the side of the house. When she reached the last couple of feet from the ground, she pushed off from the house and landed next to Devlin. She set the book bag down and unzipped it. Instantly, the vines traced their way into the bag, leaves retracting, until it became a power cord once more. A quick downward motion of her hand and her bedroom window slid shut.

"Shh!" Ivy warned Devlin as she collected the book bag, and the two took off down the darkened street as fast as their sneakered and padded feet would carry them.

Chapter 20

Only a vampire could stand directly under a streetlight and still blend in with the surrounding shadow.

"Who knew you had it in you," Raven said, shoving away from the lamppost. Like Ivy, she had dressed in all black. Unlike Ivy, Raven didn't need to wear black to be stealthy.

"I just hope this works," Ivy replied. "I feel guilty, though. Shayde is going to kill us when she finds out we didn't ask her to come along."

Raven waved a dismissive hand. "If we get caught, she'd be in big trouble. The way I see it, you're a good friend. Besides, you didn't ask Shayde because she would have thought this was another one of your bad ideas. I, on the other hand, happen to like it."

Ivy scanned the park. It was quiet, with a slight hint of breeze rustling the dry leaves. Raven was right about that much. Shayde would never have agreed to this. But, good thing Bane did. Well, he at least agreed to sneaking out in the middle of the night when he heard Raven was in on it. "Where's Bane?"

Raven grinned. "Behind you."

Although he could be anywhere, Ivy didn't see him. She peered at the trees, bushes, and benches. Devlin saw him first. He let out a little gruff and bounded forward, tail wagging. Ivy saw two gold eyes blink as the black wolf stepped out into the open from his hiding spot in the shadows, the tiniest wisps of chilled air coming from his nostrils.

Ivy smiled. "Hey, Bane. Ready?"

Bane nodded his huge, furry head.

Ivy sighed deeply. "We're probably going to be grounded until Christmas, but this is our best chance. With Devlin and Bane's sense of smell and your hearing, we should be able to find Spike and nab him while he's sleeping." She turned to Bane and Devlin. "Okay, guys, do your thing."

Devlin sniffed the ground and Bane sniffed the air. They exchanged glances and other body language too subtle for Ivy to understand. As much as the twins had taught her about canine posturing and body language, it was too complex and too fast for Ivy to take it all in. Still, she understood that the movement of the tail (to the left or right, high or low), the ears, mouth, even the tensing of certain muscles had meaning. If Shayde had been here, she could have translated Doglish or whatever it was that Bane and Devlin were saying to each other.

Bane and Devlin set off toward the woods. Ivy and Raven followed.

"It's a shortcut," Raven said. "Before Bane changed into wolf, I told him what you said about Tara probably hiding Spike on her family's estate."

"The sooner we get there and nab Spike, the better," Ivy replied. "The property is pretty large, so as long as he isn't in her house we'll be good to go. It's a long hike to Tara's though. We'll be up half the night."

Bane grumbled, his ears flattened sideways against his head, clearly unhappy about losing sleep. It wasn't making Ivy exactly happy, either.

"So," Raven said as they ventured from the open field and into the woods. The grass had grown tall here before dying off. Long strands of grass stood clumped together. "You want to tell me how you came up with this idea about the Prescotts, Spike, and Dean?"

In the pale moonlight, Ivy could see that Bane and Devlin each had one ear turned backward, obviously listening in.

All the better to hear you with, she thought.

Ivy adjusted her book bag. "Spike's too hard to catch during the day. He'll be sound asleep now. I'm betting he's staying outside somewhere. Maybe in the gazebo out back. Tara's Grandmother lives with them and I've heard Tara complain that she's an insomniac and wanders the halls all night, which means he can't be staying inside the house."

"O*kay,*" Raven said tentatively. "Sounds reasonable. Tara's family would have nothing to do with the likes of Spike in their house. We nab him, you change him and put him in the shoe box. I'll take him back to Gareth. But, do you want to explain what catching Spike has to do with Dean?"

"If we catch Spike, Tara will want Dean back."

"Have you been sniffing potions?" Raven asked.

"He'll never leave himself without a girlfriend. He's too vain. He thinks I'm too hung up on Nick, so he'll try to get Tara back. So, all I have to do is get Spike away from Tara."

Raven gave a wide, Cheshire cat grin, and Ivy felt uncomfortable.

"So, you *finally* admit there's a thing between you and Nick. Spill. I want *all* the sordid details."

Ivy felt heat rise in her face and hoped the darkness concealed it. "Yeah well... No! There aren't any sordid details. It's just that I'm not as interested in Dean as I thought. And, well, Nick is *sorta* nice. Don't go jumping to conclusions. It's not really like *that* between us."

Especially with Phoebe still in the picture, Ivy thought.

Raven smiled and bit her lip. "Too bad. Sordid could be fun. You don't know what you're missing."

"Ugh! I don't feel *that* way toward Nick," Ivy said, brushing off a web she walked through.

"Denial, much?" Raven asked, as she hurried past,

twirling in the moonlight that shone through the trees.

Bane coughed, a sound akin to Devlin hacking up hairballs. Or Guinea pigs. It didn't take lessons in Doglish to understand he was agreeing with Raven.

"Can we change the subject?" Ivy asked, and everyone held their tongue, although she swore the occasional heavy panting ahead was Bane's way of laughing.

The remainder of their walk, no one said another word about Nick. When they finally exited the woods, Ivy was the only one winded. Vampires didn't sweat and Bane and Devlin were none the worse for wear at all. Once again, when it came to anything physical, she was the wrong type of Kindred—built for spells, not a fast-paced, forty-minute hike over varying terrain and obstacles.

They continued their silent trek two blocks over to the Prescott manor. The brick and stone house was huge, at least five times the size of Ivy's house. A four-foot stone wall with iron spikes enclosed the premises, and lights illuminated parts of the house and the surrounding shrubbery.

"Let's go in from the far side of the property," Ivy said. "I don't want to take a chance that Spike will hear us coming."

Raven huffed. "You're traveling with Kindreds with padded feet or undead stealth and grace. The only one he'll hear coming is you. Got a spell for that?"

Ivy groaned. "Probably. If I'd brought a normal spell book."

"You mean to tell me you didn't bring anything other that the *bad* spell book?" One moment, Raven was five feet away, and the next, she was standing eye to eye with Ivy. "Good thing I'm not hungry," she said, tapping Ivy's forehead. "Because there's no blood flow."

"Let's just get in there and get him before anyone wakes up," Ivy said, walking off, leaving everyone to trail behind her. When they were far enough away from the lighted gates and the driveway, Ivy stopped alongside the stone wall and retrieved her book bag.

"Are you kidding me?" Raven said. "You're not using anything in that book on me! Think of some other spell."

With that, Raven stepped back several feet from the wall, got a vampire running start, and using a nearby tree for leverage, she scaled the wall. Once at the top, she spun, balancing on the iron spikes. "See you guys on the other side!"

Raven wiggled her fingers in goodbye fashion and disappeared into the shadows on the other side of the wall.

Bane and Devlin looked warily at Ivy. Raven was right—she shouldn't use the book. There had to be another way over the wall. But the lure of the book inside her book bag was too tempting. It'd be faster. Certainly, there was something there she could use—a levitation spell perhaps.

Ivy unzipped the book bag and slid out *The Rise of the Dark Curse.* The vine trick she'd used on Devlin wouldn't be enough to lift them all over the wall at the same time. But, maybe the tree could! She stared at the massive oak for a moment. The whispers from within the book beckoned to her. Yes! The tree...

The book opened, the pages turning on their own. It slowed near the middle of the book, a single page hovered upright, then turned back a page. An Animation spell. Devlin whined, sounding far off and distant. Ivy read the spell on the page, not really sure it was her voice she heard or if they were coming from the book *through* her. She wanted to yell at Devlin, to tell him to shut up, that she knew what she was doing.

It isn't right. You're using the book on Devlin and Bane.

But that wasn't entirely true. She was using it on herself, too. Guilt still washed over her.

Just get everyone over the wall and then close the book. One spell. One hopefully harmless little spell.

A single voice from within the book seemed to laugh at

this.

The air around Ivy sizzled with unseen energy. Tree limbs resembling gigantic gnarled hands reached from the other side of the wall. They snatched Bane and Devlin off the ground with enough force that they both yelped in surprise. They struggled to free themselves from the tree's tight grasp, and the tree held them tighter.

"*NO!*" Ivy called out.

The book was calling to her, telling her she shouldn't care how they all got over the wall, just that they did.

Another branch reached down and Ivy scrambled to grab the book and her book bag just as the tree snapped her up, knocking the wind out of her. All three branches hurled them over the wall, depositing them onto the ground like rolled dice. Devlin whimpered once before getting his feet under him. Bane growled and snarled as he trotted off and Ivy was glad she couldn't hear what he was saying.

She couldn't blame him, really.

Raven was in her face, shoving her. "How much longer, Ivy? How much longer before that book gets someone hurt? Before you bring back something as bad as Vlad or the Blood Countess? You want to mistreat Devlin like that, well, that's bad enough. I never would have thought you'd ever harm him. But Bane isn't your dog. Touch him again with another spell like that and I'm off my diet, so help me."

She shoved Ivy once more and Ivy landed on the ground with a thud.

Raven turned and walked away. She glanced over her shoulder. "Get rid of it. Soon."

After a few more creaks and groans, the tree returned to normal. Ivy shoved the book into her book bag. "I'm sorry," she barely managed to say.

Raven glared at her again as she checked on Bane.

Ivy sat, stunned, horrified, and ashamed that she'd

actually used a spell from the book on anyone she cared about. But, it was as though she couldn't help herself. "I know. I have to get rid of it. As soon as I find a safe spot for it. Someplace no one will find it."

Devlin belly-crawled over to Ivy, ears down, tail down in submission. He licked Ivy's hand.

Ivy rolled over on the ground to kiss him. That was twice she'd let Devlin down. "Never again, buddy. I promise. I won't open it again." She scratched the side of his head. "I really didn't mean to hurt any of you. Please, believe me."

Raven came to stand above Ivy and extended her hand. "Burn it if you have to," she said as she helped Ivy to her feet. "Rant over. Let's go lizard hunting."

Somehow, Ivy didn't think the book would burn. Ivy believed that *The Rise of the Dark Curse* had a built-in defense mechanism. It was dangerous enough that it would prevent *anyone* from destroying it. And, if the *The Book of Lost Souls* was even worse, then she might almost feel sorry for the person who had it.

Shadows from an abundance of trees and shrubs dotted The Prescotts' lawn.

Raven, Bane, and Devlin wasted no time hurrying away from anything else that might grab hold of them and waited for Ivy by a sundial in an open area twenty feet away.

Ivy dusted herself off. "Maybe we could bury—"

"*Shhh!*" Raven said. She pointed to Bane and Devlin, who's attention had become heavily focused on something around the corner of the house.

They had picked up a trail and were trotting off across the massive lawn. Ivy and Raven followed, temporarily losing them in the topiary garden. It was difficult to tell which was a manicured bush and which was just a shape in the darkness. The moon had clouded over and wasn't any help.

Raven paused, listening again. "There," she whispered.

Two sets of gold eyes glittered ahead of them. Ivy retrieved the pair of hexed sunglasses from her book bag, leaving the top unzipped. The landscape took on an eerie black and green appearance. It was much easier to see everything now.

Raven motioned for Ivy to follow. This was why Raven was the better choice to bring. Raven's night vision wasn't as good as Shayde's but she could hear just as well, and, more importantly, Raven was the risk taker.

They hadn't gone far, maybe another couple hundred yards, when even Ivy's ears picked up on the faint voices. Bane and Devlin crouched low, slinking into the shadows. Raven and Ivy darted the short distance from the wide open to the shadows along the house. The voices were getting closer. Too close.

Raven dropped to the ground, camouflaging herself in a small section of shadow and Ivy followed suit.

Ivy didn't need the night-vision sunglasses to see who was there. Tara and Spike rounded the corner, laughing. Their hands were entwined, and they were spinning each other around in circles like children. They crashed to the ground not twenty feet from where Raven and Ivy lay. Neither of the girls dared to move a muscle. Bane and Devlin were thankfully hidden in the bushes farther away.

"That was fun!" Spike said breathlessly as he lay on the ground next to Tara. "Let's do it again!"

Tara curled up next to him, resting her head against his chest. "Can't we just lie here?" She gave him an affectionate squeeze.

Spike's eyes diverted to a low flying moth. He snagged it, shoved it into his mouth, and chewed slowly. He looked at Tara guiltily, but she hadn't seen.

"Uh, okay. But can we play on the trampoline again later?" he asked cheerfully.

"Do I need to give you another Maturity potion?" Tara asked, snuggling into him. "You're much more fun that way."

So *that's* why he was acting so human! It's wasn't entirely the Intelligence spell, although that had been bad enough. Tara was doping Spike up with a Maturity spell. She couldn't believe it. Tara? A *Maturity* spell? Well, Tara had to be going through it like Kool-Aid in order to get Spike past her own maturity level.

Ivy moved slowly, trying to reach her book bag without making noise or drawing attention, but Tara and Spike were too close. She had to be careful.

Tara leaned across Spike and kissed him. He held her in his arms and they continued to make out noisily. Ivy thought about the moth and felt her stomach lurch. Raven made soft gagging noises beside her.

Ivy sought out the bushes Bane and Devlin had ducked into. Gold eyes flickered from the dark and Bane took a tentative step out. His gaze swept between Ivy and the large gates in front of the wide and extensive drive.

Go back! she wanted to tell him. *They'll see you!* Finally, Ivy understood he wanted her to see something important. Bane shifted nervously, his gaze darting between where she and Raven were hiding to the direction of the gates and the street beyond them. Ivy peered through the gates and saw a car—*Dean's* car.

"Dean's here," Ivy whispered into Raven's ear.

"Hmm. This could be fun," Raven whispered back.

Hardly.

When it came to capturing Spike, if it weren't for bad luck, she'd have no luck at all. It was bad enough Tara had snuck out to see her boyfriend in training, but now Dean was here, too.

This wasn't going to go down easily.

With Tara so close to Spike, Ivy didn't dare recite the incantation. If she went with plan B and captured Spike as is, they'd never make it over the stone wall before Tara could cause enough commotion to wake the entire household, much less bring Dean running.

The *good* thing was that Dean was spying on Tara, which meant he still had an interest in his ex-girlfriend. Still, they couldn't lie here the whole night. Ivy knew she had to do *something*. With Dean watching, Bane and Devlin couldn't venture too far from the safety of the bushes. Well, Bane at least.

Devlin poked his head out. Luckily, with his earthy colors, he still blended in with the autumn colored shrubbery. He yawned and looked around, indicating he was bored. It was only a matter of time before Devlin would find something else to do.

There weren't many things Beezlepups enjoyed more than getting into mischief. She had to come up with something soon before Devlin blew their cover.

Chapter 21

Devlin blinked, his adorable little face making her smile. He was nothing if not lovable and the very definition of cute. It was why she spoiled him with toys the way she did. She felt around inside the book bag and retrieved the hexed toy squirrel.

In between Tara's squeals and groans and all the disgustingly loud kissing, Ivy surveyed the situation. If Devlin saw the toy, he'd charge from the bushes at full throttle. Devlin never could resist anything that squeaked. But, maybe she could use his fetish to distract Spike and Tara.

Ivy decided the best course would be to hover the toy high enough off the ground so that it wouldn't *immediately* attract his attention. She also needed to keep it along the backside of the row of trees they'd come from where the toy would be concealed in shadow most of the time. For a second or two, the toy would be in plain sight to Tara and Spike, should they break from their marathon kiss and look up. There was also the chance Dean might see it. If he saw the toy, he'd also know Ivy was there. No one else carried dog toys with them. She also had to consider that the toy would be out of her sight for a few seconds. If the toy hit a tree then, she'd lose control of it *and* her only chance.

Slowly, she levitated Devlin's toy. It sailed along, hovering about ten feet in the air and moved slowly toward the trees, keeping to the shadows until the last possible second. It went flawlessly. Tara and Spike were still too involved with each other to see the squeaky toy drift behind the trees.

Raven tapped her urgently.

"Not now," Ivy hissed. Almost there, almost there. The toy should be popping out from behind the trees and toward the bush Bane and Devlin were hiding in just a second or two.

Raven was not to be ignored. "Dean's not in the car anymore. I don't know where he is, but…"

At that precise moment, Dean stepped away from where he'd been standing—the trees. He scanned the yard and Ivy watched his hand tighten around Devlin's toy squirrel. Devlin pelted from the bushes like his tail was on fire. Tara and Spike broke from their embrace, startled.

Upon seeing Devlin charging toward him, Dean tapped the squirrel, reversing Ivy's Silent spell. He squeezed the toy again, and it let out an audible squeak.

"Plan C," Raven said, getting to her feet.

"But, we don't have a Plan C!" Ivy replied.

"It's called improvise!" Raven said, running for Spike.

Dean shot out a spell that knocked Raven off course, sending her into a tree.

"What the hell did you do that for?" Raven shouted.

"Lizard breath is *mine!*" Dean growled. "I'm going to rip him apart."

Devlin was a blur as he raced toward Dean, with Bane right on his heels. Dean was so focused on Spike and Tara, he didn't see it coming.

But Ivy knew it was going to hurt. Big time.

Devlin and Bane slammed into Dean at the same exact moment. Dean hit the ground with a hard, "*Ooompf!*"

"This is your fault, Ivy!" Dean shouted. "That kiss was supposed to be between just us."

Ivy shook her head. "Spare me the break-up speech, Dean. It never would have worked anyway."

Tara was frantically smoothing her clothes and her hair. "It was a Kissing spell, Dean. I swear. I didn't want to be with him." She pointed to Spike. "Ivy showed up and hexed me," she blubbered.

"What a little liar!" Raven scoffed. "You were unbuttoning his shirt, and *that* wasn't part of any Kissing spell!

Tara fell to the ground and hugged Dean.

"It's okay, Tara. She tricked us both. But, I'm still going to kill that lizard." Dean's next spell missed Spike entirely and hit the ground instead. A dirt clod exploded, showering Spike. Spike cowered, raising his hands to shield his face.

Ivy grabbed the power cord from her book bag, and with a quick wave of her hand, the cord changed into the vine, spreading out in Spike's direction. The vines raced up Spike's body, binding his arms and legs at his sides. He yelled for Tara, but Tara ignored him.

Devlin wrestled the squeaky toy from Dean and took off with it across the lawn, squeaking it loudly.

Great. Now the whole house would wake up.

Please let the grandmother be deaf.

"Devlin!" Ivy called after him. But, Devlin had already vanished around the corner of the house and out of sight.

"Bane!" Ivy called. "Go get him and make him be quiet."

Bane darted off after Devlin.

The vines pulled the frantic Spike toward her. He cried out again for Tara's help. The cacophony of barks, squeaks, voices, and screams was enough to wake the whole house. Ivy expected Tara's parents to come running outside any minute.

This mission was about as stealthy as Godzilla at a petting zoo.

"*Nooooo!*" Spike wailed as Ivy started her incantation. "Not the terrarium! I know stuff. I have a note for you. It's very important."

This had to be some sort of lizard trick. "A note? From who?"

"A man gave it to me while I was in the woods hunting for bugs," Spike explained.

Ivy gave Spike a suspicious glare. "Who gave it to you? What does it say?"

Spike tried to shrug. "I've never seen him before. And I don't know what it says. I can't read. Tara said she'd teach me."

"Give it to me, then," Ivy demanded.

Spike rolled his eyes. "Duh! I can't. You've got me tied up."

Ivy stared at him for a moment. "You're lying."

"No I'm not. Look!" He eyed the vines binding him.

"I mean about the note!" Ivy snapped.

"Oh. Yeah. It's about the books," Spike said.

After a moment's standoff, Ivy undid the vine spell, all except for a section around Spike's left wrist.

Another clump of dirt exploded near Spike.

"Run!" Raven shouted. She nearly slammed into Ivy and Spike, grabbing them both by the arm and dragging them with her. "Unless you can out duel Dean *and* Tara."

She could, maybe. But not while keeping control of Spike. Besides, all the racket would bring out half the neighborhood at this rate.

"Bring back that lizard!" Dean demanded. "I'm gonna skin him for moving in on my girlfriend."

Raven laughed. Ivy hardly found any of this amusing.

"Well, if nothing else, your plan to put the two of them back together worked, but I wouldn't advise matchmaking as a living," Raven said as a sprinkler head went flying past them.

Ivy didn't release her hold on the vine as she ran. Great. Now the mission to change Spike had become a *rescue* mission to keep him from becoming boots. What next?

Unless there was some other way off the property,

Devlin and Bane couldn't be far. Ivy and Raven ran, dragging Spike with them, finally coming to a wooden gardening shed the size of a small barn. Bane and Devlin were involved in a tug of war match with the squeaky toy.

Raven pulled Ivy around the corner of the shed just as Dean blew off a piece of siding with another spell. Bane let go of the toy and he and Devlin scrambled to take cover with them.

"Geez, Bane. If you really want, I'll get you a squeaky toy for Christmas," Raven quipped.

It earned her a raised lip and a growl from Bane.

Ivy poked around the corner and fired off a Repelling spell. "We've got to get off the property."

"You take left, I'll go right," Ivy heard Tara say to Dean.

"Behind the Cypress," Spike said. "There's a gate."

"There's a *gate?*" Raven said. "You should of thought of that before you used that stupid book."

Ivy shrugged. "Yeah, well, I didn't think I needed blueprints for this, you know?"

Tara rounded the corner, taking aim at Ivy. "Gotcha!" she said.

Ivy ducked, letting the spell completely miss her.

"Dean's coming," Raven warned.

"Run," Ivy said. She took off for the gates, Spike in tow, although he didn't seem to need any coaxing. Lizard or human, Spike understood he was in serious trouble with Dean.

Bane and Devlin made it to the gate first, both whirling about to defend Ivy and Raven if they needed to. The gate was locked.

Ivy raised a hand to the gate. "Unlock!" She handed the vine holding Spike to Raven. "Go, I'll hold them off. Get to the woods."

Raven snatched the vine and dragged Spike through the gates. Bane and Devlin whirled around after Raven just as a tree limb crashed to the ground. Ivy raced out of the gate behind them, turning to fuse the latch shut with a hex.

Secure in the knowledge that the spell would give them time to escape, Ivy ran, following her friends into the woods and the relative safety of darkness.

Chapter 22

They didn't stop running until they were well into the woods and Ivy could no longer keep the same pace as the others.

"Slow down, guys. I don't think they're behind us anymore." She stopped, rubbing at the stitch that had developed in her side. "Bane, are they following?"

Bane looked about carefully, nose in the air, sniffing. Puffs of his breath hung in the cool air like ghosts. After a second or two, he relaxed and blinked, signaling that he thought they hadn't been followed. He turned and walked onward, nearly disappearing into the darkness.

Raven shrugged. "I don't hear them, either."

"We got lucky. I can't believe no one in the house heard all that racket," Ivy said.

Spike snorted. "That's because Tara cast a Quieting spell so no one would hear her sneak out." He frowned deeply. "Dean was really mad, wasn't he?"

A Quieting spell? Tara put a *Quieting* spell around the perimeter of her own house? Ivy was almost impressed. "Yeah, Spike. He was."

"Guess I can't go back to hiding in the gardening shed or down by the river," Spike said with a mournful shake of his head.

Somewhere in the woods, an owl hooted, followed by the fateful scream of a small animal. Walking in the woods may have been routine for Bane, but not Ivy. Sounds carried out here, and Ivy was aware of every noise around them. Much of the forest was nocturnal, as evidenced by the hooting owl. Thin threads of moonlight weaved around barren hardwood trees and fragrant Evergreens, finally pooling here and there on the forest floor in patches of faded silver.

Raven laughed, filling the air with human sounds for which Ivy was grateful. "She kept you in the gardening shed? The one Dean took a chunk out of? Wait until the Prescotts' see all the damage."

Ivy shrugged. "They probably won't know. If Tara and Dean hurry, they can fix most of it and blame the rest on moles or something. The one thing I'm betting on is that Tara won't tell anyone we were there. That would be admitting she was out with Spike and her parents think she's perfect. Spike isn't exactly the type of dating material the Prescotts' would approve of, much less have the town know about."

"Hey!" Spike protested. "I resent that!"

Ivy looked at Spike. She needed to change Spike back into lizard form before something else happened. Or, before the Intelligence spell and whatever else Tara had done made matters worse.

A twig snapped somewhere around them, indicating something larger than a rabbit or field mouse was afoot. Bane and Devlin froze, listening. They exchanged a quick glance then continued on. Ivy wondered if it was just a deer or something... *else*. Like two murdering souls from a particular book.

"It's nothing, right guys?" Ivy asked, hoping she was being silly and that nothing other than the five of them and maybe a raccoon lurked in the cloak of the forest. Ivy peered into the blackness, unable to see much except the skeletal branches of trees. Bane and Devlin came to a halt.

A dull ripping sound, similar to falling timber, broke the

silence. Ahead, a medium-sized tree uprooted itself, scooted to its right about twenty yards and plunked itself down. The air suddenly smelled rich and musty as writhing tree roots burrowed back into the soil like oversized worms. The tree's branches creaked as it bent forward, frantically smoothing the surrounding soil. Another tree busily tamped down the upturned earth its neighbor had vacated.

"Oh. Well, that explains it," Raven said.

Ivy sighed, relieved it was just the stupid Trekking trees. "Knock it off, okay? We're Kindred."

The trees stopped their forest floor housekeeping and bowed. With a few final creaks and groans, they stood still. A lone root wriggled in the dirt.

"What was *that?*" Spike asked, clearly alarmed. "Trees can *move?*"

"*Some* of them," Raven clarified. "Just Trekking Trees. They like to confuse hikers—get them lost. It's sort of a game to them. Back when a lot of trees were harvested it also saved them from being chopped down and made into furniture."

Ivy smiled. "My grandmother had a table made from one. Of course, she didn't know what type of wood it was when she bought it at a garage sale. She had to get rid of it. The crazy thing kept darting across the house one too many times during dinner."

"They can see, then?" Spike inquired, sounding equally horrified and intrigued.

"Yeah," Raven said. "If you get close enough, you'll notice the knots in the tree are really eyelids."

Ivy turned to Spike. "Look, Spike. I've got to turn you back into a lizard now."

"NO!" Spike yelled. He tugged hard on the vines binding him. Despite his best efforts, Spike was no match for Raven's vampire strength.

"The note!" Spike said.

Ivy stopped to get the shoebox from her book bag. "I'll

read it when I change you. Once you're safely tucked away."

"But...but you won't be *able* to," Spike said. "These aren't really store bought clothes. They're charmed. Tara did it. You turn me and the clothes disappear. Maybe the note, too."

Ivy considered this. "Very smart, Spike. Too smart."

Spike stood tall with a triumphant grin on his face. "Well, thanks to you and the Intelligence spell you cast." Spike tapped the side of his head. "That, and lizards have a high survival instinct. Besides, Tara told me how the spell worked."

Ivy walked up to Spike, palm extended. "Fork over the note. If there really *is* a note."

Spike grinned. "The man who handed it to me said he needs more time. I promised him I'd give you the note." Spike cocked his head. "I lied."

Ivy and Raven exchanged glances.

"Who are you talking about? He needs more time? For what?" Ivy asked.

Spike waggled a finger. "*Not* telling. You'll turn me into a lizard."

Ivy took the vine from Raven. "Fine. Raven, search his pockets."

Raven shot Ivy an incredulous look. "No way!"

Ivy sighed. They really didn't have time for this. "Since when did you get all modest?"

"Geez! He's my brother's pet lizard. That's just a little too weird, even for me," Raven replied.

"Besides," Spike said. "The note isn't in my pockets. It's in my underwear."

Bane let out a series of barks that sounded almost like a hyena.

Ivy slapped her palm to her forehead. Next time, she'd be more careful and pay attention to spell warnings. Spike might not be Einstein, but he had been under the Intelligence spell long enough to think this through, juvenile as it was.

"Wait," Spike bargained. "Let me stay human for a little while longer and I'll give you the note." He scanned the area around him and frowned. "Hey, where are all the bugs?"

"It's fall," Ivy said, irritated. If it weren't for bad luck, she wouldn't have any luck at all. His *underwear*? "There aren't many bugs out anymore, Spike. You got lucky with the moth. Nice snack, by the way. And when the next hard frost hits, there won't be *any* bugs."

Spike looked oddly nervous. "Moth? What moth? And I don't *eat* bugs. Not anymore. Um, I was just curious about what happens to the bugs. You know, just filling the old noggin with more knowledge. Really? None?"

"Anyway," Ivy huffed. "Maybe I'll make you tell me *without* a deal.

Spike swallowed hard and diverted his attention to the surrounding woods and thick underbrush.

"Don't even think about it, Spike," she warned.

"She'll zap you into next week," Raven said.

"You wouldn't. Gareth would be very upset," Spike said.

"He'll get over it when we get him another lizard. Something less scaly," Raven replied, easily maneuvering over a large, recently fallen oak. There was just enough room between the trunk and a thick branch that partially propped the tree off the forest floor, allowing Bane and Devlin to crouch down and scoot underneath it.

Spike easily hoisted himself on top, and he offered Ivy his hand, helping her across. "I'm being reasonable," he said. "Just for a few days. Tomorrow, I'll tell you even more."

He shuffled some leaves away from the fallen log. "Say, do you know if these woods are where Gareth used to find Tiger beetles to feed me? Um, I mean, did you know that they taste *almost* like sweet and sour chicken?"

Ivy's stomach lurched. Tiger beetles? She'd never eat

sweet and sour chicken again.

"Never mind me! Just spouting off odd facts. Still, it's sad. Maybe I could catch all the bugs and save them from whatever is making them disappear." He took a deep, steadying breath. "Anyway, about keeping me human in exchange for the note and some information. Deal?"

"And why would we believe you'd actually help? Why should we trust you?" Raven asked. "Is there a code of ethics among lizards?"

Spike frowned, considering her question. "Why should you trust me? That's simple," he said with a snort. "Because I'm betting Ivy *won't* hurt me. She saved me from Dean back there. *She* has a conscious. That doesn't take smarts to figure out, you know. That's a lizard thing. Animals are better at studying their environment than humans. Humans talk. Animals observe. I want to be human for a while longer. Just until the end of the week. Then you can change me back. This is your fault, you know! Unless I can stay human until the end of the week, I'm not telling anyone anything! Besides, I'm the outcast here. Gimme a break."

Unbelievable! Gareth's pet was giving her a guilt trip. "I'm really starting to not like you."

They emerged from the woods and back into the park. Without the chirp of the summertime crickets it was eerily quiet. Even the wind had long called it a night. Glistening dew sparkled the tips of the now dormant grass like miniature prisms.

Ivy glanced at her watch—two fifteen. Today was going to be hell.

"So," Raven piped up. "Since you've been suckered by Catcher of the Flies here, what are you going to do with him?"

They'd reached Bane's house and Bane ambled up the steps, head and ears hanging low from exhaustion.

Ivy shook her head. "Keep him in the guest bedroom, I suppose."

"Interesting," Raven said. "But, it's your funeral when your mom finds out. Not that I'm turning into Shayde on you or anything. Just thought I'd throw that out there. Don't get caught, okay? Takes the fun out of everything. Wouldn't want that, would we?"

"It's only until Saturday night," Ivy replied with a yawn. Fatigue had taken a toll on her, because she distinctly heard herself say, "How hard can that be?"

Chapter 23

Ivy woke with a start, nearly flinging Devlin from the foot of the bed when her alarm went off at six the next morning. He grumbled and chose another spot to lie down.

Her muscles ached, protesting movement this early after only a few hours of sleep. Bringing Spike back hadn't been easy.

Spike...

Ivy sat up in bed. "Oh, no! Devlin, tell me I didn't really tell Spike he could stay in the guest bedroom."

Devlin raised his head and looked in the direction of the hallway. He whined and scooted under the blanket.

She tossed the covers back and flew from the bed, practically tripping over the shoes and clothes she'd left haphazardly on the floor in her rush to get into bed. She wrenched her door open and shot down the hallway.

The guest bedroom door was closed, like always. But, her mother's bedroom door stood open and Ivy froze at the sight of the empty bed. Her mother *never* got up before six-thirty since she didn't have to be at the library until eight-thirty.

"Ivy?" her mother called from downstairs.

Devlin ran past Ivy, crouched low, head shifting left and right, ears pinned sideways against his head. He took refuge in her mother's room, disappearing under the bed. He whined faintly.

Raven's words echoed in Ivy's head. *It's your funeral when your mom finds out.*

"Be there in a minute," Ivy called back, wondering if her funeral would be open, or closed casket.

Quietly, she opened the guest room door, her eyes taking in the whole room at once. It wasn't difficult. The room contained a twin-sized bed with an old, dark headboard that needed refinishing. Her grandmother's antique lace bedspread covered the bed. On either side of the bed were two small off-white square night tables.

What the room didn't contain was Spike.

Neither did the closet.

Closed casket. Definitely closed casket.

She ran to her mother's room, knelt next to the bed, and lifted the dust ruffle. Devlin peered up at her, his ears still slightly down and sideways. Usually, this behavior meant he'd done something wrong, like peeing on the roses, digging under the fence, or regurgitating rodents on the living room carpet.

This time, however, it was as though he were agreeing with Raven's prediction last night of Death by Parent.

"Hey, buddy. Can you pick up Spike's scent anywhere?"

Devlin retreated further under the bed.

"What was I supposed to have done? Leave him outside?"

Devlin cocked his head. "*Gerrrr.*"

"Yeah, well, does it *sound* like Mom's found him? I don't think she's using her happy voice." Her mother didn't sound angry, but sometimes, when she was really mad, she tried to sound calm. Still, it could mean she'd found Spike and wanted an explanation on why he was still human.

Devlin scooted backward.

"Come out of there and help me!" she whispered.

He crawled to the far side of the bed and turned his head away from her, tucking his coyote-like tail beneath him.

"*Ivy?*" Her mother's voice was louder this time and Ivy heard the bottom stair creak.

"Chicken," Ivy muttered. She quickly got to her feet, hurried out of the room and dashed down the stairs, nearly colliding with her mom who met her halfway.

"Are you okay, sweetie? You look pale."

"I didn't sleep well last night," Ivy replied honestly.

Okay, she said sweetie, so maybe she hadn't found him. Yet.

Her mother sighed heavily. "I know the feeling." She turned and trudged down the stairs like a much older woman. "I've put on some tea. Looks like you could use some, too."

Ivy patted her leg and clucked for Devlin to follow them. She heard a shuffling noise and a slight whine from her mother's bedroom, but Devlin wasn't budging from his hiding place under the bed. For a moment, Ivy considered joining him.

The good news was that Spike might have escaped. Of course, that was bad news, too. What if Spike was downstairs in the kitchen? Then, bad news didn't begin to cover it.

Her mother waved a hand as they passed through the living room and the blinds opened, letting in light from what promised to be a clear, sunny autumn day. "There's a Council meeting at the library at seven o'clock."

Ivy stared out the window and sighed with relief. Her mother was up and about already because of a Council meeting. Not because she'd found Spike.

Outside, Mrs. Bennett from across the street was watching her seven-year old son, Josh, walk to the bus stop. Two women wearing fleece jogging suits traveled briskly past the house. Mrs. Quincy's cat, Midnight, stalked birds in the neighbors yard. If Spike was out there, she didn't see him. Ivy glanced around the living room to make sure Devlin wasn't looking out the window as well. Midnight needed a break. The room was as clean and neat as always.

No bulge behind the drapes. No one crouched behind the sofa. No Spike, no Devlin. Ivy joined her mom in the kitchen.

"There was a break-in last night over at the Harrisons' house on Culver Street," her mother said.

Ivy's heart skipped a beat. "What happened?"

The teakettle whistled on the stove and with a wave of her mother's hand, a cabinet door opened and two white tea cups with matching saucers flew to the table. "The Harrisons are okay. They'd just gotten home from dinner at the Wok of Life. A man and a woman ran out the back door. The Harrisons were lucky. They think the people who broke into their house were the same people Gloria saw attack her brother-in-law. Nothing was taken that they could tell, but the whole house was ransacked."

A drawer opened and spoons fluttered out, finding their way alongside the teacups. A couple of tea bags and the sugar bowl soon joined them. Milk from the fridge lazily drifted to the center of the table. The teakettle hovered above each cup long enough to pour hot water before returning to the stove.

Ivy took a seat across from her mother. "What does the Council plan to do?"

Her mother shook her head. "Form a hunt. Whoever is behind this can't hide if all the Kindreds work together. Two murders and a break-in. I've taken extra precautions and put Warning spells around the perimeter of the house this morning. If someone steps foot outside after dark, I'll know."

Good tip, Ivy thought.

Two bowls and a box of cereal floated toward the table.

"The Council is concerned that these people were..." her mother took a deep breath. "That they were looking for those...books. The ones the Council thinks your father took from Helen Skinner. Unfortunately, someone is using one of them—*The Book of Lost Souls*. The Council is saying that the people who broke into the Harrisons' house are conjured souls." She shook her head. "We've been dreading it for years. Well, ever since your father left. The Regulars never knew exactly what those books could do. I suppose that the Council will have to tell them. We just need to band together and catch whoever is using these books again. Dark magic like this always leaves a mark. Sooner or later, the Kindred using it will go mad. Hopefully, we'll catch them before something else tragic happens."

Ivy suspected that her mother would have a fit if she knew her own daughter had one of Skinner's books hidden in her room. If the town were searching for the person responsible, it'd be best to keep quiet. If anyone found out she had *The Rise of the Dark Curse*, they might just stop searching for the real culprit and blame her for what had happened. She was her father's daughter after all.

"Mad?" Ivy repeated.

"Oh, yes," her mother said. "At first, they just become a little irritable. Act out of character. It's the books. It's like an addiction. They start to blatantly perform darker and darker magic, not caring who sees them. Eventually, they just lose themselves to the book and the evil inside it. Problem is, it could take the better part of a month. If you see anything, Ivy, anything at all— someone acting odd or anyone performing illegal magic, then you let me know immediately."

"Mom?"

"Hmmm?" her mother said, raising the teacup to her lips.

"You don't think he's back, do you?"

The teacup fell from her mother's hands, spilling tea onto the table. They both knew they were speaking about Ivy's father.

"No," she said firmly. She got to her feet, took the dishrag and began to manually clean up the mess. She rubbed the table harder and harder, even though there wasn't any more tea to clean up. "Now, you listen to me, Ivy! He's *never* coming back. If someone has the books, they've taken them from your father and returned here. Northwick would be the last place I'd ever expect to see your father. The Council would find him, *destroy* him like he did Helen Skinner."

Ivy stood and tried to stop her mother from wiping the varnish off the table. "Mom, it's okay."

But it wasn't okay. Her mother had loved him. Trusted him. He'd left her with a daughter who's eyes reminded her of him. He'd left her with a broken heart and shame. Her mother had spent years regaining the trust of the Council and the town.

Ivy shouldn't have said a word about her father. Not one word. If there was any hope of telling her mother that she had one of Skinner's books, or that Spike was somewhere in the house—and still human, that hope was now gone.

Chapter 24

Stopping her mother's hurt and anger was like trying to stop a hurricane. She snatched the dishrag back from Ivy and stormed over to the sink, wringing the cloth repeatedly. "He said he just wanted to make sure Helen Skinner wasn't going to start using them again. He promised me that he was stronger than anyone else who had been allowed to see or read the books. He *wasn't*."

Her mother tossed the dishrag aside. "I'm sorry, sweetie. I didn't mean to…"

Ivy hugged her mother. "It's okay. I understand."

Devlin finally made his way to the kitchen. He stood in the doorway and barked.

Her mother turned toward him. "Well, it's about time, sleepy-head. I suppose you want your breakfast?" She made a single swoosh with her wrist and Devlin's bowl floated up onto the counter. Devlin backed up and barked again.

"I think he needs to go out," her mother said.

Somehow, Ivy doubted that the need to water the roses or chase Midnight was Devlin's problem. She was betting he'd found Spike.

Her mother glanced at her watch. "Is it seven already? I have to go or I'll get stuck sitting in the back of the meeting. Don't forget, I've got the girls night out dinner after work. There's leftovers in the fridge if you want them. I should be home around nine."

Devlin pawed at the floor. Ivy put a finger to her lips. Devlin whined, but acknowledged the need to wait and be quiet.

Her eyes darted around the room in case Spike had mysteriously shown up at a very inopportune time. Thankfully, it was still Spike-free.

"I'll be *fine*, Mom. Shayde and I were planning on studying tonight anyway."

Her mother moved from the kitchen to the small coat closet in the foyer, pausing with her hand on the door knob. Devlin cocked his head, eyes trained on the closet.

"Ivy? Would you mind emptying the dishwasher?"

Ivy held her breath as her mother opened the closet door. Inside, there were only coats, the vacuum cleaner, and a few pairs of boots. "Sure. No problem."

"You'd better let Devlin out," her mother said. "He's acting like he's going to spring a leak."

Indeed Devlin did seem rather anxious. He was standing on the sofa thrashing a pillow. Patience wasn't in a Beezlepup's nature. The front door had barely closed and her mother was still bustling down the walkway when Ivy snatched the pillow from Devlin's mouth. He'd managed to tear it. "Repair," Ivy said, dragging her fingers across the small holes in the fabric.

Devlin was now upside down and wedged between the rest of the cushions. "*Narrn, narrr!*" he said, staring up at her.

"Okay, *okay*! What?"

Devlin sprang from the sofa and raced to the cellar door. Ivy didn't particularly like the cellar. It was damp and smelled of moldy earth. In the summer, it harbored spiders and some of the largest millipedes she had ever seen. Ivy opened the cellar door and Devlin raced ahead of her. Whoever was down there, Devlin knew them. She took a few hesitant steps down. The cellar light glared cold and yellowish against the walls. "Hello?"

No answer, only a distinct rustling followed by a loud crash. It sounded like an entire shelf of who knew what—the cellar was where they stored everything from Christmas decorations to gardening supplies—had careened to the ground.

"Ouch! Oh. Hi Devlin," came a weak voice.

Ivy hurried down the steps and around the corner. Spike was slumped on the cellar floor, a few clay pots were sprawled next to him, and potting soil was spilled across his legs and lap. Devlin started to dig in a small heap of nearby dirt, sending sprays of soil everywhere.

"Devlin!" Ivy complained. He gave her a look that clearly indicated he thought she wasn't any fun, and he wandered off to show his displeasure by chewing on a plastic watering jug.

"What are you doing down here?" Ivy asked Spike, who was rubbing the top of his head and wincing.

"Er, um, I thought it'd be a good place to hide," Spike replied.

"You were fine where you *were*," she said, looking around. Several metal shelving systems lined the wall. The one in the middle had a distinct bend in it. At the very top, Ivy noticed the remnants of an old spider web.

Spike followed her gaze. "Kinda dirty down here, isn't it? I mean, all the old cobwebs and stuff. He forced a small, giddy laugh that sounded both embarrassed and forlorn.

She knelt down next to him. He looked terrible, not just because of the potting soil covering his head, but because it didn't appear as though he'd slept at all. Spike's eyes were wild and bloodshot and dark circles had cropped up under them. He ran a dirty, shaking hand through his disheveled hair.

It was hard not to feel some sympathy for him. He was right. Whatever he was going through, it was her fault.

"What's wrong, Spike?"

"*Wrong?*" Spike nearly shrieked. He cleared his throat

and forced a more normal tone. "Nothing. Everything." He scanned the cellar in his familiar herky-jerky movement before his eyes met hers.

And then it hit her. Ivy reached out and placed a hand on his shoulder. Spike was going through bug withdrawal.

"Why?" he asked, his voice trembling. "What happens to them?"

"Bugs can't live when it gets cold. I'm sorry Spike. I really am. I can change you back right here, right now if you'd like."

"But then what? What happens then? The bugs are still... gone."

"Gareth will buy you bugs from the pet store, just like he always has."

He lifted his head, a shimmer of hope on his face. "Buy them?"

Spike continued to stare at her with soft brown eyes. "Yes, Spike. You can buy bugs from the pet food store down on Main and Elm."

He wiped at his nose. "No. I can't do that."

"Why?" But she thought she already knew. Spike didn't want everyone to know he couldn't get by without eating insects. He didn't want to be seen purchasing a box the size of Chinese take-out full of crickets.

"If I can't find bugs on my own, I'm not buying them," he said with a sniffle.

"I can change you back, Spike."

"No. *Please.* Just a few more days. The man I met down by the river—the one who gave me the note—I'll tell you what he said."

"I don't get it, Spike. Why do you want to stay human? You're not doing very well. You obviously miss your...bugs."

His eyes found hers. "I'll never have another chance to be human, will I? And I'm not sure I'd want to. Anyway, it's not something the average lizard ever gets to do. It's an amazing adventure. It's like walking on the moon."

What could she say? The guilt trip he'd given her had been one thing. This was something else entirely. She didn't have the heart to turn Spike back. Not yet. Not until he was ready. She'd done enough selfish things lately. Maybe this one act of granting Spike a wish would help remind her that magic could be used for good.

Besides, he looked so darn pathetic.

"Saturday," she said at last. "Don't ask for another day past that." Ivy smiled and offered Spike a hand up from the floor.

"Thank you," Spike said. "Sorry I made such a mess."

She dusted herself off, and with a single wave, motioned for a nearby broom and dustpan. With another wave, the pots repositioned themselves back on their shelves, including the watering container Devlin had attempted to bury in the dirt without success.

"Being a witch does have benefits," she said. "Come on. I've got to get ready for school. And you've got some cleaning up to do yourself. Then I'll drop you off by the Wallace farm. Bees are still somewhat active."

Excitement flickered in Spike's watery, red-rimmed eyes and a smile slowly etched onto his face. "That's right! I forgot. Bees are sort of bland and mushy, and their stingers are tough, but they'll do."

Ivy couldn't remember ever getting ready for school so fast—less than forty minutes from shower to dress. It usually took her nearly ten minutes just to dry her hair. This morning, she'd cast more spells in under an hour than she did most entire days. While her brush and hairdryer coiffed her hair, Ivy applied what little makeup she wore. She rushed out of the hall bathroom to her room, dryer and brush flying after her, styling her hair as she went. The closet and drawers flew open, clothing collecting on her bed.

By the time she gathered her book bag and raced down

the stairs, Spike was just coming back inside with Devlin. "I've got to do one more thing," she said as she strode to the kitchen. With a few swishes and swirls of her hand, the dishwasher opened and dishes, glasses, and silverware flew out. Drawers and cabinets opened and closed as everything found its place. The cereal box and sugar bowl took their respective places in the small pantry and cabinet.

"Whew! Ready," she said. "Let's get going." She gave Devlin a hug and a kiss, telling him to be a good boy until she got home, and then she and Spike scrambled out the door to Ivy's car.

"The man who gave me the note," Spike said. "I'm smarter every day, but I can't remember every word he said because they don't make sense to me. He said he's been watching you and that you've got something the conjured souls will come looking for soon."

"Where did you meet this man?" Ivy asked.

"He was down by the river, like he usually is in the afternoons."

The river? She'd have to go down there and see for herself. She'd have to be careful. The man Spike saw could be the same person who was conjuring souls. From there, she could follow him around and then tell her mother she *had* seen someone acting suspicious. Her mother's description echoed in her head: irritable, acting out of character. All symptoms she was experiencing. "The things he told you, is that what's on the note?" she asked.

"No," Spike said. "He didn't. He says the note is for later. When it's time. Not before then. He says I'll know. I only made up the part about the bargain so I could stay human for a few more days."

Spike frowned. He looked lost, distant. "I don't get what he meant. I'll *know*? And yet, it feels like something big. Too big for a lizard to work through. But, I promised. And I really didn't lie to him, Ivy. But, I've lied a few times since I've been human and it conflicts with the animal part of me. It's like I don't know who or what I am then. That's why I'm willing to let you change me back soon."

Ivy shook her head. "I don't understand."

Spike stared through the windshield. "Because, the longer I stay human, the more I *become* human. For starters, it means things like lying will come easier to me. Raven asked about ethics. While animal's ethics aren't the same as humans, we don't lie. We're always honest. Sure, we eat other animals. We kill. But we *don't* lie. I don't want to lose that part of me. I wonder what happens when I go back to being a lizard. Will I retain some of the knowledge I have now? I think I might. It feels that way. It's probably a hard thing for you to understand."

But, it wasn't difficult to wrap her brain around at all. She'd done a few rotten things lately—putting herself, Devlin, and her friends in danger by using *The Rise of the Dark Curse*. It was as though nothing and no one else mattered right then. She'd been a bit too cruel to Tara. In fact, she'd actually enjoyed it. At the time, all those things had been easy to justify. But, it'd come at a price—trust and the risk of damaging her friendships. And, if she didn't get rid of the book soon, she'd wind up like Skinner. She'd wind up like her father. The last thing Ivy wanted was to hurt those she loved like her father had hurt her. She had to agree with Shayde—the pain he'd caused had managed to change the way she saw things. It was hurting her still.

If she didn't get rid of the book soon, if she didn't find out who was behind all this, then who knew what else she might be capable of doing—of becoming. Ivy didn't want to risk losing the good in herself.

Yeah, she understood Spike's fear perfectly.

Chapter 25

"You let him *go*?" Gareth shrieked.

Several nearby students looked his way. His voice had startled a sophomore girl who dropped her purse, and while retrieving it, she spilled her books onto the ground.

"He's tricking you, Ivy! Why would Spike go on a bee-eating expedition when he's eaten Chinese food and could be dating the whole cheerleading squad?"

There were times Ivy thought Gareth acted like a seasoned teen vampire. This, however, was *not* one of those moments. "*Chill,* Gareth. Spike really is at the Wallace farm. In fact, why don't you go talk to him? I've got a stop to make on my way home, so you can keep him company until I pick him up."

"*Whaaat?*" Gareth sounded frantic and a bit annoyed. "You mean you're not coming with me? You're not changing him back? And what do you mean you're picking him up? Where are you taking him? Don't you care about Spike? There's more than just bees out there Ivy! There's yellow jackets! Spike might not be used to yellow jackets and they sting pretty hard. What if Mr. Wallace sees him? What if he does something to Spike?"

Gareth was well on his way to a meltdown. His black eyes were bulging and the palest hint of color tinted his cheeks.

Shayde and Raven exchanged all-knowing glances as

though psychotic behavior among brothers was to be expected.

Raven pressed three fingers against her brother's forehead as though she were resetting a computer. "Reboot, Gareth. You're frying that little processor of yours."

"He's *my* pet!" Gareth complained. "Or, at least, he used to be. What if someone found Devlin and then just let *him* go?"

Ivy grimaced. Yeah, she hadn't thought of that. She'd just sort of believed that Spike wouldn't run off.

"Geez Gareth, quit *whining!*" Raven said. "I wasn't supposed to tell you, but Mom and Dad bought you another lizard. Will you calm down now?" She threw her hands up in exasperation. "Immortality with you as a brother is going to be impossible. Grow up!"

Gareth sneered at her. "Very funny. We're kind of stuck as teens forever, stupid. Or haven't you figured that out?"

"What*ever*, Gareth. Get over it already. You've got a new lizard. Can't you ever be happy?" Raven unlocked the car doors with her remote. "See what I deal with? He's the only obsessive-compulsive vampire I know. And he's been going through the same hormone crisis since we were changed."

Gareth was well accustomed to his sister's comments, and either he chose to ignore this particular instance, or his mind was set on Spike. Or, maybe it was just another Raven-Gareth sibling thing. Ivy was betting on the latter. Guess sibling rivalry never grew old.

"What kind of lizard?" Gareth asked.

"A Leopard Gecko," Raven said soothingly. "It's *really* pretty—shiny and coppery with black spots."

Gareth was all smiles again. "A Leopard Gecko? Seriously?"

"Maybe you could show it to Spike," Shayde suggested. "He'd probably enjoy that. He hasn't had a lot of lizard company lately."

"Is Bane going to join us for dinner?" Ivy asked Shayde.

She was sure Bane was well rested by now, and he would hardly turn down a Saludo's pizza with extra meat. Shayde, Raven, and Ivy thought it'd be a good night to see if they could come up with a plan to find out more about the mystery man Spike had met, and if he was the same person who had unleashed Vlad the Impaler and Elizabeth Báthory.

"No, he's got practice. Last one before the game against the Bristol Bulldogs on Saturday," Shayde said. "Bane thinks the Bulldogs look a little tougher this year."

"He's mistaking looking tough for looking ugly," Gareth commented. "The Bulldogs don't stand a chance against the Wildcats." He tugged on his sister's coat sleeve. "Can we go now?"

Raven rolled her eyes. "I'll pick up dessert. See you guys later." She and her brother got into Raven's red Saturn and drove away.

"Mind if I tag along?" Shayde asked Ivy.

"No problem. I need to talk to Nick, if that's okay. I figured I'd pick up pizza for our dinner."

Ten minutes later, they arrived at Saludo's. It was a lot more crowded than Ivy thought it'd be for a Wednesday night. Usually, there wasn't as much traffic most weeknights. The place was filled with more Kindreds than Regulars. Most were picking up orders to take home, and the line stretched out the door. Both she and Shayde couldn't help but listen to the conversations around them.

"Well, they're shaken, naturally. Can't blame them. Mrs. Harrison wants them to go to her sister's for a week," someone said.

"Well, we'd better figure this out before midnight, Halloween."

"If we don't find out who's behind all this before Friday... well, I hate to think—"

"How hard can it be? We've got nearly every Kindred in

town on the lookout."

"Who'd do this? Who'd open *The Book of Lost Souls?*" One of the women said as they walked out with their order.

Mr. Evans sat at the counter, his foot tapping impatiently against the stool's rung. Why hadn't anyone ever told him his pants were always too short and that white socks didn't go with dark slacks? Like Shayde and Ivy, Mr. Evans seemed to be listening to the conversations around him.

"It's almost impossible, but I think Mr. Evans looks worse than us," Shayde said as they waited in line at the counter.

Now that Shayde mentioned it, Mr. Evans didn't seem well at all. He was pale, and his hair, if possible, looked greasier than normal and hung in limp strands across his forehead. He rubbed at his temples as though he had a headache or was seriously stressed. She couldn't blame him. The whole *town* was stressed.

"Here's your order, Mr. Evans," Nick said, sliding four large boxes of pizza in front of him. "Sorry it took so long. Hope the other teachers aren't starving."

"Thanks," Mr. Evans said distractedly as he collected the pizza boxes and pushed past Ivy and Shayde.

"That's a lot of pizza," Shayde mentioned to Nick as Mr. Evans scurried out the door.

"Says he and some of the teachers are working late grading papers. He offered to get dinner." Nick's eyes caught Ivy's. "What can I do for you two?"

"Two medium pizzas, half pepperoni, half extra meat," Shayde said, stepping aside and pushing Ivy closer to the counter.

"Hi, Nick," Ivy said simply, only mildly aware Shayde had plunked down the money for the pizza on the counter.

Three more people joined the line behind them and Ivy wondered if Nick would be able to get away long enough to talk.

"You okay?" Nick asked, his voice far less harsh than it had been earlier. Only the slightest hint of edginess remained.

Ivy shrugged. "Yeah." But she couldn't quit staring at him and she didn't feel okay. Her heart thudded painfully in her chest. This was horrible! What idiot ever said that if you really liked someone it was comparable to walking on clouds? It felt more like dodging traffic on a New York freeway.

Nick's face softened. "Give me a few minutes." He motioned toward an empty booth.

Shayde pulled Ivy away from the counter toward the booth. They slid onto the vinyl seats to wait for their order.

"Hey, guys!" Raven said sliding in next to Shayde. "Just saw you guys here and thought I'd say hello. Gareth is down at the pet store picking up bugs for his new lizard."

Nick strode toward them with two sodas in to-go cups. "While you're waiting," he said, scooting in next to Ivy.

Raven nodded to Shayde. "Gareth wants your opinion. On the... Oh, never mind. Just follow me."

Shayde followed Raven's lead. "Be right back." Shayde snagged her soda. "Thanks for the soda, Nick."

Ivy waited until they'd gone outside. "I'm really sorry, Nick," she gushed. "I'm not any good at this."

"Good at what?" he asked, the cold tone back in his voice. Even his dark eyes had an icy look to them Ivy hadn't thought possible.

He's still hurt and still putting distance between us, she thought.

"Dating. Figuring out if it's the right guy or not. If I really like someone, or I just think I do." She hoped he'd say something to let her off the hook, but he just sat there, staring at her like she hadn't finished speaking.

"Don't do this to me, Nick. What do I have to say? Look, I think what you said to me the other night was right."

He raised his eyebrows. "What was that?"

Ivy swallowed hard. "That, we may not be who we end up with, but I think we're both what we need."

She couldn't meet his eyes for fear he'd see how nervous she was. She would not beg for forgiveness. Not even from Nick Marcelli. She waited. It felt like eternity although it was probably less than ten seconds.

"Fine. Never mind then," she said. "Is our pizza ready?"

"In a minute," he said softly. When Ivy finally met his gaze, he offered a slight smile and slid out of the booth. "What makes you think all the sudden I'm really the one? That this is the right thing for you?"

Ivy's insides were in turmoil. Part of her wanted to stand up and kiss Nick in front of everyone. Another part wanted to storm past him and put him out of her thoughts. This wasn't an audition! How could it turn out like this?

"I don't know, Nick. I have no idea when it's really right between two people. I only know when it's wrong. Dean was wrong. All I could think of was you."

Nick's uncle held up two pizza boxes and called hers and Shayde's name.

A smug little grin appeared at the corner of Nick's mouth, but he still didn't say anything.

"Like I said, never mind." Ivy took her soda and shoved past Nick, brushing up against him. She turned, startled at how that single moment of contact made her feel. Nick seemed just as puzzled.

Why couldn't he say anything? Had she spoken up too late? Oh, this was so humiliating and... painful.

She spun around, feeling the weight of his stare— possibly everyone's stare. Snapping up the pizza boxes, she ran blindly out the door, hoping Shayde hadn't wandered too far off with Raven.

Phoebe was in the parking lot leaning against her silver Mazda Miata. Her arms were folded loosely across her chest, but Ivy found nothing casual about the hatred on Phoebe's face. "You should have stuck with Dean."

"Don't mess with me right now, Phoebe. I'm not in the mood," Ivy shot back, feeling a crackling, tingling sensation within her. A low humming throbbed in her ears.

"Or what?" Phoebe jeered. "You might just have some of those new powers everyone thinks you do. That is, if last night's third-rate carnival event when you sent your friends over the Prescotts' wall was any indication. Where did you ever find a spell like that? Still, you have no idea what black magic is until you tangle with me. See, I really *do* practice black magic." Phoebe laughed and placed a finger across her lips, which were curved sardonically. "Shhh! Don't tell."

Phoebe? *Phoebe* was the one who had followed them last night? Where did she think Ivy was going? If Phoebe really did practice black magic, she might be the one behind all this. Come to think of it, she couldn't remember seeing Phoebe the night of the dance. She might have been in the cemetery.

Phoebe grinned. "I see you've put together a little piece of the puzzle, Ivy. You always were so smart. You were so busy paying attention to Dean and the rest of your little friends that you never noticed me. If Bane and your miserable dog had been upwind, they might have known I was less than a hundred feet from Dean. Even he didn't know I was there. The spruce tree hid me and my scent pretty well, I think."

"You *followed* me?" Ivy said, furious. The tingling in her body felt worse; it was moving outward into her legs and arms. A spell came to mind, and Ivy couldn't quit thinking about it.

Snakes. She remembered it having to do with snakes. Lots of them. Page two hundred nineteen, *The Rise of the Dark Curse*. She wondered how Phoebe would look with a head full of writhing, venomous snakes.

Don't, a voice echoed in her head.

She set the pizza boxes on the hood of her car, barely aware she was preparing to duel Phoebe if she had to, and yet she felt sure she'd lose in such a silly display of anger. Whatever was happening to her, even if she were going dark herself, Ivy thought Phoebe was darker. *Way* darker.

Okay, Ivy thought. No snakes. But she couldn't just let Phoebe walk away. Not untouched, anyway. Phoebe had to know who *she* was dealing with. Another spell from *The Rise of the Dark Curse* came to mind.

Phoebe laughed again, a high and bitter sound. She stood taller, hands tense at her sides. "Bring it on Ivy, if you think you've got what it takes. But no matter what, Nick is mine. How many ways do I have to spell it out for you? I suppose I could wipe you off the face of the earth, send you to the very depths of hell itself. But, I'm going to make you a deal—"

"Nick will make his own decisions. If he chooses you it won't be because of any deal." Ivy feared Nick had already made such a choice, but she wasn't backing down now.

Ivy softly uttered a curse from the book, pausing long enough to raise her hand and block one of Phoebe's spells.

In near zombie-like fashion, Phoebe raised her hand to her mouth and tore off the end of a perfectly manicured nail. Then, she began to gnaw on the ragged edges of it. Ivy noticed a small trickle of blood. It was mesmerizing. She could stand here and watch until Phoebe chewed the whole nail from her finger and start on the next.

"Ivy!" Shayde and Raven were hurrying toward her, breaking her concentration.

Raven stared, speechless at Phoebe, unable to say a word. Like Ivy, she was momentarily fixated on the blood.

"Stop it!" Shayde demanded, shaking Ivy. *"Stop it right now!"*

The buzzing in Ivy's head had vanished. Phoebe was still worrying at the nail bed of her index finger. The sight no longer held Ivy in a trance and she recanted the curse. Her friends had to intervene. If they hadn't come when they did, how much longer would she let the hex go on? What if someone else had seen?

It's that damn book!

"What's this?" Phoebe said, spitting out a bloody piece of nail. "You need backup? A werewolf with absolutely no powers over me and some vegan of a vamp?"

Shayde growled, low and guttural, sending the hairs on Ivy's neck on edge. It was a sound she'd only heard when Shayde hunted and was going for the kill. But that was as wolf, not human.

Raven didn't look any happier. "I normally don't drink low-grade, but I'm off my diet," she said.

Phoebe grinned, the blood making her red lips even more crimson. She licked the blood off the end of her finger. She examined the nail bed for a moment or two. "Nice," she said. "I wonder where you learned such a spell. But, if you want to play rough, MacTavish, then we'll play rough. Next time, leave your friends at home." She gave a quick glance at someone approaching from the restaurant, but Ivy didn't dare turn to see who it was. Phoebe pivoted on her four-inch heels and got into her car.

"That book has to go, Ivy," Shayde said quietly.

"Ditto," Raven agreed. "I don't ever want to see you use that book again."

Ivy forced herself to nod. They were right. "Thanks, guys." She looked to see who was approaching. It was Nick.

"Isn't there a Bitch-Be-Gone spell?" Raven asked a bit loudly.

Despite her use of a spell from the book, Raven was trying to cover it up. For now. But, how much longer? Ivy shook her head. "Don't I wish."

"Too bad," Raven said.

Nick erupted into laughter. Thankfully, he hadn't seen the whole incident. "*Bitch*-Be-Gone?"

"Just looking out for your girlfriend, Nick," Raven said. Her tone had an edge of sadness to it.

Nick shook his head and sighed heavily. "Ivy's not

exactly…" His eyes locked with Ivy's.

Not exactly? Not exactly what?

"Fine!" Ivy said. A tangle of emotions overwhelmed her—fear, shame, and now, total embarrassment. "See you at the house, Raven. Come on, Shayde, let's go." Ivy snatched the boxes off the hood of the car and shoved them at Shayde. The pizza was probably cold by now and they'd have to heat it up when they got home. Or, they could eat it cold for all she cared. It had been stupid to come here. They should have gone over to the Wok of Life and had Chinese. If Phoebe wanted Nick so badly, she could have him.

Good riddance, Ivy thought, and felt more miserable than she ever had in her life.

Chapter 26

"I don't know which one of you is more depressed," Shayde said to Ivy and Spike.

Ivy adjusted from her slouched position at the kitchen table and pointed to Spike. "He is. I'm okay, really. Just deep in thought about the missing book." There were a lot of things going on in her mind, and the book was at least part of it. But Nick took center stage. His comment to Raven had hurt more than she'd expected.

Ivy's not exactly my girlfriend.

Okay, he hadn't finished the sentence, but that's what he was *going* to say. There was an empty ache in her chest unlike anything she'd ever experienced. What was she thinking? How could she let someone into her heart like she had Nick? Stupid, stupid, *stupid!*

Spike sighed heavily. Ivy detected a small hitch in it that sounded more like a sob. "She's beautiful," he said. "I don't blame him."

Ivy's head jerked in his direction. Yeah, Phoebe was rather pretty, but beautiful? Who's side was Spike on, anyway? "You weren't there! You didn't see her. I didn't think she was that hot. I don't know *what* he sees in her."

Spike didn't know what he was saying—it was the bug withdrawal. But Phoebe… maybe she could think of a way to turn Phoebe into a slug or make her butt the size of Texas.

Spike and Shayde both put down their pizza slices. Raven took a sip of her soda. The grandfather clock ticked loudly in the other room.

"What?" Ivy said. "You guys think she's beautiful?"

Spike fidgeted with his pizza slice. "But I *did* see her," he said, his eyes now a bit watery. "Gareth showed her to me. I was only hanging out in the parlor when you came to get me because I couldn't stand to see her in my old terrarium any longer. Her skin is amazing—so sleek and coppery with the darkest, most perfect black spots."

Raven burst into laughter. "Oh, this is too freaking funny."

"What? What spots?" Ivy asked.

Raven could barely contain another outburst of laughter. Even Shayde snickered.

Ivy glanced at her friends. "Oh. You're not talking about Phoebe, are you?"

Spike picked up his pizza and stared at it. "Phoebe? He named her already?" He devoured the last of his pizza in three bites, belched, then searched the pizza boxes for more. All that remained were crumbs.

"Spike's talking about Gareth's new lizard, isn't he?" Ivy asked, embarrassed.

Shayde laughed. "Yep. *You're* the only one thinking about Phoebe."

"Yeah, I'm sure Nick isn't even thinking that much about her," Raven added.

"That *much*?" Ivy said.

"Oh, geez Ivy," Shayde said. "I'm really sorry it didn't work out for the two of you tonight. I was hoping it would."

Raven nodded in sympathetic agreement. "It had all the potential of being hot."

Ivy stared at the floor. Spike eyed the pizza crusts on her plate and she shoved it toward him.

"Dessert. We need dessert and a different topic." Raven

slid the chair back and skipped to the fridge. She pulled out the caramel and chocolate sauce and a small container of sprinkles from the bottom shelf.

Shayde nudged Ivy's arm. "Yeah, ice cream will cheer you up. Nothing like a bunch of empty, sweet calories to make a girl happy."

Ivy flicked her hand at the cabinets and four bowls and spoons made their way to the counter. The freezer door opened and a large carton of vanilla ice cream floated lazily through the air. Spike caught it and opened it, tossing the lid into the sink.

Devlin whined at Ivy's feet.

"Fine, why not?" she said. A smaller bowl made its way next to the four larger ones. Devlin barked in delight.

They made heaping bowls of ice cream drizzled with chocolate and caramel sauce and topped with sprinkles.

"Are you sure?" Shayde asked as Ivy set a bowl with half a scoop of ice cream on the floor for Devlin. "It'll give him hiccups."

Spike gave Devlin a pat on the head. "Hiccups?"

Raven took her finger and wiped away the extra chocolate from a spoon. "Yeah. Too much sugar does it do him. And, like all Beezlepups, he hiccups spurts of fire." She licked the chocolate from her finger. "The last time Devlin set the living room drapes on fire."

"I wonder if it's Phoebe," Ivy said, earning her a quizzical look from everyone. "The book. Phoebe said she'd been studying dark magic."

Shayde took a mouthful of ice cream. "Makes sense I suppose. But why is she attacking the Regulars?"

"I don't know what her motive is. I don't know a whole lot about Phoebe." Ivy added extra chocolate syrup and sprinkles on her ice cream. "What I *do* know is there's something not right about her."

"Besides the fact she's after Nick?" Raven teased.

Ivy shot her a half-playful, half-serious, *don't go there* glare.

"So how do we find out if she's got the book or not?" Shayde asked.

"I make a little trip down to the river," Ivy said.

"Huh?" Shayde said.

"Spike says the guy who gave him the note hangs out by the river. Maybe he's meeting Phoebe there."

Spike nodded in agreement.

"And you just happen to think they'll have *The Book of Lost Souls* with them?" Shayde asked.

Raven gave Ivy a hard stare. "Sure. Just like Ivy carries around its twin everywhere *she* goes."

It would have been difficult not to notice everyone looking at her, and it didn't take rocket science to figure out both of her non spell casting friends weren't thrilled about the book. They just didn't understand.

"Well, I can't leave it in the house," Ivy said, feeling more than a bit defensive. "And what if I just happen to stumble upon the dead and the damned? Maybe there's a spell in *The Rise of the Dark Curse* that can send them back."

"You are *not* going to go through that book again!" Shayde said. "Tell me you're not!"

Raven folded her arms across her chest. "I'm with Shayde on this one."

"It's the only way, guys! Do you think that whatever spell Phoebe cast to bring back Vlad and Countess Báthory has a generic counter-spell?"

Shayde narrowed her eyes. "You're not bringing that book. And we'll know because we're going with you."

Ivy realized she should never have said anything about going down to the river. "If I promise to leave the book here, then you two are staying behind. I'm not risking anyone else."

Raven and Shayde exchanged knowing glances and it made Ivy wonder what they'd been discussing. She didn't have to wait long.

"We've been talking," Shayde admitted. "We've agreed

that it's time for us to step in. We want you to give your mom the book."

Both her friends stared at her, waiting for a response. A flash of anger welled inside her. They didn't trust her with the book any longer. They didn't think she could handle this on her own.

Spike's gaze shifted uneasily among them.

"See?" Shayde said. "You're upset. You've got to get rid of it, Ivy. Can't you see what it's doing to you? No good can come of this."

Raven leaned forward. "We'll make you a deal. We'll stay behind if you give your mom the book. We'll even give you until Friday night. That's two whole days. And, we'll be with you when you do tell her. Fair?"

It didn't go unnoticed that ever-cautious Shayde didn't bat an eye. They'd planned this.

Ivy felt her hands clench into fists. "I can't believe you guys! I can't believe you'd do this to me!"

Raven slammed her palm onto the table, making Spike and Devlin jump. "And *we* can't believe the things you've done to your friends *or* to Devlin! Do we really need to go over all of them? Do we? It's controlling you, Ivy. You can't go one day without reading it or touching it, can you?"

Ivy shook her head. It hadn't gone unnoticed they hadn't mentioned the incident with Phoebe. They were right. She didn't want to admit it, but they were. Every day, the book had a stronger hold on her. There were times when all she wanted to do was ignore everyone and sit in her room with the book. There were times when she wondered how a particular curse worked. It had to stop now while she still had control.

"Deal," she said finally. They didn't have to know that she'd take the book with her, or that she would get rid of it somewhere in the woods before she'd ever admit to her mother that she'd been hiding the book from her all along. It would devastate her mother if she learned her daughter had followed in her father's footsteps. As Ivy saw things, she was behaving no differently than *he* had. She gritted her teeth. Even without his influence, she was still like him. Was there no way to fight genetics?

Still, it hurt to think her friends would give up so easily on going with her. Had she hurt them that much? She couldn't look at them because the truth was too painful. Ivy had a feeling that neither Raven nor Bane had told Shayde they'd gone to the Prescotts' the other night. If she had, Shayde would have been really hurt and totally furious. Ivy had jeopardized them all, and in more ways than one. Her friends were keeping secrets for her and it was starting to strain everyone's relationships.

If she kept the book, she would hurt them again.

But, she needed *The Rise of the Dark Curse* one more time—tomorrow.

Shayde got up, bowl in hand. "It's settled then. The deal calls for more ice cream."

"And more chocolate syrup," Raven said as she collected her own bowl.

Spike, who had remained eerily quiet and sullen, was already ahead of them. He'd made himself a second bowl of ice cream and was frantically scooping the spoon around the sides of the bowl. All three girls grimaced at the same time.

"Spike, your sprinkles are moving," Raven said.

Shayde peered harder at the bowl. "Um, they've got legs!"

Ivy saw exactly what her friends had noticed and her stomach lurched. "Spike, are those—"

"Yeah," he said with a sigh. "Gareth bought me a carton of meal worms." His voice hitched again. "Look at me! I'm a bug addict! I'm drowning my sorrows in food!" Tears glimmered in his eyes. "And... I'm so...*emotional!*"

He set his bowl of ice cream on the table with a clatter and placed his face in his hands. The mealworms that weren't stuck in caramel or frozen were escaping down the sides. Ivy swirled a finger at them and the bugs returned to the middle of Spike's bowl.

Yeech! she thought. *We may never use that bowl or spoon again.* For that matter, Ivy didn't feel like finishing her ice cream. She nudged the chocolate sprinkles around in her own dish and pushed the bowl away.

"I thought that was another carton of Chinese food!" Shayde opened the refrigerator and peered inside. "You mean I put a carton of bugs in the fridge?"

Raven glanced at Ivy's bowl. "You're not going to finish that?"

"No. Spike's right," Ivy said. "I'm eating out of frustration." Great. First she couldn't finish the pizza, and now the ice cream. Couldn't she even eat the wrong things correctly?

Raven returned to the table, taking Ivy's bowl. "Apparently, Shayde and I are the only ones without relationship issues."

"I don't know what to do anymore!" Spike said, his face still in his hands. "Did he give me the box of meal worms as a send off? He's got a new pet now. Oh, you should have seen her, guys. The way her skin glistened like glass, the way her big black eyes shone like polished beetle shells. And the way Gareth stared at her! I hate her." Spike belched heartily again. "And I... I love her."

In a way, it was sad to see Spike so upset. Guilt weighed heavy on Ivy, not only for Spike's feelings, but because she was glad that he'd managed to guide the conversation away from the book.

Shayde put down her bowl and placed a comforting hand on Spike's arm.

"Excuse me," Spike said, wiping his eyes.

Spike got to his feet and shambled out of the kitchen. They all listened as Spike shuffled down the hall, past the living room and to the small half-bath located under the stairs. The door clicked shut and then they heard Spike blowing his nose loudly.

Shayde leaned toward Ivy. "He worries me. I think I'll go check on him." She hurried from the kitchen and out of sight.

"Men!" Raven said. "Lizards. They can be so weird, don't you think?"

Ivy nodded. "Yeah, well, in Spike's defense, he's suffering from bug withdrawal."

Truth was, she understood Spike's feelings about rejection. True, there was probably quite a bit of difference between a pet-master relationship than a boyfriend-girlfriend one, but it didn't change the heartache of rejection. Not that Nick had ever *been* her boyfriend. Spike hated that he could be replaced so easily and Ivy just hated Phoebe for stepping in so quickly. It took one emotion to escalate the other. Who'd have thought love and hate could have so much in common?

Raven nervously glanced toward the hallway. "You've got to change him back soon, Ivy. He hates her *and* loves her? He's gone completely mental."

How strange, Ivy thought. Raven showing this much concern was rare. Not unheard of, but rare. "I'll change him back anytime he wants." Ivy got up from her chair. "Maybe I should go talk to him. Convince him that Gareth really wants him to come back now—"

"No! Just let him be. We can't all go coddling him, can we? Knowing Spike, it'll only convince him we care more than Gareth. Let Shayde handle him." Raven began to collect the bowls and spoons. "Let's just clean up."

Ivy waved a hand and the dishes floated from Raven's hands and into the sink. The water turned on and a dishrag hovered as the detergent bottle squirted liquid into the bowls.

"So," Raven said. "If you're going to the river to find this guy, you'll have to cut classes."

"Yeah," Ivy replied with a sigh. She had never cut class before. She actually *liked* her classes.

Raven leaned against the counter. "You'll be fine. How exciting! But, unless you want your mom to ground you until graduation day, you'll need a note. How good are you at forging her signature?"

Ivy hadn't given it much thought until now. Luckily, Ivy had never felt the need to individualize her penmanship. Her handwriting was a lot like her mother's. "I think it's close enough that no one will notice."

"Good," Raven said, giving the kitchen doorway another glance. "We won't mention the note thing to Shayde, okay? Just be careful out there. Use that Quieting spell on your shoes or something. You don't want this guy to hear you."

Ivy nodded. "Good idea. Thanks."

Spike trudged back into the kitchen, still looking dejected, but overall, much better than when he'd left. He opened the fridge and took out the carton of bugs. With a deep sigh, he sat and ate the last of his mealworms like popcorn.

"Where's Shayde?" Ivy asked.

"Here," Shayde said, entering the room. She seemed a little pale.

"You okay?" Ivy asked.

"I'm not feeling so well," she said. "If it's okay, I think I'll just go home."

From behind her, Devlin hiccuped. Ivy whirled to see a small flame erupt from his mouth before quickly disappearing into a tiny puff of smoke. "You're not the only one."

After Shayde and Raven left, Ivy sent Spike to the guest room to get some rest. She returned to her bedroom in time to see Devlin hiccup and set the bedspread on fire.

"Yikes!" The fire went out quickly, thanks to the Fireproofing spells her mother had painstakingly put on everything flammable in the house. It had taken her months.

"Looks like you need acidophilus." Ivy fetched a bottle she kept in her nightstand, just for this purpose. She handed a couple of capsules to Devlin who readily ate them.

"I don't care if Phoebe's been studying black magic or not, she can't be that much more experienced with spells," she said. "I mean, she's my age, right?"

Devlin's eyebrows shifted. "*Nrrrrrgh.*"

"Okay, okay! So she's seventeen. She's only a few months older. How good could she be?"

Devlin hiccuped again. This time, only a wisp of smoke came out his nostrils.

"Much better!" she said. "So she's better at being a dark witch. I'm okay with that."

Devlin licked her face, then cocked his head toward the doorway.

"Spike? Oh, yeah. Wouldn't want a repeat of the other night." Ivy got out of bed and kissed Devlin's head. "Thanks."

She walked down the hall and opened the door. Spike was sound asleep. Ivy charmed the window shut in case Spike decided to wander off. After closing the door behind her, Ivy repeated the spell, then added one more—the Quieting spell just in case Spike woke up and went off on another crying jag. She could only imagine the start it'd give her mother in the middle of the night.

Just a couple more nights and Spike would be safely back in his terrarium.

Ivy sighed. She only wished that finding out who had *The Book of Lost Souls* could be half as easy.

Chapter 27

For the second time in a week, Ivy slept very little. Fortunately, her nerves kept her alert the next morning. She had to admit she was nervous about going without her friends, especially Shayde who was familiar with the woods and had senses to detect things and people that Ivy did not.

Before leaving the house that morning, Ivy tried the Quieting spell on her shoes. Sure enough, it worked—even over the squeaky floorboard in the upstairs hallway. She'd have to apply the charm again once she got to the woods just to be on the safe side, but all in all, she couldn't thank Raven enough for the idea.

Ivy spent a few extra minutes with Devlin in the backyard, wondering if she could really go through with burying *The Rise of the Dark Curse* somewhere in the woods. Her choice seemed simple—get rid of the book or tell her mother about it. Her friends weren't going to let her keep quiet any longer.

Then, tell them you buried it. Slide it under the car seat and show them the inside of the book bag...

Ivy tried to ignore the idea. Would they believe her? Could something that simple work?

"You sure you're okay?" her mother asked as Ivy came back inside. "You look a bit tired."

"Just studying a little too hard I think," Ivy assured her. Even though it wasn't a real lie, Ivy felt horrible about it.

She told herself it was for her mother's own good and that she'd worry if she knew what her daughter was really up to. Worry? She'd freak out.

Her mother smiled brightly, "I never thought I'd tell a child of mine that they studied too much." She shrugged into her jacket and blew a kiss to Ivy as she grabbed her purse and keys from the table in the foyer and headed off to work.

Ivy watched out the window as her mother drove away. Then, she and Devlin raced up the stairs to let Spike out of the guest room. Spike was dressed and waiting for her, looking tired and depressed, but still much better than the distraught Spike from last night.

"Ready to go bee hunting?" she asked.

He shrugged half-heartedly. "I'm not that hungry."

Ivy sat on the bed next to him. Devlin jumped up and sat on the other side. "Gareth misses you, Spike. Even if the new lizard is everything you say, she's not a Horned-Toad lizard. I think he'll be thrilled with two lizards to care for."

"You think so?" Spike said, sounding slightly happier.

"Yeah, I do."

Spike's soft brown eyes found hers. "Are you sure you don't want me to come with you? You've been a good friend. Aside from Gareth, I love you the most."

Ivy put her other hand on top of Spike's. "Not this time, Spike. Gareth would kill me."

Spike nodded. "If it's all the same to you, then, I'll just hang around here today. I promise I'll hide if your Mom comes back. I'll keep Devlin company."

Devlin barked happily.

"I guess that would be okay," Ivy said. "But, I have to go. I'll have Shayde check on you as soon as she gets home from school."

Spike nodded.

Devlin followed her down the steps and sat at her feet.

Ivy shrugged into her jacket and knelt down in front of him. His ears were half-mast, as though he was uneasy about being left behind.

"Don't be scared. I'll be fine," she said, giving him a hug. "I'll see you when I get back."

Ivy stood and grabbed her car keys, snatched up her book bag, and rushed outside. As she closed the front door, she heard Devlin barking and scratching against it. The way he always worried about her was so cute.

She tossed the book bag into the back seat and slid behind the wheel as the engine cranked to life. As she drove to school, she thought of how pleased Gareth would be to have Spike back. He had to be really missing him by now, even though he knew Spike was okay. At least Spike wasn't with Tara anymore, which made Ivy feel a lot better. If Spike wasn't already scarred for life, he would have been after a few more days with Tara. She could just see Gareth contacting a pet psychic who could translate Spike's trauma to a psychiatrist.

Shayde met her at her locker first thing. Like Ivy, she seemed a bit tired, and like Devlin, she also looked very worried. "Before you say anything Ives, I'm really sorry."

Ivy frowned as she opened her locker. "What are you talking about?"

Shayde seemed to consider Ivy for a few minutes. "We were a bit hard on you about the book. You do know it was for your own good, right?"

Leave it to Shayde to worry about their friendship and every little disagreement.

"Yeah. I understand," Ivy said. "And you'll be happy to know that I didn't touch the book once last night. I promise, if I don't get rid of the book by Saturday, I'll hand it over to mom. It's just that...it's just that I know what this is going to do to her."

Ivy hung up her jacket, aware that Shayde had grown

quiet.

"I've been thinking," Shayde said at last. "Give it to Nick. He'll turn it over to his dad and you'll be in the clear."

Ivy closed her locker and leaned against it. If Nick really would give it to his dad, she might consider it. But, Nick would have to tell who he got it from, and she wasn't ready to trust Mr. Marcelli.

Ivy smiled. Yesterday, she wouldn't have given up the book at all. Today, she felt better about the decision. It still felt uncomfortable, but not like she was giving up an heirloom or her right arm. Although Raven hadn't realized it when she'd lashed out about Ivy's slowly growing dependence on the book, a challenge had been laid down. Ivy hadn't touched the book because Raven had said she couldn't go a single day without seeing it.

"I'll think it over. It could work. I just have to deal with the whole trust thing with his dad a little more, okay?"

Shayde gave her an easy grin. "Good to know this means you're starting to trust Nick."

"I'm not," Ivy replied as they walked toward their first class. "What I mean is, what if Nick is back with Phoebe? It wouldn't be good if Phoebe ended up with *The Rise of the Dark Curse*, would it? Especially if she already has *The Book of Lost Souls.*"

The thought of what Phoebe could do with both books made Ivy shudder.

Shayde shook her head. "I don't think there's anything between them anymore. He wasn't real happy with her the first time.

Ivy didn't feel so sure. "Well, *she* looked happy with him. And, he wasn't exactly chasing her off. You were there. You heard what he said to Raven."

"Yeah," Shayde replied. "I did. So I um, I sort of asked him about all that."

The hallway spun, and Ivy wanted to crawl somewhere and die of embarrassment. "You asked him? Great! Now I look pathetic."

"Stop looking at me like that. Just listen, okay? I called him last night."

Pathetic wasn't the word. Now, she just looked stupid, desperate. How long before this bit of news got out? "Does Bane or anyone else know about this?"

"Well, yeah. He walked in and heard me talking to him. So, it's just Bane and me. Unless he told Raven. He probably told Raven. She's been saying all along that you and Nick—"

"No. No, no, no!" Ivy wheeled around in a state of panic and confusion. She wanted to run down the hallway and out the doors. She'd call her mother at work—tell her she was sick. Maybe she'd say she had some incurable, rare disease and that her dying wish was to never step foot in school again.

"Ives. Get a grip so I can tell you what he said."

Ivy took a deep breath. "Okay, tell me. He's seeing her again, isn't he?"

"No. He's not. They've hung out a few times since you've been so stuck on Dean. I think Phoebe just flatters his ego. He wants a chance to talk to you. You've got class together after lunch, right? He wants to straighten things out. And, he's still willing to take the book. *Very* willing. He's worried that something bad will happen to you if you keep it much longer."

Of all the crazy ideas Shayde ever had, calling Nick had to be the dumbest. "*Talk* to him? No. I can't. I won't be in class."

"You're still going to the river this afternoon, aren't you? You're actually going to cut class?" Shayde wanted to know.

Ivy sucked in a great gulp of air. "Yep. I'll be *fine*, Shayde." She glanced at her watch. If they ran, they'd each make it to their classes. "So, that talk with Nick is going to have to wait. Gotta go." With that, Ivy turned and ran down the hallway to her first period class.

If she hadn't been cutting class before, she sure was now. The trick would be to not even return to her locker today—just in case Nick was waiting for her there.

Now what? She couldn't manage to talk to Nick much less give him the book. And, if he and Phoebe were getting all buddy-like, she couldn't risk it anyway. Not until she could prove to Nick that Phoebe had *The Book of Lost Souls*. Unless he already knew. What then?

Like she had most of the morning, Ivy kept checking out the hallways to make sure Nick wasn't anywhere around. She made her way through the lunch line, expecting Nick to walk up any minute. What would she say? Sorry my friend decided to try matchmaking? I didn't really put her up to it? He wouldn't believe that. *She* wouldn't believe that. Even so, where did that leave them with the books? She'd only sound worse if she asked Nick to stop hanging around Phoebe.

Someone slammed into the back of her and Ivy nearly dumped her tray onto the kid standing in front of her.

She steadied herself and turned to see who had been so rude. She should have known. Speak of the devil and there she was. Phoebe looked less than happy, which brightened Ivy's mood considerably.

"Good timing," Ivy said, taking a fork and pushing aside something brown and gelatinous on her tray. "I was just thinking of something revolting and here you are."

Phoebe clearly wasn't amused. She stood with her hands firmly on her hips, teeth clenched. And that expression! Nothing said, *if looks could kill* more than that scrunched up face and fire-rimmed eyes. As pretty as Phoebe normally was, her current look was far from attractive. A grin tugged at the corners of Ivy's mouth.

"You have something I want," Phoebe spat. A lone vein stood out on her forehead. For a moment, Ivy was sure Phoebe's head would explode.

Phoebe jabbed a finger at her. "Don't mess with me, MacTavish. In the end, I *always* get what I'm after." Without waiting for a reply, Phoebe stormed off.

The kid behind her smiled sheepishly. "Man, that was some face, huh? What do you have that she needs that much?"

Ivy shrugged. "I took something from her gym locker this morning. It was just a joke, but apparently she really needs them." As she left the line, she looked over her shoulder and replied, "Laxatives. Who knew, right?"

She scanned the cafeteria, finding her friends sitting at a nearby table. Thankfully, Nick was not with them. She wasn't sure if Nick told Phoebe about Shayde's phone call, but Ivy felt certain of one thing—Phoebe knew she had *The Rise of the Dark Curse*. Nick was now the last person she'd give the book to.

After a Phoebe and Nick-free lunch, Ivy made a beeline for the principal's office. She pulled out her forged note, holding it in shaking hands. Hopefully, her mother wouldn't find out. So far, she'd been able to hide a lot of things, why not one more?

Why? Because one of them was bound to catch up with her. Funny how one lie, one secret kept spiraling into the next. If she could just go back in time to one week ago, she'd have listened to Shayde and just gone out with Nick instead of changing Spike into her date. Then, she never would have found those books and wouldn't be caught up in the middle of this.

And Nick wouldn't be so close to Phoebe. Why had he told Phoebe she had one of the books?

Ivy opened the door to the main office and stepped inside. Mr. Evans was rifling through a filing cabinet and talking to Mrs. Olsen, the school receptionist. Mrs. Olsen sat behind her desk typing away on her keyboard, pausing every once in a while to peer at the computer screen. She was a thin woman with thin lips and a wide face.

"Well, anyone who's anyone and lived in this town long enough knows that the Harrisons have visited that old gravesite every month, good weather and now good health permitting. They weren't up to anything, and *certainly* not desecrating any of the old Kindred graves, Gerald. Why would they?" Mrs. Olsen said.

The subject clearly had Mr. Evans worked up. "Because," he said rather curtly, "The ancestor they visit was killed during the Kindred-Regular conflict. They're secretly holding a grudge, I'm sure of it!"

He stopped rummaging through the tall filing cabinet behind Mrs. Olsen, his fingers curling tightly around a drawer handle. He pursed his lips, and then he saw Ivy. For a moment, he looked like a frightened rat—he was still standing on the balls of his feet, and he wrung his hands. His beady black eyes darted between Ivy and Mrs. Olsen.

"Why, Gerald, you *are* in a foul mood. That's nonsense," Mrs. Olsen said. "The only grave touched was the Laughton grave, and that was just crazy old Lucas digging for bones again. Other than the Gray children and their friends, no one has been up to that section lately. And those children were clearing out weeds. Such a nice thing for them to volunteer for on weekends."

At this, Mr. Evans turned to stare at Ivy as though she were under a microscope. He flexed his hands into tight fists at his sides. Mrs. Olsen's back was still to Mr. Evans or she might have found his behavior as unsettling as Ivy did.

Mrs. Olsen reached across her desk to fetch a paper and noticed Ivy standing just inside the doorway. She lowered her bifocals and peered over the top.

"Well, hello Ivy dear! I was just thinking of you. Come, come!" She waved her hand vigorously. "What can I do for you today?" The corners of Mrs. Olsen's mouth did their best to turn upward. The result looked more like a grimace than a smile.

"Hello Mrs. Olsen. Good to see you." Ivy glanced at Mr. Evans who was still leering darkly at her. His fists were now so tightly clenched they appeared to be shaking. She'd never seen him so angry, so upset before.

She turned back to Mrs. Olsen. "I've got a note to be excused the rest of the day."

"Oh!" Mrs. Olsen exclaimed softly. "Is something wrong?"

"I woke up with a migraine. My mom said I could come home if it didn't get any better. She wrote this note just in case."

Mrs. Olsen made a few tsking sounds. "So young to have migraines. I hope you feel better soon, dear." She took the note from Ivy and read it. "Well, okay then. Did you need someone to drive you home?"

"Yes," Mr. Evans said, still eyeing her suspiciously. "I could drive you."

"Uh, no. I can drive home," Ivy answered. Had Mr. Evans always been so creepy? Nerdy, yes, but now he was outright scary. She smiled weakly and turned to leave.

"Tomorrow's Halloween, Mrs. Olsen called out. "Wouldn't do for a Kindred to be sick on Halloween, would it now? Only a half-day!" she said cheerily.

"No, it wouldn't. Thanks." Ivy left without looking back at Mr. Evans. Why was he acting so strangely? Did he detect her lie?

As soon as she closed the door behind her, Ivy bolted down the hall toward the exit.

Chapter 28

It took ten nerve-wracking minutes to get to the park just outside the woods. Luckily, Ivy didn't pass anyone who might tell her mother they'd seen her on the road during school hours. She didn't think Mrs. Olsen would say anything to her mother since they didn't see each other often. Hopefully, the same could be said of Mr. Evans.

Ivy pulled the VW into the most remote spot she could find—a shady, heavily treed area. She grabbed her book bag, and then thought better of it. In the twenty-four hours she'd refrained from reading *The Rise of the Dark Curse*, she'd felt better—less irritable, less moody. It might be best to leave it hidden in the car just in case things went wrong. She wouldn't want someone to catch her in the woods and find the book on her. She set the bag on the rear floorboard and threw a blanket over it that she'd kept in the car for Devlin. If she had time, she'd come back for the book and bury it in a briar patch or someplace else where no one would be likely to stumble across it.

Ivy briskly walked to the path leading into the woods, feeling all the while like someone was watching her. A crow cawed loudly from a nearby branch, startling her.

Ivy took a deep breath. "Quit being so jumpy," she muttered.

"Who says I'm jumpy?" called the all-too familiar male voice behind her. It looked like she wasn't the only one cutting classes.

Nick strolled up to her, an easy grin on his face. A lock of dark hair fell over one brow.

Ivy opened her mouth to explain why she was out here. "I—"

"Cut classes to spy on some mystery guy by the river. You're hoping he'll be the one who's got *The Book of Lost Souls.*"

Ivy shook her head. "Who told—"

"Shayde. Raven knows I'm here, too. They said you didn't want them going with you—part of a deal to get you to surrender the other book." His mouth crooked into a smirk. "They never said they wouldn't send someone else."

Ivy gave him a dark look, but the truth was that she felt better not going alone.

Not that she'd ever admit that.

"What about Phoebe?" If she was going into the deepest, darkest part of the woods with Nick, she needed to know where they stood. Until then, she'd just have to keep close watch on him—stay on guard. If anything happened to her, Shayde and Raven knew where to come look. They'd also know whom to suspect. She pulled out her phone to text Shayde.

"Phoebe doesn't know I'm here. She's been pretty jealous," he said. "And, she's got a right to be."

Ivy sent Shayde two words: *Nick's here*. If Shayde hadn't told Nick, then Ivy could expect a text back. She pocketed the phone and started for the woods again.

"Such lack of trust," He said.

Ivy kept walking. "Shayde should never have called you, Nick."

He caught up to her. "I'm glad she did. Look, there hasn't been anything between Phoebe and me for a long time. I can't stop her from what she thinks—"

"She *thinks* I've got something she wants," Ivy finished. Her heart was pounding hard, and she tried to tell herself it had nothing to do with Nick, but that would be a lie.

"I have no idea what that is," Nick replied.

Ivy looked at him. "She knows I've got *The Rise of the Dark Curse.* You didn't tell her, did you?"

He actually looked shocked. "She doesn't think you have the book. Phoebe thinks whoever has *The Book of Lost Souls* also has *The Rise of the Dark Curse.*"

The sky had been overcast all day and it made the woods darker and gloomier, than normal. "So, Phoebe *doesn't* have *The Book of Lost Souls?*"

Nick nearly burst out laughing. "No, she doesn't. I'd know."

"Uh-huh."

"I *mean* that if Phoebe had the book, she wouldn't be wasting her time with me or anyone else. She's as hung up on her powers as Tara is on her looks. There is nothing that would appeal more to Phoebe than having either of Skinner's books."

"Hmmm," Ivy said. "I don't know. I think it's her or this mystery guy."

"So," Nick said. "This guy Spike saw. Has anyone seen him before?"

Up ahead, Ivy heard the sound of water rushing over rocks.

"Not that I know of. Just Spike," Ivy answered. "Says he's some tall guy in a suit."

They both came to a stop when they reached the clearing just before the river.

"A suit? Here? That's weird. So, now what?" Nick asked. "Do we just wait?"

Ivy shook her head. "No, we cross over. At least, that's what Spike said. We must have walked too far south. There's supposed to be a bridge, then a clearing of some sort."

Nick motioned to their left. "I bet I know exactly the area Spike is talking about. Everyone hangs out there."

Ivy didn't know the precise spot, but she'd heard some

of the kids came down here to party on weekends. Of course, Nick being part of the group in question, she had no doubt he could find it.

"It's just a few hundred yards or so down," Nick said. "The clearing is just on the other side of the river."

"We can cross here." Ivy pointed to a large fallen log closer to the bank of the river.

Nick followed her gaze. "That log isn't budging, Ivy. And those stepping stones are spaced too far apart. We'd have to wade through the water over the first section. The bridge is easier."

"What if this guy sees us coming from that direction?" Ivy asked. "Follow me."

Nick sighed, but followed her down to the river. Water rushed past river rock in an angry swirl. Large, flat gray rocks rested in the middle, and on the other side, a much gentler flow of water. It was hard to tell about the depth from where she stood. On the other bank, large trees flanked the shoreline.

Not too far from the bank, a rotting log lay in a patch of overgrown grass. The jagged edges of the trunk still in the ground had become weatherworn and hollow.

Ivy knelt next to a small patch of red clover and chanted a spell she'd memorized from *A Botany of Spells—Magic for the Garden*:

From this soil of earth and clay,
Seeds of beauty shall make their way
Flowers bloom, where once was none
'tis nature's gift, from earth to sun.

Pea-green sprouts with tiny leaves pushed from the soil like choreographed dancers, lifting their heads in unison, leafy arms rising skyward. Their tiny stems swayed to the rhythm and music carried in on a sudden breeze. Even the small amount of sunlight from a break in the clouds joined them, radiating golden swirls onto the young plants' new growth unfolding from their stems like silk scarves.

As they matured, their dance quickened to the wind's song. The breeze even whistled through blades of grass, like tiny horns and trumpets. Some of the grass blades beat against the earth like a drum. To Ivy, it appeared as though Mother Nature liked jamming to jazz. Little plant heads bobbed forward and back, leaves in tune with the motion.

In a brief growth spurt that looked like each plant had done a short pause then a hop, their buds blossomed in a flowing wave of gemstone colors. Each full-grown flower furled and unfurled their petals. The dance of the forest flowers continued onward, enveloping everything within their path in vivid splendor. Leaves shot upward and downward in time to the music, stems twisting from side to side. The flowers spread to the fallen log, pressing themselves against its weight. In turn, the log began to bounce to the beat and then started to roll down to the stream's edge. The flowers took little notice as they continued on with their melodious expansion.

The log tumbled forward, gaining the momentum Ivy needed for her next spell to work. She swirled a finger in a clock-wise motion and the log spun outward on the flat rocks.

"Stabilize," she commanded the log with another wave of her hand. Tiny white sparkles hovered around the log before flickering out of existence. The water was most chilly this time of year and it wouldn't do if the log shifted while they were crossing.

Nick hopped up and offered Ivy a hand. "Not too bad."

Ivy smiled and took his hand. They only had to leap from one of the stones to the next before making it safely to the other side of the river.

"Not bad?" Ivy inquired as they made their way upstream. "That was awesome!"

Nick was running now, and Ivy ran behind him.

"If you say so," he said grinning over his shoulder.

Ivy pushed herself harder, catching up to Nick just as

they came into an open area slightly larger than the science lab at school. The surrounding area was crowded with large oaks still clinging to most of their leaves. A massive Trekking tree stood in the middle of the area, its leaf-covered branches adding to the umbrella-like canopy. Another downed log along the edge was lined with quite a few discarded beer bottles.

Nick had stopped and she nearly ran into him. She gave him a punch on the arm.

"Ow! Okay!" he said with a laugh. "You're spell was...cute."

When he turned to face her, she realized she was standing far too close.

They stared at each other for what felt like an awkward minute.

"I could get lost in those eyes of yours," Nick said.

She should have turned away, but couldn't.

His hand lightly touched her arm. "How do I prove to you that all I want is you?"

She wanted to hear this, and yet, she didn't. She had to stay strong, she had to be sure. His words weren't enough. They were, after all, just that. Words. He'd been here before. Maybe with Phoebe. She felt her head shake slowly. "Nick—"

He took a few steps away from her. "You want to see some real magic?"

Nick bent down and picked up two empty liquor bottles. He slammed them against the fallen log, shattering them into hundreds of small, glistening shards. The broken glass rose into the air and swirled above their heads, glowing like small fireflies. A breeze stirred through the clearing, and the brown leaves at her feet rustled, folding over on themselves before unfurling into red rose petals.

Nick extended his hand, and Ivy's heartbeat sped up a few notches. Nick took her hand into his.

"I don't know what you want to hear or what you want

to know. Just give me a chance," Nick said.

A warm breeze filled the clearing, stirring the leaves and the trees into some sort of song. Vines tightened around the trees, sounding like guitars. The melody was more rock than ballad, which clearly suited Nick's rock 'n roll style.

"Dance with me," Nick said, pulling Ivy to him.

She wanted to tell him not to hold her so close, that she could feel his heartbeat against hers.

"This doesn't have to end here, Ivy. I'm serious about you."

She raised her eyes to meet his, "Why me? You could have Phoebe or anyone. I bet you could even steal Tara from Dean if you wanted."

"I don't need glitter or special effects, Ivy. I just need someone who's *real*."

He spun her around and Ivy felt dizzy with the feelings inside her.

"Remember when I asked if you wanted to see real magic," he whispered into her ear as he cradled her back against him. "This is magic. Us."

Could anything ever feel so frighteningly wonderful? It was like Nick could promise her the world without saying a word. "You've done this before."

His laughter felt soft against her hair. "No. I might have known what to do with anyone else. But not you. With you, I'm not sure what to do at all. I haven't a clue if I'm doing any of this right."

He wasn't sure if he wasn't doing anything right? Was he kidding? Her heart fluttered like the rose petals and the crystalline fireflies.

He twirled her so she was facing him again. Nick stopped dancing and Ivy was aware that the music from the trees had stopped even though her heartbeat felt like it was still keeping tune. Why hadn't it exploded by now?

Run. It's just demon charm. Don't fall for him.

She gazed up at him, knowing it was too late. "Do you

still want the book?"

He gave her a lazy grin. "Later."

His face was so close and she felt the pull of her lips toward his.

I'm in serious trouble here, she thought, and her very soul wanted to agree.

A hawk screamed overhead and both Ivy and Nick froze, their impending kiss hovering between them. A twig snapped and crows resting in a nearby tree took flight, cackling loudly.

The moment was gone. The bits of glass fell from their twinkling orbit and the rose petals blew on the ground, turning back into dead leaves.

"Quick! Hide!" Ivy said, still feeling breathless.

Nick grabbed a low-lying branch of the Trekking tree and hoisted himself up with ease. "Here!" he called to her.

She took his hand and climbed up after him. They scaled higher, taking refuge in a cluster of fall foliage. From their vantage point it should be easy to pick out anyone in the clearing.

A squirrel in one of the neighboring trees chattered angrily. Another twig snapped and voices broke the eerie serenity around them. A flash of crimson appeared below. Nick hunkered down on the branch to get a better look. Ivy held on to the trunk of the tree and knelt lower, peering through the leaves. They'd expected only one person—a man. Below, both Vlad and Countess Báthory strolled into view.

"He must be dealt with," the Countess said as she took a seat on the fallen log. "After all, we did him a favor with...what was his name? Nash? *Nicely* done, Vlad. I don't believe I've seen an impaling before. How delightful! We must do it again."

Ivy and Nick exchanged glances. Nick was right. It wasn't Phoebe. Whoever they were looking for was male. Maybe the mystery man.

Vlad paced beneath them. "And we *will*, my Elizabeth. We will. First, we must find who has the other book. Until then, he remains our master. And I answer to no one!" he finished angrily.

The Countess fanned herself. "And that despicable food he fed us the other night. Pizza is not a proper feast for such royalty as us. We must kill him soon. Besides, I'm tired of coming here to discuss our plans."

"Patience, my dear. Patience," Vlad said. "He has charmed his house to listen to what we say while he is at that school."

Pizza. Irritable. School. Ivy worked with this information. Student, or teacher? For that matter, it could be anyone who worked at Northwick High. Still, it nagged her, like the answer was on the tip of her tongue. Across from her, Nick seemed to be making sense of this bit of information himself.

"Are you sure he didn't leave it behind in the cemetery?" the Countess asked.

"We've looked!" Vlad snapped. "Someone else has it. Someone who's been to the cemetery since then."

"Perhaps we should pay another visit to the Harrisons," the Countess suggested. "He did seem to think it was them. They had been to the cemetery recently to clear an ancestor's grave. Perhaps we need to be more persuasive."

Vlad waved her off. "It isn't the Harrisons. It has something to do with the *other* one, the tall wizard who followed us here the other day."

Ivy couldn't stop thinking about the clues. Pizza. She'd been to Saludo's a few times since the dance. She searched her memory for anyone who stood out. Someone not acting right, someone at the school who seemed nervous or on edge.

Below, the Countess laughed softly. "The *other* wizard? Darling, if he had the other book, he would have tried spells a lot darker than what he used."

Vlad stopped pacing directly beneath them. He rubbed his chin.

Ivy shifted on her branch. There were *two* wizards. And the one who had *The Book of Lost Souls* was at the school. Her mind went through a list of possibilities. Lately, only one wizard had been so bad tempered—the same one who had bought four pizzas just the other night—and they weren't for the other teachers. Nick looked at her. Was he thinking the same thing? Why hadn't she noticed it before? She recalled the look she'd gotten in the principle's office. Still, it was so hard to believe. As teachers went, he was usually so meek, so mild-mannered. So...nerdy.

There was a flash of silver light below. The Countess held up a mirror, turning her face left and right. Her hand paused over one cheek. She let out a gasp. "A wrinkle! I need the blood of another girl. Quickly!"

"You shall have as many as you like," Vlad said. "But first, I must have the book. Then, our master must die."

The Countess laid the mirror down on her lap. "The book! Then death to him! Death to Mr.—"

"Evans!" Ivy and Nick both whispered precisely at the same time they heard the Countess and Vlad speak the name of Northwick High's geekiest science teacher.

There was a moment of silence as Vlad and the Countess stared at each other. Then they looked up. Nick placed a finger over his lips, a pointless gesture since Ivy had already stopped breathing, fearful that the tiniest amount of breath might be heard rustling a dried leaf.

There was a flash of silver again as the Countess adjusted her mirror. The Countess looked up once more and grinned. It was the most horrible grin Ivy had ever seen.

"There," the Countess said. "Do what you want with him. The girl is mine."

Chapter 29

Vlad removed something from a pouch at his waist.

The Countess rose to her feet and stood beside him. She smiled up at Ivy. "Won't you come down, my young lovely?"

"Nah. I'm good," Ivy eeked out. She mouthed to Nick, "What do we do?"

Nick didn't look like he had any more ideas than Ivy did. "I'm working on it," he said.

"They'll come down," Vlad assured the Countess. He struck a match and placed it in a pile of dry leaves at the base of the tree.

The flames lapped at the leaves and spread up the trunk. The Trekking tree swatted at the flames with a few branches while taking aim at Vlad and the Countess with others. The swinging limbs knocked the Countess to the ground and Vlad helped her to her feet.

Nick cast a spell at the flames, snuffing them out.

The victory was temporary. Vlad stuffed a wad of discarded paper into a bottle. He lit the paper and flung the bottle into the Trekking tree. Flames raced up the trunk, catching dried leaves on fire. Frantically, Ivy and Nick cast one spell after another to douse the fire.

The Trekking tree, which had other ideas, had had enough. It uprooted itself and shuffled over. Ivy toppled forward, breaking a small branch. Another bottle hit the tree, the flames racing through the dry, brittle leaves. Branches began to beat at Ivy and Nick. The tree probably figured the only way to stop Vlad's fiery assault was to rid itself of the two things he wanted.

The flames were too close and the smoke grew thick. "We can't stay up here," Nick said as he extinguished more flames.

Vlad and the Countess circled below, grinning triumphantly.

Ivy and Nick extinguished more flames as they climbed down. Ivy paused when she was just out of Vlad's reach. *"Repel!"*

The effort knocked Vlad back a mere foot or two. Nick's spell had managed to do about the same to the Countess.

Ivy hurled another spell, giving it everything she had. *"REPEL!"*

Vlad staggered backward, but remained on his feet.

"Why isn't it working?" she asked Nick.

The Trekking tree shuffled another few feet and turned, tilting its branches downward. Branches beat at them, tossing them both from the tree.

"Ow!" Ivy exclaimed as she hit the ground. The Countess was on her, grabbing her by the hair and yanking her to her feet. Ivy felt her knees want to collapse. The Countess planned on killing her and bathing in her blood as she had Angela's.

"Go on," the Countess dared Nick who was taking aim at her. "Your spell will do little, and I'll be forced to rip her hair out."

Vlad grabbed a long spear from behind the fallen log and rammed it into the ground with very little effort. Then, Vlad eyed Nick with a cold and soulless stare.

Nick slammed another repelling spell into Vlad, the spell having even less effect this time.

"Why aren't our spells working?" Ivy cried out to Nick.

"Your magic isn't working because we're growing

stronger everyday. We're black magic, my sweet. Conjured from the spells written by a highly practiced black magic sorceress." The Countess put a finger to her cheek. "Although, I must admit, we did come across one wizard who tried to banish us. Very strong, very old magic from the sting of it. I must say, it was rather unpleasant."

"Without *The Book of Lost Souls* he can't send us back." Vlad explained. "And when we find the book's mate, we're *never* going back. We'll be able to do a little magic of our own."

Another flock of crows scattered from a nearby tree, flapping their wings and sending out startled warnings. Both Vlad and the Countess turned to see a sable-colored wolf sail over the fallen log. The wolf landed within a few feet of them, snarling and yet careful to keep distance.

Shayde's diversion was enough to make the Countess release her hold on Ivy.

Nick grabbed Ivy's arm. "Run!"

They turned and fled the clearing, Shayde raced alongside them. They ran upstream, Vlad and the Countess right behind them.

"Faster," Nick called to Ivy.

"It's the curse," Ivy huffed as she picked up the pace. "It's like they're super villains!"

Ivy didn't dare look back again. Standing their ground wouldn't work. Whatever spells Ivy and Nick had would do little to thwart their attackers, and other than a Repelling spell, she'd never learned much defensive magic. Living in a town like Northwick, there wasn't a lot of use for it. She could use a spell from *The Rise of the Dark Curse*, but which one? Even so, she doubted she'd be quick enough.

The bridge Nick had mentioned was just ahead. If they could get to their cars, they could get away. She had to think of something to buy some time. Ivy took aim at a fallen branch. "*Propel!*"

Without looking behind her, it was hard to tell if the

branch had hit either Vlad or the Countess.

Rocks, some rather hefty, lifted from the riverbank and flew through the air toward Vlad and the Countess. Nick was good—she'd never seen him cast a spell or say a single word.

"Gah!" came the pained Countess' cry. Vlad's curses were enough to tell Ivy the rocks were working.

Shayde made it to the bridge first. Nick and Ivy made it right behind her and followed as fast as they could. Vlad and the Countess were still further back.

The planks ahead on the bridge shifted and began to buckle. Shayde ran faster, and was now nearly across the bridge. With each step Ivy and Nick took, the boards beneath them fell away to the rushing water below. They didn't stop running full-tilt until they reached the other side and reunited with Shayde.

Only then did Ivy slow enough to see what had happened. Vlad and the Countess were clinging to the rails of the bridge and sounding none too happy about it.

Nick and Ivy followed Shayde through the woods at a jog, eager to make it back to the park before Vlad and the Countess could figure out a way to follow them. With any luck, they wouldn't find the fallen log for a few hours.

When they reached their cars, Nick cast a spell that opened the doors to Ivy's VW Bug.

"I'll call you when I get home," Nick said.

"You can't mention I was out here," Ivy said. "Even though Mr. Evans has *The Book of Lost Souls*, the Council can't know I've got Skinner's other book. Give me a chance to get rid of it first."

"Waiting isn't a good idea," Nick said.

Ivy reached for his hand. "Please. Just a few hours. Besides, I don't think Vlad and the Countess are exactly on good terms with Mr. Evans. They're not likely to tell him we saw them."

Nick squeezed her hand and sighed. "Why are you so

stubborn?" He pulled away and chirped the alarm to his own car. "I'm going to regret this, but okay. I'll call you. Now, go. I'm not leaving until you do."

Shayde hopped into the passenger side and Nick closed the door behind her, then he ushered Ivy to the driver's side.

"By the way," Nick said. "I left you something. You'll see. When you get home."

Her heart fluttered, excited at the thought of a surprise.

"Now, go." He closed her door and trotted over to the Mustang.

Ivy twirled a finger at her window and it slid down. She leaned her head out. "Hey, what you did back there with the rock throwing was quick thinking. The collapsing boards were a bit scary, though."

Nick took a few steps back to her. "I thought that was you. That means..." Nick frowned and scanned the area around them.

Ivy glanced out through the windshield and into the woods. Nothing stirred. Other than the three of them, no one else seemed to be here.

Yet she knew differently.

He was here. Watching. He'd probably been watching ever since she took her first step into the woods. Who was this mystery guy and what did he want with her? Why had he helped them at the bridge and then chose to remain in the shadows? Ivy rubbed her arms as a chill came over her. She wanted to be home, and it suddenly had nothing to do with the surprise Nick mentioned.

"Yeah," she said. "I know exactly what it means. It means that someone else was out there with us."

Chapter 30

Ivy pulled into the Connors' driveway and let Shayde out. Shayde hopped down from the car and padded across the lawn toward the back of the house, where Ivy knew there was a doggie door large enough for werewolves. Changing back hadn't been an option. Driving with a naked passenger would draw too much attention. After seeing Shayde off, Ivy got back into her car and drove next door to her own house.

When she went to retrieve her book bag, she found Nick's surprise. He'd gotten into her car and left her a small book. It was one of those pocket-sized ones that people often bought at checkout registers at bookstores—no more than ten or fifteen pages. This one had probably been bought at Pages and Sages, a bookstore and potion shop over on Hawthorne Street. The title was *Simple Spells for the Suburban Girl*. Cute. Nick had a sense of humor knowing the other book she carried with her.

The thought of Nick and their almost kiss would have normally made Ivy dance with joy. And, if she thought finding out who was behind this would solve all her problems, she was wrong. How long before Vlad and the Countess figured out where to find them? True, they couldn't just ask around, and they stayed hidden in the woods most of the time. Still, she had to get rid of *The Rise of the Dark Curse* before Nick told his dad.

She retrieved her book bag and after glancing around, hurried to the front door and went inside. She had to figure out where and how she was going to get rid of the book. She'd be glad to be rid of it. The idea of touching the book again scared her. It'd be like walking into a dark alley full of everything nightmarish.

Devlin met her with his usual exuberance and tail wagging. Spike bounded down the stairs, nearly as happy as Devlin.

"You're home!" he said, nearly shoving Devlin aside to give Ivy a death-grip of a hug. "Geez, it felt like you were gone forever and ever!"

When he finally let go he stood and stared at her—just like Devlin. Both of them were waiting for her to do or say something. She half expected Spike to cock his head to one side when she asked Devlin if he needed to go outside.

"I wasn't even gone a full day," she said to Spike.

Spike was happy enough to go outside with Devlin for a few minutes. Ivy stayed inside, trying to decide what to do next. It would be easy enough to say she didn't want to be grounded for ditching class, but that wasn't it. Not really. All she could think about was protecting her mother from the whole ugly truth. Because, no matter what Ivy told her, what excuse she might have, her mother would be horribly hurt. And, she'd fear that Ivy really was like her dad. And that was something Ivy just couldn't bear.

She thought of calling Raven and asking if they could use the funeral home's incinerator, though she doubted the book would even burn. *But*, she could go back and hide it someplace in the cemetery. After all, when the Council questioned Mr. Evans, he'd have to tell them where he'd found *The Book of Lost Souls*. She could put *The Rise of the Dark Curse* in an area they hadn't cleared weeds and vines away from yet.

If she were going to do that, she needed to hurry. She wanted to be home before her mother. Spike could stay here with Devlin or they could both come with her. She weighed which place would be safer for them. The last thing she wanted was to run into Vlad and the Countess in the cemetery and put Spike and Devlin in any danger. The thought of ever seeing the Countess and her evil grin again made Ivy shudder.

She felt the side of the book bag. Funny, when she touched the bag, she no longer felt that weird pulse of energy she used to. She no longer felt agitated or even the need to lock herself in her room to read the book.

Ivy let out a sigh of relief.

And then she started to wonder why she didn't have the usual *craving* to read it. There had been no other word for it. Ivy reached for the zipper on the book bag, hesitating for a brief moment.

Let it be. Maybe it's just... sleeping. Don't touch it until you're ready to dump it in the cemetery.

Her traitorous hand unzipped the bag anyway, and she carefully reached inside to remove the book.

Which was when she realized it had been switched out with another. *The Rise of the Dark Curse* had been replaced with a large, hardbound thesaurus.

Frantically, Ivy searched the bag, although there was no other place it could be. Heart pounding, she raced up to her room and searched there, nearly ransacking the drawers in her panic to find the book.

The book wasn't anywhere to be found.

She collapsed onto the bed. *Think, think. Who would have switched it out?*

Her first thought was the mysterious man in the woods. If he had just wanted the book, then why stay and help her? She hardly thought someone like that would have a guilty conscience. And why even swap it out with another book? Then, her heart sank and Ivy thought she might just be sick. There was one other person who was with her today who knew she carried *The Rise of the Dark Curse*. And, not only had he replaced it with another book, he'd left her a token gift.

As if that would ever make up for it.

Nick had played her. He actually managed to not only break down every last bit of her defenses, he'd taken the book, just like he said he would. It's why he didn't think there was any need to wait and tell everyone that Mr. Evans had the *The Book of Lost Souls*. In fact, she bet Nick wasn't going to tell anyone other than his father. She'd also bet money the two of them were over at Mr. Evans right now.

It's why he hadn't called her yet. And, even if he were home, Nick never had intentions of calling her.

She didn't know if she should be angry, or hurt. As much as she wanted to be angry, hurt won out. The pain she felt where her heart had been, the burning of tears threatening to spill from her eyes was beyond what she could keep in. Images flashed through her mind again—the leaves turning into rose petals, the glass fireflies, how she felt in his arms.

Now, she couldn't even breathe.

This was more than just the pain she'd experienced when her father left. This was how betrayed her mother had felt.

She'd like to say she'd never seen this coming, but hadn't she? She wanted to tell herself that at least her mother would never know she had the book, never know how involved her daughter had been in all this. Nick and his father had what they wanted.

Let it be.

Could she? Already, part of her was afraid of what they might do with both books.

Maybe Vlad and The Blood Countess would hunt them down. Maybe when they did they'd...

But, Vlad and the Countess belonged to Mr. Evans. Nick and his father would certainly get rid of them. Wouldn't they?

Shaking and unable to control her emotions any longer, Ivy hung her head and let the tears flow.

"Ivy?"

She couldn't look up at Spike and yet she didn't care to make him go away, either.

Devlin padded across the floor, head down. He lay at her feet and rested his head on her hiking boots. No crazy antics this time. This time, Devlin's instincts must have told him that whatever was wrong wasn't something he could fix with his puppyish charm and mayhem. This time, the ever-devoted Devlin knew all he could do was wait it out—to be there for her. She wondered what a Beezlepup's life expectancy was.

"Ivy?" Spike repeated, his voice soft and uncertain. He gently sat on the bed beside her. "Did you have a bad day?"

His naivety almost made her laugh. Almost.

The next morning, Ivy got herself ready for school, doing her best to put on a perfectly normal face in front of her mother. All she could really think about was how to avoid seeing Nick Marcelli ever again. And how to tell her friends how foolish she'd been in losing *The Rise of the Dark Curse*.

When Shayde caught up with her at school, she couldn't even manage to tell her best friend, which made Ivy feel even worse, more isolated.

"You don't look so good," Shayde said. "What's wrong?"

"Nothing. I don't want to talk about it," was all Ivy could manage to say as the two walked to their first period classes. She had never withheld anything from Shayde before.

For a moment, Ivy swore Shayde might burst into tears. "I just want you to know how really sorry I am," Shayde said. "You know I'd never do anything I thought would hurt you, Ivy. Never. Please always believe that."

The sentiment choked Ivy up, and so she simply nodded

as the two parted ways. Shayde turned left to go to her World History class, Ivy turned right to go to Calculus. Of course Shayde wouldn't ever do anything to hurt her. Over the years, they'd disagreed on many things, but through it all, Ivy knew that next to Devlin, Shayde was the most dependable and loyal of any of her friends.

Between the next couple of classes, Ivy avoided her locker entirely. Twice Nick texted her, asking where she was and why she hadn't texted him back or returned his call from late last night. She'd wanted to ask why he hadn't called when he got home like he'd promised. The call hadn't come in on her cell until after ten.

She wanted to ask why he felt the need to trick her the way he had.

Before darting into her last class of the day, Nick texted her again.

She stared at the message, which wanted to know why she was avoiding him. Then, she turned her phone off.

"You're going to have to talk to me sometime," Nick said, causing her to jump. He shouldn't be here. He had class downstairs, at the other end of the school.

All the pain from last night returned. And so did the anger. "What's the point? You got what you wanted!"

She turned to walk away. Nick tugged at her book bag and she spun around to face him, furious. He was still smiling. The jerk was still *smiling*.

"Did I *really* get what I wanted?" he asked.

She folded her arms defensively. "The book, Nick. Stop pretending you don't know what I'm talking about."

"Cute, huh? I was hoping you'd like it."

Ivy stepped forward. She wanted to pound him, but now that she was standing so close, she couldn't do it. "*Like* it? You—"

"Hey guys!" Shayde rushed up and snatched Ivy by the arm. Ivy hadn't been aware that Shayde was among the small crowd staring at her and Nick. "Don't mind if I borrow Ivy for a minute, do you Nick?"

Nick shook his head and before Ivy could say more, Shayde was briskly leading her away.

"Wait!" Nick said, catching up. "Geez, Ivy. I'll pick poetry or something next time. It was a joke, I didn't mean you were only capable of simple spells. We've got to get rid of that damned book. It's really getting to you."

Despite Shayde's grip, Ivy turned to face him. "Funny, Nick. Since you've already got it."

Shayde went white. Nick stared at Ivy in disbelief for a minute, then to Shayde and back to Ivy. "I don't have the book. You mean, you thought I took it?"

"No!" Shayde said. "She doesn't mean that at all. I'll tell her. Gotta go," Shayde said, dragging Ivy away. Nick stared after them looking more than a bit angry.

"Witch's Curse," Ivy said as she finally followed Shayde into the classroom. "For taking the book, I hope he gets everything that's coming to him."

There was an uneasy moment of silence before Shayde spoke again. Probably because it had been a long time since Ivy had invoked the Witch's Curse on anyone. She thought it was much nicer than any of the hexes she'd cast lately. The Witch's Curse was barely a curse at all. It hardly even qualified as a jinx. It simply was a wish that those who'd meant good received good things in return, and bad things to those who meant harm.

"Then, that'd mean you two get back together," Shayde said quietly. "See, Nick didn't take the book. I did."

Ivy turned to face her. "You? Why? The book doesn't do you any good. You can't cast spells. You're not making any sense."

Shayde seemed miserable. "It makes perfect sense! I did it to keep the book from hurting *you*. It did all the good in the world. Until now. Nick doesn't know anything about this."

"Uh oh," Ivy said, realizing what she'd just accused Nick

of doing. "He really has to hate me by now."

"I'll fix it. I'll explain," Shayde said.

Ivy sighed. "Not this time. I need to apologize in person." She didn't think any apology in the world would fix things between them now. Lately, she'd been more trouble to him than she was worth. If she were in Nick's shoes, she'd find a new girlfriend.

"The book. Where—"

"The book is safe," Shayde assured her. "I was going to tell you, I really was. Tonight. Raven and I were going to tell you. Then, we figured we'd dress up in costume and go back out to the cemetery after dark and get rid of it. No one would know it's us. We wouldn't be the only ones in the cemetery on Halloween. Don't be mad. We did it for your own good."

Part of her wanted to be mad, but she couldn't. The book really had been one of the worst things that had ever happened to her. An apology might not ever get Nick to talk to her again, but she still needed to get rid of *The Rise of the Dark Curse*. She'd apologize and ask if he wanted to help them.

Ivy managed a smile. "It's a good plan. Count me in."

Shayde smiled back. "I'm glad you aren't mad. You're my best friend, Ivy. I'd do anything for you."

The bell rang, and Ivy whispered, "I'll need to find Nick first. You and Raven wait for me at the house, okay? Spike will be there with Devlin."

"Ahem!" Mrs. Willis said from the front of the class.

Shayde nodded to Ivy. "I'll be there."

The mood of most of the students was unusually upbeat, even for the end of a Friday. People laughed and raced across the parking lot, catching up with friends. Some were even dressed up for Halloween. An eclectic bunch rushed by—a mime, a cowgirl, and a grim reaper.

In her hurry to find Nick before he got to his car, Ivy

shouldered past Frankensteins, ghouls, rock stars, and a few real zombies who hadn't bothered to try and camouflage themselves; their skin was pitted and grey. For them, dress-up was every other day in the year. There was a break in the crowd and Ivy took the opportunity to run, turning the corner and slamming straight into Mr. Evans, knocking a textbook from his hand. She hurriedly bent to retrieve the book.

"Sorry!" she said, hoping she hadn't made him angry enough to hex her right there on the spot. He'd been using *The Book of Lost Souls* so there was no telling what his frame of mind was in. She should've seen how weird he'd been acting all along. How bad had the book affected him by now?

She stood and handed him the textbook. At first, she thought Mr. Evans *was* going to hex her. At least she figured he'd give her detention for daring to even speak to him in the hall. His eyes were mere slits that matched the thin line of his mouth.

"Careful, Miss MacTavish," he said, a hint of a sneer appearing now. He held something in a closed fist. "You never know what you'll lose." He handed her the object he'd been holding. It was a dog toy—a squirrel much like the one she kept in her book bag or jacket pocket for Devlin.

"Thanks," she said as he walked away. After he was gone, she let out a sigh of relief. She'd gotten off lucky. And his attitude meant that Vlad and the Countess hadn't told him anything. Yet. She pocketed Devlin's toy, frowning now. She hadn't realized she'd dropped it.

Ivy walked into the crisp autumn afternoon, wishing she could join her classmates in carefree celebration. The sky was a pale, cloudless blue. Students were piling into cars, heading to Saludo's for pizza before going to the movies or driving down to Burlington. It appeared to be a perfect Halloween day, except for the small fact that there were two murderers on the loose and a crazed teacher who'd brought them back from the dead. She had to tell her mother about Mr. Evans. Vlad and the Countess were still out there, waiting. Ivy decided she'd call her once she apologized to Nick. Then, maybe all this would be over.

Unable to find Nick or his car in the lot, Ivy called and left two messages on his cell phone before driving home. Raven, Bane, Gareth, and Spike were outside on the front porch talking loudly and pacing when she parked her car in the driveway next to Bane's SUV. Spike ran down the steps toward her. The others were right behind him. Something was wrong. Very wrong. Spike's eyes were wide, frightened. Bane didn't look much better. In fact, his eyes were golden, as though he were close to shifting. Other than when the change was voluntary, werewolves sometimes shifted out of anger or fear.

"Spike, what's wr—"

"I couldn't stop them," Spike cried. "I'm so sorry, I just couldn't."

"Who?" Ivy asked, already afraid of the answer.

"*Them*! Vlad and the Blood Countess! You have to meet them at the old textile plant with *The Rise of the Dark Curse*." Spike closed his eyes as though trying to block out some awful memory. "If you don't, they'll kill them. They've got Shayde and Devlin."

Chapter 31

Ivy's knees buckled and Bane rushed forward to steady her. She shook her head, unable to let loose the scream trapped in her throat. They couldn't have taken them. Not her best friend, not Shayde. Not Devlin, her little Beezlepup. Her vision swam and it felt like her heart had plunged into her stomach.

"Tell us again, tell us exactly what they said, Spike," Bane urged.

Ivy forced herself to breathe.

"They said they'll be at the textile mill at sundown. That Ivy is to meet them there if she wants to see Shayde or Devlin again." Spike took a deep breath. "She can't tell anyone what she knows about Mr. Evans, either. And, if they see anyone from the Council, they'll kill Shayde and Devlin."

Raven put her arms around Ivy. "We'll get them back, Ivy. We're going with you. They said they didn't want to see anyone from the Council. They didn't say anything about us."

Ivy tried to smile. If she went alone, she didn't stand a chance of saving herself much less Shayde or Devlin. With her friends there, maybe there was a remote chance. Maybe.

Stay positive.

Shayde was tougher than nails and had handled the whole situation back in the woods much better than Ivy.

But Devlin, her little Devlin... He had to be terrified. If they hadn't already...

Surely they wouldn't kill either of them without getting hold of the book first.

"Were they okay when..." Ivy couldn't manage to say it.

"Yeah. The best I could tell," Spike said, sheepishly. "Except Devlin had the hiccups."

Ivy looked at him. "Hiccups?"

"Um, well, I had another bug withdrawal and all the mealworms were gone. So, I ate the rest of the leftover ice cream from the other night. And I sorta gave Devlin a small bowl. There were flames shooting from the crate they stuffed him into."

"I'm amazed the house is still standing," Bane said. He'd started to pace. "We've got to do something. If they hurt one hair on Shayde's head, I'll rip them apart."

Clearly, Bane hadn't dealt with Vlad or the Countess yet. He had no idea what they were up against.

"No chance Devlin caught them on fire?" Raven asked rhetorically. She knew just like everyone else that if Devlin had barbecued his captors, then they wouldn't be coming up with a rescue plan.

"Which direction did they go?" Ivy asked. She had to stop panicking and think this through. Shayde and Devlin's lives depended on it.

"They ran off toward the park. I think they went into the woods," Spike said.

"Bane, you can find them, right?" Raven asked hopefully. "Before they get to the mill? Maybe we can ambush them."

Bane shook his head. "They already have too much of a head start."

"I've got to get them back. I've just *got* to. Let's do this. Right now." Ivy felt anger diminish some of the shakiness in her voice.

"I'm in," Raven said.

"You know I am," Bane added.

"I'm in," Spike said breathlessly.

"Me too!" Gareth announced.

"We can't all go," Ivy said. "Someone has to stay here, in case...in case we don't come back."

Raven nodded and turned to her brother. "I think that's going to have to be you."

"Are you nuts?" Gareth asked. "I'm a vampire! We're freaking fast and we're strong!"

"Ivy has to go," Raven said. "And Shayde is Bane's sister. That leaves you or me."

"No, it leaves you, me, or Spike. I say Spike stays," Gareth replied.

Raven took her brother by the shoulders. At first, Ivy thought she might shake him. Instead, Raven's gestures said what Ivy knew she never would—that she loved her brother very much and she wanted to know he'd be safe.

"He's a lizard, Gareth." Raven sighed and rolled her eyes a little. "Even though he looks human. And, sometimes acts human. Who are Mom and Dad going to believe? You, or Spike? Besides, if someone sees Spike and changes him back, we're screwed. If we're not back by sundown, get help."

Gareth didn't look too happy, but he agreed. "Be careful."

Raven gave her brother an affectionate punch on the arm. "I'll be fine. They're just conjured wannabes. I'm the real thing."

Ivy hoped Raven was right. They'd need her speed and Bane's stealth and strength. And Spike had a way of being a bit hard to catch himself. All of this was good because Ivy wasn't sure what use her spells would be against Vlad and the Countess.

"Raven," Ivy said softly. "Do you happen to know where Shayde hid the book?"

"You're thinking of using it to get them back, aren't

you?" Raven asked, although it was more of a statement. "It's in the truck. Spare tire storage."

Ivy looked at her, then all of them. Truth be told, she was as afraid of the book as they were. She'd just gotten used to the idea it was gone, and Ivy had never felt more normal. Looking back, her time around it had been like a sickness, a dark fever she'd rather soon forget. And now, she was going to have to use it, at least one more time.

"Yeah," she said before turning and heading for Bane's truck. "Unless anyone has a better idea."

Bane wasted no time getting onto the highway. "It'll take forty minutes to get down to the mill. We've got that much time to come up with some sort of a game plan. Start thinking."

"Will it really take that long to get there?" Spike wanted to know.

"Yeah. The mill has been shut down for over ten years. The road going in has deteriorated. We'll have to do some off-roading," Bane explained.

"Do we *have* a plan?" Spike asked. "Even the start of one?"

Ivy ignored Spike's look of concern. "I'm working on it." She placed *The Rise of the Dark Curse* on her lap, and flipped it open. Her heart had started to pound so hard that she could feel her pulse in her temples. She couldn't believe she was holding it again, watching creepy things move beneath the pages. She heard the familiar voices that were both repulsive and yet so hypnotic and...*addictive.*

Spike eyed the book as through it might suddenly grow teeth. Ivy wanted to tell him it wouldn't. The book's ability to control, to *consume* its readers was far more subtle and much more effective.

"Isn't there some other way?" he asked.

Ivy shook her head. "I wish. But, my magic isn't strong enough. I need to fight dark magic with dark magic, Spike.

In the woods, Vlad said that *only* dark magic works on them. He also said the only thing capable of banishing them—" She jerked her head up from the book. "That's it! Bane! We need to make a short stop."

"Name it," he replied. Bane had the truck doing at least eighty by now.

"First, slow down. I want Shayde back as much as you do, but we don't want to draw attention. Second, we're going to go visit Mr. Evans. We've got to get *The Book of Lost Souls* from him. It's the only way to banish Vlad and the Countess."

With great restraint, Bane let off the gas a little. As calm as he normally was, Ivy could tell he was ready for action and before the night was over, Ivy figured he'd have it. They all would. Question was, would they live to tell about it?

"That book gives me the creeps," Spike said as he scooted as far from Ivy as possible. "I don't know how you can read it. Don't you hear those voices?"

The car fell silent as everyone strained to hear. Bane cocked his head and Ivy heard the faintest hint of whispering.

"*Rejoice! She's back. Little one loves us.*" The voices murmured. "*Little one is starting to see, just like her father.*"

"What are they saying?" Raven asked.

"Nothing. Gibberish. I can't understand them," Ivy lied. There was no sense in getting everyone more freaked about the book than they already were. What did the voices mean? She didn't love them, whoever *they* were. Starting to see? See what?

The thought of actually finding and using *The Book of Lost Souls* when she was already in over her head with its twin made her stomach ball into a knot. Even if the stranglehold had started slowly, *The Rise of the Dark Curse* had managed to cause its share of erratic mood swings and a few fits of anger. And, if it could cause a compulsive need to not only read it page for page, but an irresistible need to try the spells within it regardless of who she might hurt, then what would *The Book of Lost Souls* do? It had turned Mr. Evans into a murderer, a kidnapper, and all-around psychopath in less than a week's time. What happened when someone had control of both books?

Bane turned down Glenview Street. The beauty of living in a small town all her life was that everyone knew practically where everyone else lived. Mr. Evans's house sat at the end of the block—a white, 1930's arts and craft style cottage with a two car garage around the back that was missing a garage door, making it easy to see Mr. Evans's car inside. He'd probably left school right after she'd run into him in the hallway.

Careful, Miss MacTavish. You never know what you'll lose.

She recalled Mr. Evans handing her Devlin's toy. She hadn't dropped it. By then, Vlad and the Countess had already taken Devlin. If Vlad and the Countess hadn't told him about her, Nick and possibly Shayde, then he had somehow figured out she had *The Rise of the Dark Curse.*

Mr. Evan's house was in equally rough shape as the garage. The roof sagged in the middle and one of the front windows had a long, jagged crack in it. A notice of some sort had been taped to another window and the entire railing was missing on one side of the porch steps. The property was large, though—a nicely shaped lot with mature hardwood trees.

Bane pulled to the curb. "Now what? Do we just go knock?"

Ivy closed *The Rise of the Dark Curse.* "Yeah, something like that. Let's go."

They didn't have a lot of time—the sun would start to set just before six o'clock and it was almost two. Even if she were successful in getting the book, she had no idea how long it'd take to find the counter-spell. Then, they needed to get to the textile mill, find and free Shayde and

Devlin, and finally send Vlad and the Countess back where they came from. If nothing else, they at least needed to get Shayde and Devlin safe before the cavalry showed up. Ivy had no doubt that Gareth would stay true to his word. If the sun went down and he didn't hear from them, Gareth would tell everyone within earshot.

Please let Shayde be okay, she pleaded. *And, I'm coming for you, Devlin. Don't be scared. Hang in there.*

Ivy pushed the book under Bane's seat and hopped out. She strode to the front porch, fists clenched, prepared to do whatever it took to get the other book. No one threatened to hurt her friends or her dog and got away with it. She rapped on the front door, not really expecting Mr. Evans to answer.

The door creaked opened and Mr. Evans peered out. His eyes were wild, angry. Fearful. "Give it *back!*" he hissed at her, "Or—"

Without further warning, he shot a spell at Ivy.

A huge flash of light erupted in front of her. She raised a hand defensively, and deflected the hex. The doorframe shattered, sending pieces of splintered wood everywhere.

"*REPELL!*" Ivy shouted. Mr. Evans flew backward onto the floor with a huge *umpfh.*

Bane pushed past Ivy. Before Mr. Evans could sit upright, Bane shoved him back to the floor and stomped down on his hand.

Mr. Evans let out an angry cry. "You don't know how to put them back, do you? You can't find the right section in the book and your friend and your precious dog are going to die now."

Bane pushed down harder and twisted his shoe into Mr. Evans's hand. Mr. Evans cried out in agony. Raven caught Mr. Evans's other arm as he tried to strike out against Bane.

"Don't even *think* about touching my boyfriend," she snarled.

The search for *The Book of Lost Souls* wouldn't be easy.

Books were strewn throughout the room, some lying open and face down. There had to be hundreds of books. Strangely, they were the only thing out of place. Everything else was neat and tidy.

"How dare you! That's my *friend* Báthory has," Ivy said, "You know what she'll do! And how dare you jeopardize an innocent little dog!"

"You would have told," Mr. Evans said. He started to laugh. "I knew you had it figured out. I couldn't let you tell anyone in the Council, could I?"

His comment made Ivy think. Vlad and the Countess hadn't told him they'd seen her, Nick, and Shayde in the woods. Mr. Evans had figured out who had the book on his own. That meant Mr. Evans's conjured souls were still planning on doing him in. Ivy wanted to blame the time she'd spent with *The Rise of the Dark Curse* on the way over here, but it wasn't entirely true. Desperation was the other part of this—she'd do anything to get Shayde and Devlin back safe. Even if that meant putting Mr. Evans in harm's way. And, why not? Look what he'd done to them.

Mr. Evans continued to laugh.

"I don't find your situation funny," Bane said, twisting his foot on Mr. Evans's hand again.

Mr. Evans howled in pain. After a moment he managed to speak. "You see, it *is* funny. Ivy thinks she's so smart! She gets all of you to help her break into my home and find the book, only she can't use it so she has to come back and beg me for her friend's and her dog's life. Everyone thinks she's like her father. She's *nothing* like him. He'd know where the counter curse was. He was stronger, more powerful, and so willing to *use* that power."

Not like him? Had it been anyone else, Ivy would consider Mr. Evans's words a compliment. On the other hand, had she been more like her father she would have used any number of curses from *The Rise of the Dark Curse* on Mr. Evans by now. She wanted to, now that the book was back again.

Take the higher road, she thought.

Bane's eyes had completely changed to amber and his teeth had started to become more wolf than human. "Why did you do it, you freakin' slime ball? Why did you have your scumbags attack the Harrisons and then kill Mr. Nash and Angela?"

Mr. Evans leered at him. "Nash was nothing more than an overgrown bully. No one liked him. I did all the Kindreds a favor. Did you *see* what he taped to my front window?" he nearly shrieked. "He was trying to condemn my house! He wanted the property for himself. I've never met anyone who hates Kindreds the way he does! And the Harrisons had been out to the cemetery. I thought they might have the other book. So, I *had* to threaten them. I didn't know about Angela until after the murder. I never planned for that to happen. It was inconsequential. A small sacrifice."

Ivy heard what Mr. Evans had been saying, but it was what he'd *already* said that stuck with her. "Wait. We didn't break in earlier."

Mr. Evans paused for a moment, then laughed even harder. "Someone *else* beat you to it? Oh, now that's even better."

Spike, Raven, and Bane exchanged glances with Ivy. Someone else had beaten them to the book?

"What now?" Raven asked.

Ivy felt her heart surge, and panic threatened to consume her.

No, she kept telling herself. *Think, Ivy, think! It won't help Shayde or Devlin if you come apart.* So, who'd have the book and what would they be doing with it right now? Where would they go with it?

Two thoughts came to her mind—it was either Phoebe, or...

"Bane, do you smell the presence of anyone else?"

He sniffed the air carefully, then nodded. "Yeah, although it's not anyone I recognize. It's like it *should* be familiar. I can't figure it out. But, it's not Phoebe. I'd know her perfume anywhere. It's a bit overwhelming."

True. Even Ivy would have smelled Phoebe's perfume by now. "It's him," she said to them all. "It's our mystery guy —the one Spike saw in the park. The one who followed us into the forest. He's been following me all along. Come on, we've got to go."

She could only hope their mystery guy was still following her around.

Raven and Bane let Mr. Evans sit upright. He cradled his injured hand against his chest and he shifted his eyes between them. "Go ahead. Run along. I'll call the police before you're on the main road."

"Oh yeah. About that," Ivy said. "You're coming with us."

A very large book hurled through the air and smacked Mr. Evans across the forehead. He wobbled, his eyes rolling back in his head before he passed out.

Bane gave Ivy a surprised look. "He is?"

Chapter 32

"I can't believe we're kidnapping a teacher in broad daylight!" Spike said incredulously, his eyes wide. "And look at his front door!" He paced back and forth in Mr. Evans's cramped living room like a caged animal searching for a means of escape. "Oh, I wish I'd stayed with Gareth."

Leave it to Spike to point out the obvious. Kidnapping made everything else Ivy had done so far seem childish and insignificant. Ivy figured there wasn't *any* explanation good enough to cover this, even if she managed to do away with Vlad and the Countess. Kidnapping a teacher made the forged note look like cheating at solitaire.

"Well," Bane said, forcing a smile. "On the bright side, we can't be charged for breaking and entering. He let us in fair and square."

"I thought that was for vampires," Spike stated.

"You've been watching silly Hollywood horror movies, haven't you?" Ivy sighed.

"Then you mean like COPS!" Spike said, a hint of exhilaration returning to his voice. "Tara's grandmother watched that."

Ivy did *not* want to think about Spike peeking through Grandma Prescott's window and what else he might have seen. *Yeech!*

"Hate to spoil the fun, but how are we going to get him out of here without being seen?" Raven asked.

"I've got an idea," Ivy said, surprised by how calm she was about kidnapping Mr. Evans. "Spike, get some sheets from the bedroom and see if he's got anything that we can use for costumes. Raven, see if you can find a pair of scissors and maybe a marker somewhere. Try the kitchen. It's Halloween, so maybe with a costume no one will notice what we're doing. Bane, can you guard Mr. Evans while I fix the front door?"

Raven and Spike went off in search of the objects she'd requested, Spike muttering under his breath. Bane stood watch over Mr. Evans while Ivy did her best to repair the doorframe with a Mending spell. It wasn't perfect, and anyone who came as close as the porch would certainly see the door had been trashed. They'd just have to hope no one would notice from a distance, or at least assume that since the rest of the house was in such bad condition the frame had always been damaged.

Raven and Spike returned a few minutes later. Raven had found two black markers and a pair of old scissors that Ivy hoped would cut through the sheets Spike had given her.

In less than ten minutes, Spike and Bane had Mr. Evans hoisted upright while Ivy and Raven slid a white sheet over him. Bane drew black ovals over where Mr. Evans's eyes and mouth were. Cheesy costume, but it'd work. The sheet also hid that his hands were tied behind his back. There wasn't much Ivy could do about the way his head kept lolling from side to side.

"Too bad he's not like a Horned-Toad lizard," Spike said. "We often flip over onto our backs and stiffen up when snakes or something look too threatening."

Raven tried to right Mr. Evan's head once more. "Isn't there something like a rigor mortis charm?"

"No, unfortunately." Ivy cocked her head to one side as Mr. Evans head lolled back onto his chest. "Oddly, for the first time in my life, I can honestly say something like that would be useful. Anyway, he'll have to go as he is. We've got to go. The trick-or-treaters will start to come soon."

Raven opened the door for Spike and Bane who were pulling Mr. Evans to a standing position. Mr. Evans didn't look like a ghost as much as he looked like a dead body with a sheet over his head. Or, maybe a giant moth.

"Yeah," Raven said. "That's not going to draw any attention. Put your arms under the sheet to steady him," she coached.

Spike lost his grip and Mr. Evans fell to the floor. "Sorry," he whispered, as though he might awaken Mr. Evans. "He's a slippery one. He's all sort of...jiggly. It's hard to get a grip on him."

"That's because he's all sweaty," Bane said, sounding rather disgusted.

After one more false start, they finally had Mr. Evans upright again.

Ivy nodded her approval. "Much better. Now, let's get him to the truck as quickly as possible."

"I'll walk in front," Raven offered. "Block the view as much as I can."

Spike and Bane grunted as they squeezed through the doorway with Mr. Evans. They were out the door and halfway down the front porch steps when Ivy realized people might see Mr. Evan's feet dragging along the ground.

"Elongate!" she whispered, aiming at the length of sheet hanging around Mr. Evans calves. Ivy held her aim until the sheet reached his shoes. Then, she scanned the street as they made their way to the truck.

Three little girls dressed as ballerinas and carrying treat bags gawked as they passed by. Raven opened the hatch, and Bane and Spike shoved Mr. Evans into the cargo area. Raven dusted off her hands as she smiled at the little girls who seemed mesmerized by what was going on.

"Reaction to all that candy," Raven told the girls.

Then everyone scrambled into the truck, leaving the

little ballerinas to stare after them.

"Well, that went well," Raven said. "You can wipe memories, right Ives? Does it work on small children without giving them nightmares?"

Ivy didn't reply because Raven wasn't really expecting an answer.

Bane took the corner onto the main road a little hard and Mr. Evans rolled around in the cargo area. If he hadn't brought back Vlad and the Countess, Ivy might feel sorry for all the bumps and bruises he'd feel tomorrow.

She reluctantly retrieved *The Rise of the Dark Curse* from under the seat. She forced herself to stay focused and flipped through a few pages. There had to be some spells she could use against Vlad and the Countess.

"Why even bother with that book if you think we can find the other one? I mean, *The Book of Lost Souls* will send them back, right?" Bane asked.

Without taking her eyes off a promising, if not a very grisly spell, Ivy replied, "Because the guy who has it might not want to give it up without a little coaxing. And if, I can't get hold of *The Book of Lost Souls*, this is all we've got."

"So, you're going to use it on another Kindred?" Bane said.

"Do you want your sister back?" Raven asked him. "I know Ivy wants her back. Devlin, too. Tell me you aren't going to use whatever talent your wolf-half has."

Bane glanced at her, but Raven didn't flinch. "I'm using my vampire talents. Just sayin'."

Whatever guilt Ivy had on using black magic, Raven's statement had a profound, freeing effect. She still didn't like using black magic because of the way it wanted to consume her. But, at least she felt more justified. And, the more Ivy read, the more the pages whispered to her, the more they chanted and cheered her on. With each page, Ivy felt the overwhelming urge to never let the book out of her sight again.

Little one loves us, she does!

Reading the book was like a drug. She needed it, true. But this time, she told herself, this time, it was only because she needed it to save her friends.

Mr. Evans stirred from the cargo area and Ivy closed the book and whacked him on the head with it. He immediately went back into his state of unconsciousness.

"Where to?" Bane asked.

"The textile mill," Ivy replied. "We don't have time to try and find who this other guy is. We've got to rescue Shayde and Devlin." Ivy glanced over Bane's shoulder. He was doing eighty-five. She leaned back and closed her eyes, not bothering to tell him to slow down. Of all the things Ivy could conjure, time wasn't one of them.

They sped down the highway heading farther away from town toward the deserted industrial park as the afternoon sun journeyed across the sky, the bright light of the afternoon giving way to the more muted glow of early evening.

Ivy looked about the truck's interior. "What do you keep in the glove compartment?" she asked Bane.

"The usual. A flashlight and the owner's manual. Why?" He looked up briefly into the rearview mirror at her.

"We'll need the flashlight. Anything else you carry in here?"

"A spare change of clothing, a tire iron in the back and some jumper cables," he said.

Ivy resumed reading and didn't stop until they'd reached the textile mill, folding over pages of interest here and there. The ride got a bit bumpy as they made their way over the broken asphalt and gravel that had once been the entrance road. The pavement had buckled in some areas and had sunk in others, making large potholes that tested the truck's suspension. She heard the scrape of tires against the wheel wells more than once.

When the factory shut down, a chain link fence had

been erected around the property as a deterrent for trespassers. A chain and lock had once been installed across the gate leading into the main entrance. Now, the heavy chain had been broken, and the gates were wide open. A pickup truck Ivy had seen before, but couldn't place, was parked at the front door.

"We've got company," Bane said, driving in and choosing to park a short distance from the other vehicle. "It looks familiar. I just can't remember where I've seen it."

They all got out of the Suburban, everyone taking care to quietly close their doors—except Spike.

"What?" he asked, taking in everyone's stares.

"Nothing," Ivy replied.

"I take it we're bringing Mr. Evans?" Raven asked.

"Well, it's cruel to leave animals in the car," Spike retorted.

Bane popped the cargo door open.

"Don't worry Spike. He's going with us," Ivy replied.

Bane hauled the semi-conscious Mr. Evans over his shoulder. Ivy rummaged through the cargo storage and stuffed the jumper cables into her book bag, leaving the top unzipped. Raven handed the tire iron to Spike and the flashlight to Ivy.

"Thanks." Ivy wedged the flashlight down next to *The Rise of the Dark Curse.*

Ivy slid the book bag over her shoulder. "Well, this is it, guys. Shayde and Devlin are here somewhere."

"Let's do it." Bane set off ahead of them.

Half of the thick boarding covering the mill's front entrance had been ripped away. It reminded Ivy of the doorframe on Mr. Evans's house. The metal doors leading to the lobby were rusted shut, but entering would be easy—the plywood that had been installed over the door and the glass behind the plywood had been shattered as though with great force. Or a spell.

Ivy stepped through first, mindful of her surroundings.

The roof had collapsed in several places and huge sections of roofing material hung down. The steel rails on the second floor walkway had disintegrated. Old, rotting office furniture sat in heaps, smelling of mold and cat urine. A rat scurried behind a dilapidated copier. What walls remained upright were crumbling or bloated with black decay. Beyond that, only darkness.

They were all inside now, listening and alert. The sounds of their shuffling feet echoed faintly. Mr. Evans groaned and Spike bonked him on the head with the tire iron, and he went limp once more.

The murmur of water dripping from an unknown source resonated in the blackness. Something metallic clunked audibly. Everyone stiffened and listened.

"Rats?" Spike inquired in a whisper. No one answered him. It was a rat, all right. Two legged or four was the real question.

Ivy moved onward, prepared to strike if necessary. She heard more scuffling and as she approached an open doorway. Inside were gloomy shadows—one in distinct human form.

Ivy drew a steady breath, ready to blast whoever stood there into oblivion with a spell she'd read from *The Rise of the Dark Curse*. But, it was better to be sure who it was first. It could be Shayde.

"Retrieve flashlight—on," she whispered. The flashlight flew from her book bag, hovering a few feet over her head and switched on, illuminating the person lurking in the shadows.

"Nick!" Ivy shouted in surprise.

Nick exhaled sharply.

"What are you doing here?" Ivy asked.

"Good to see you too, Ivy," Nick said.

"How did you know we were here?" Raven asked.

"Gareth," Nick explained. "My uncle had a large catering order down the street from Ivy's house. After today, I wanted to stop and have a face-to-face talk with Ivy. Hey, I'm sorry to hear about Shayde and Devlin. I thought I could help."

The flashlight switched off and returned to Ivy's book bag. Her happiness to see Nick was overwhelming. She hugged him tightly. He hugged her back, although somewhat tentatively.

Ivy would have given almost anything not to detect the change in Nick's attitude toward her. He might be here to help, but his awkwardness in returning her enthusiasm clearly meant anything between them was over. The blame was all hers. It was too easy to remember the hurt in his eyes when she had basically accused him of playing her in the woods and stealing *The Rise of the Dark Curse*.

She straightened, feeling the uncomfortable moment shift to Raven, Bane, and Spike as well. She cleared her throat softly. "Well, thanks. We could use the help. I won't be the only spell caster."

Nick nodded. "That's what I thought." His attention focused on Bane. "Who's that?"

"Mr. Evans," Raven said, matter-of-factly. "We kidnapped him."

"Mr. *Evans?*" Nick repeated incredulously. He scrubbed his face with both hands. "You thought bringing the *one* person who started this to begin with was a *bright* idea? He's just one more for their side!"

And, some things with Nick never changed. Once again, they were at odds about how to deal with all of this. "That's why he's tied up," Ivy said. "And we couldn't leave him, he said he'd call the police as soon as we left."

Nick stepped out of the shadows and into the other room where there was more light. "I'm afraid to ask *why* he was going to call the police."

"Then don't!" Ivy hissed. She was becoming impatient, agitated. It was *The Rise of the Dark Curse*—probably. Thinking of it sitting in her book bag, saying or thinking or *whatever* the book was doing should have made her skin crawl. Instead, it was almost...*comforting.*

"Okay, lovebirds," Raven said. "This isn't helping us find Shayde or Devlin."

"Who's truck is that outside?" Bane asked.

"My uncle's," Nick said. "Good thing I had it for the delivery, too. Ground outside was too rough for the Mustang. Well, let's get rolling. We've got enough people to split up and search for them."

"Split up? Are you nuts? We're stronger as a team," Ivy said.

Nick closed his eyes and took a breath. "Listen, okay? We'll all stay real close, but not *too* close. Demons are good at hiding in the shadows. Raven can stay with Spike. Bane should change into wolf. He's far more agile and stealthy that way. Not to mention his teeth might come in handy. Leave Mr. Evans tied up and gagged under a table in the lunch room down the hall."

"And what about me?" Ivy asked.

"You enter the factory floor first," Nick said. "You and *The Rise of the Dark Curse* are the distraction, the bait."

Ivy shook her head. "No way! We need to blindside them."

Bane stepped forward. "Nick's got a good plan. They won't know how many of us there are. And you've got the greatest attention getter of all—the book."

"Speaking of," Nick said. "You'll only pretend to have the book. "I'll take it."

Ivy took a step backward. "I need it."

"Precisely why I don't want you with it," Nick countered. "It's done enough to you, don't you think?"

She blinked. "Are you saying that after all this you still want the book, or are you saying that you don't trust me because of what I've done with it?"

Nick didn't answer. Great. It still came down to the book, one way or the other.

Raven touched Ivy's arm. "He wants to be sure you'll remain on our side."

"They've got my friend *and* my dog in there! How can anyone think I'd do anything to jeopardize them?" Ivy didn't dare look at anyone. It was true—she had done some not-so-nice things in the past and now the stakes and her emotions were higher. Who knew what *The Rise of the Dark Curse* might coax her into doing next.

"It stays with me," Ivy said. "I'm already under the book's influence. No one else needs to be. Don't look at me like that. I'm getting them back. I don't care what it takes. I promise. If anyone starts to think I've gone too far, I'll hand it over then. Okay?"

Everyone nodded.

"Then I'm good with Nick's plan. But, no one moves until we see they're safe." Ivy readjusted the book bag. "Come on. We've been standing here for so long they probably already know we're here."

Nick's plan didn't sound half bad, but Ivy wasn't convinced he knew what he was doing. It was her dog, her friend. They weren't his.

When Bane reemerged as a wolf, Ivy had to admit he was definitely harder to spot in the dark. Other than when light hit his tawny eyes, he blended perfectly with the shadows.

"Who's dragging Mr. Evans?" Ivy asked.

"Got him!" Raven stuffed Bane's car key's into her pocket, then grabbed Mr. Evans by his ankles. His head smacked against the ground as she headed down the darkened hallway. Spike followed her.

Ivy and Nick set off next. They walked down the hall, careful to be as quiet as possible. As it was, every noise seemed to amplify the farther they went into the dark heart of the building. Ivy glanced over her shoulder into the deserted corridor.

It's not really empty, she told herself. Her friends were

close. But where were their enemies?

Ivy could hear her own heartbeat as she walked out of the hallway and onto the factory floor. Light trickled in from the many holes in the roof high above them like dull spotlights. Sunset wasn't too far off. She straightened and held her chin up. "I'm here," she called out.

Silence. It was as though the building itself had quieted, taking notice of the young girl who dared breach its core. A rat squeaked from somewhere on the metal grating above Ivy's head.

"I have the book," Ivy called out.

Vlad's voice boomed from somewhere—everywhere. "Then come closer, my child."

Chapter 33

Ivy stepped forward, her heart pounding. At first, she didn't see Vlad—the dust filtering through the sunlit holes in the ceiling obscured her view. As her eyes adjusted, however, and as she walked further into the massive room, she caught sight of him. Vlad sat at a long table that must have been moved from the cafeteria. On the table were skewers upon skewers of rats, some of them still wriggling. The Countess sat next to him. As Ivy approached, the Countess dabbed at the sides of her mouth with a napkin.

"So delightful of you to bring the book," the Countess said. "Now, HAND IT OVER!"

Vlad rose to his feet and placed a hand on her arm. "Manners, my sweet. Our guest has just arrived." He picked up a skewered rat. "Have you eaten?"

"Where are they?" Ivy demanded. It took everything she had not to step backward from Vlad's outstretched hand and the impaled rat-kabob.

Vlad waggled the rat and its lifeless tail swung limply. "Well, perhaps your friends are hungry." He grinned. "Come now. You don't think we know you brought friends? We heard you arrive."

Vlad took a seat. "Tell them to show themselves or we'll commence with the pleasantries."

He tugged at a rope. There was a sliding, grating sound—metal against concrete as a large, wire crate came into view. Inside, was Devlin. He was wedged up against the far side of it, as far from Vlad as possible, trembling.

"Devlin!" Ivy cried out.

Devlin whined as Vlad reached under the table and retrieved a long, wooden stick. The end was sharply chiseled.

"No!" Ivy cried out.

"No!" echoed another voice. Spike stepped from his place in the shadows. Raven, Bane, and Nick emerged from their own darkened places.

"Don't hurt him," Ivy pleaded. Never had she felt so scared, so helpless. "I've got the book. Release him and my friend and...and I'll give it to you. Then we'll all leave."

She didn't want to think of what Vlad and the Countess might do when they discovered Mr. Evans didn't have *The Book of Lost Souls* anymore.

Vlad placed the spear on the table, although his hand never left it.

The Countess let out a bark of laughter. "Leave? Whatever gave you the idea you could do such a thing? Why, your male friends look rather tasty, my sweet. Much better than rat. And you! You are like your wolf-girl friend —so young and vibrant! I'll need your blood. And then I'll need *her* blood." She pointed to Raven. "I'll save hers for last. A young vampire's blood should surely bring me eternal beauty!"

Raven came to stand near Ivy. "If you want me, then come get me."

"Yeah. You're aging by the minute," Spike said nervously.

"*SILENCE!*" The Countess rose to her feet huffing so hard Ivy thought she might pass out. "I'll not tolerate insults! Kill him, Vlad. I demand it! Impale him where he stands!"

"In due time," Vlad said, assuredly. "*All* in due time."

The Countess grew quiet, but her jaw remained set and

her breathing was still shallow.

"Where is she? Where's Shayde?" Nick demanded.

Vlad glanced around in exaggerated fashion. "Here. Somewhere."

Ivy straightened. "You're not getting the book until we see her."

Vlad took hold of the skewer. He rolled it from one hand to the next. "You care to choose between your dog and your friend? Care to watch me run your precious pet through? Give me the book and I'll open the cage door and free your pet. Refuse, and not only will I kill him and feed him to the rats, but Elizabeth shall still bathe in the blood of your friend, Shayde."

Ivy, Nick, and Raven exchanged glances.

The Countess retrieved her mirror and looked into it, gasping. "A wrinkle! Enough of this! I need one of these girls' blood."

"Blood?" Spike said, rather hoarsely. "How about something less severe? Have you tried hemorrhoid cream? Tara's grandmother swears it reduces puffiness and fine—"

"*GAHHHHH!*"

The Countess grabbed a skewer from the table, and ran at Spike. Spike was just standing there, frozen. He must have thought his suggestion was helpful. The Countess clearly didn't agree.

Bane leaped, grabbing her dress in his teeth. The fabric ripped, but the Countess didn't seem to care. Her face contorted, she tugged at the hem of her gown, the skewer still raised in her other hand.

"*Fragment!*" Ivy commanded, aiming for the skewer in the Countess's hand.

The skewer splintered in half. The only problem was that it was still a weapon. Only shorter. Raven's speed was amazing—in a mere blur, she had tackled Spike, getting him out of harm's way. Spike had barely righted himself by the time Raven was back on her feet. In a series of flips and kicks, she managed to get several good shots to the Countess's face.

The Countess wiped a finger under her nose and came away with a small trickle of blood. Had she been anyone else—Regular or Kindred, she wouldn't be standing.

"You little bitch!" the Countess said.

Vlad grabbed the spear from the table and turned toward the cage, spear held high. Devlin howled.

"Devlin!" Ivy screamed.

Nick aimed at Devlin's cage. "Repel!" The cage shot back five feet, nearly toppling Devlin over.

"*Aduro inimicus!*" Ivy shouted at Vlad. A feeling, something akin to a jolt of electricity ran through Ivy. She'd used one of the spells in *The Rise of the Dark Curse*, one meant to incinerate someone to ash. She didn't care. Vlad was nothing more than a conjured soul. He had tried to kill Devlin. For that alone, he had to die. She could hear the book agreeing with her, praising her for the spell she'd used.

For a brief moment, flames engulfed Vlad. The fire rushed over him in one direction, incinerating his skin down to a bare skull. The flames retreated in the other direction before going out all at once. Bone regrew muscle and flesh in such a rapid rate that at first Ivy wasn't sure she'd seen a skull there at all. Although the spear he'd held was gone, there was nothing more than soot on Vlad's cloak. Ivy raised her hand again, trying to muster all the energy in her body for one more spell.

Do it! Do it, little one! Show us that you love us! the book encouraged.

"*ADURO INIMICUS!*"

Again, the flames washed over Vlad, imploding and going out as soon as they changed direction. His flesh regenerated just as quickly as it had before.

Vlad laughed heartily. "You can't kill me. And without *The Book of Lost Souls*, you can't banish me."

He moved toward her. "But *I* can kill *you!*" He grabbed another skewer, ripping the wriggling rat from it and hurling the animal into the wall.

Ivy raised her hand as a shield, but Vlad threw the skewer past her.

"Or, maybe one of your friends," he said.

Ivy and Nick turned as Raven dropped to the floor. She hadn't seen it coming—she was far too intent on the Countess and her back had been turned. Bane raced over to her, whining and licking her face. Ivy ran to Raven's side.

Raven managed to raise her head. "Pull it out! Pull it out!"

Ivy took hold of the wooden spear and tried not to think about what she was doing. She gave it a hard tug, pulling the stick from Raven's back.

Raven turned her head to Bane. "I'll be fine. It didn't go all the way through. Give me a minute." She leaned back into Ivy. "Or maybe three."

Devlin barked from the other side of the room. Spike had managed to slip over and was trying to free him.

"Stand aside," Nick called to Spike. Spike stepped back, shielding his face. Nick hurled a ball of red light across the room, hitting the lock. It flipped over and popped open, then fell to the floor, freeing Devlin.

Vlad sneered, striking out with his boot as Devlin raced across the floor toward Ivy. She met his Beezlepup kisses with open arms and then hugged him tightly, covering his soft, furry head with kisses of her own.

The Countess laughed maniacally. She gathered her dress in her hands and ran across the factory floor. "How heartwarming. Stay with your mutt, or try and stop me before I kill Mistress Shayde. Care to play a game? I'll even count to a hundred. Or not." She raced up a set of metal stairs, her laughter echoing off the metal.

Nick nodded to Ivy. "It's either you or me. Shayde's best hope is someone with spells."

Bane growled, signaling he disagreed.

"I need you here," Nick told Bane. "It's you, me, and Spike. And someone's got to keep Raven safe until she recovers."

Ivy didn't wait to see if Bane stayed or was behind her. She took off after the Countess with Devlin on her heels.

The railing shifted uneasily. Ivy caught a glimpse of the Countess running toward a gutted hallway. Devlin raced ahead and Ivy followed. The hallway was dark and Ivy had to use the flashlight to see where they were going. Shadows danced off the decaying walls.

"Shayde!" Ivy called out. "Shayde? Where are you?"

Devlin growled, the hackles rising on his neck. Ivy stopped and bent slightly to pat him. Devlin stared down a corridor to her right.

"Well," came the Countess's distant voice from someone down the corridor. "There's no one down *this* hallway."

Even though the Countess was somewhere up ahead, Devlin's attention remained on the corridor to the right.

"Is someone in there?" she asked him.

Devlin bared his teeth.

"Stay! Watch." Ivy made a V with her fingers and pointed to her eyes, then back to Devlin, indicating he should stay on guard.

Devlin sat and looked up at her with uncertainty.

"It'll be okay," she said, not really sure it *was* okay. "If you hear anything, bark." Ivy walked off into the corridor alone. Someone was here, she could sense it. It was like yesterday at the woods.

"Shayde?"

After several steps, she doubted it was Shayde. Had the ties binding Mr. Evans been tight enough?

Dim light shone at the end of the hall from another hole in the ceiling. Ivy's blood grew colder as she took a few more tentative steps.

Almost there, almost there.

She could see a doorway at the end, just to the left.

Turn around. Shayde isn't here. You're wasting time.

The thought was overwhelming. Yet, going back required turning her back on whoever or whatever was down here. Ivy began her retreat, keeping her back to the wall. Devlin was still waiting for her in the open hallway. At the darkened end of the hallway, something hit the floor with a loud thud. She jumped and let out a little scream. She whirled around, sure it was Mr. Evans or maybe that the Countess had found a way to circle around.

It wasn't a person at all. It was a book.

Devlin barked, worriedly.

"Stay!" She warned him.

The book was one of the largest she'd ever seen. It was leathery and black with a blood-red gem in the center of it like the eye of a dragon. It wasn't just *a* book. Ivy knew it was *the* book.

"It's okay," she said to Devlin in a shaky voice. "I'll be right back."

She eased her way back to the end of the hallway and knelt. The book's cover rose and fell.

It was *breathing*.

She read the title, written in gold.

The Book of Lost Souls.

It flipped open and Ivy nearly shrieked. Pages turned, leisurely at first, becoming a blur as they turned faster and faster. It stopped abruptly three quarters of the way through the book. She couldn't believe what she was reading—the counter curse to banish lost souls. She was so mesmerized by what she read, that it took the sound of footfall and movement from the shadows to draw her attention away from the page.

Slowly, her eyes traveled along the stained and dirty floor caked with years of scum and who knew what, stopping when she saw a pair of men's black dress shoes, perfectly polished. Her eyes continued upward, over the dark slacks and long, expensive-looking black overcoat.

This was who had been following her. The mystery wizard, the one who had positioned *Magic for the Garden* and *The Rise of the Dark Curse* in the graveyard for her to find. She wasn't sure how her mother's gardening book fit into all this, but it did. Then, he'd helped her in the woods. He was the one who had thrown stones at Vlad and the Countess. He'd been the one to disintegrate the boards on the bridge. He'd ransacked Mr. Evan's house and taken *The Book of Lost Souls*. The only question left was what he wanted with her.

Ivy looked up to see the mystery man's face and stared, bewildered, into grey eyes that were so much like her own —her father's.

Chapter 34

After all this time, all the years she'd spent imagining him coming back, all the nights she lay sleepless in bed, thinking of what to say to him, Ivy was utterly speechless.

How often she had wanted to tell him how badly he'd hurt them, to tell him how many nights she'd awoken to her mother crying in the other room. She wanted to know how he could leave his family—those he'd sworn to love above everything else. How could he have held his daughter in his arms that day so long ago and profess she and her mother meant the world to him, and then simply walk out of their lives?

If only her words could be weapons against him, inflicting the pain he deserved.

Rage boiled inside her and yet her tongue remained silent. It was the shock of seeing him *here*, of all places. Her own father was the mystery man she and her friends had talked about.

They stared at each other for a long moment. She saw something in his expression—anguish? Did it hurt to look at her? Was it so awful?

"Shayde is okay," he said softly. "I've charmed the room she's being held in. The doors will hold until you get there. I'm sorry I couldn't do more. She was awake, and she'd see me. That can't happen. Not yet. So, the rest is up to you, Ivy. Read the spell. I'll be close."

Ivy glanced down at the page.

The counter curse required four ingredients: the plants ivy, Wolfsbane, and Nightshade, and the blood from Vlad and the Countess. The blood might be one thing—she'd already seen that the dead and damned were capable of bleeding. The question was, where was she going to get plants inside the ruined textile mill?

"Where—" Ivy looked up to ask him, but he was gone. Just like that day in the cemetery when he'd left the books for her to find before vanishing into thin air. He'd left her clues all along. He'd shown himself to Spike of all people. And, Spike had told her where to find him. Except, she'd found Vlad and the Countess instead. Of course, that had led her to Mr. Evans.

And, Spike still had a note from her father. One Spike couldn't give her until it was time.

"N*ow* would be a good time," she whispered, but the words seemed louder than she'd intended. She read the spell's ingredients again. Besides them, what else was she missing?

The answer was in one of the books. Just not in either of Skinner's books. Her father had left her more clues in the form of little penciled-in stars inside *Magic for the Garden*: ivy, Nightshade, and Wolfsbane. She didn't *need* the plant versions.

From inside her book bag, the voices started up again.

She sees! Little one sees! Use the ingredients wisely. Yesssss... do use them wisely. Then, come to us. Come to our side...

Words swam into view beneath the ingredients and Ivy felt her stomach rebel. The rest of the counter curse was horrible. And, even if she succeeded in doing the atrocities the book required, there was a warning Ivy wasn't sure she wanted to ignore. She hadn't been very good at paying attention to warnings so far. Unfortunately, this one didn't tell her of a way *out* of the consequences.

She tentatively touched the book, expecting something

to reach out from it and grab her. It didn't. Instead, it felt cool and smooth against her fingertips. Like the skin of a large snake.

Don't let it get to you, she thought. She slammed the book shut. Her head began to throb. How long before the books took control?

Ivy shrugged off her book bag. "Maximize!" she held her hand over the canvas until it grew large enough to stuff *The Book of Lost Souls* inside it. Then, she gathered up her book bag and ran down the hallway toward Devlin.

"Find Shayde," she said. "She's here, inside one of these rooms."

Devlin whined.

"Yeah, I know buddy. Both books. It can't be good. It'll all work out, somehow. Right now, we've got to find Shayde."

Devlin trotted off down the hall, nose close to the ground. He paused at the next hallway, turned, and waited for Ivy.

"Where?" she asked, looking around. The hallway was short, no windows and no closed doors. The only thing around was an open intake vent. "Devlin, she's behind a closed door. You've got to be wrong."

Devlin turned and disappeared into the large vent. His bark echoed inside.

"I am not going in there. There could be...spiders. Large ones. Or rats the size of rabbits."

Devlin grumbled in frustration.

"Fine," she said, climbing into the vent. "But there just better not be any spiders."

On hands and knees, Ivy followed Devlin's barks and the sound of his nails against the piping. At least, she hoped those were Devlin's nails and not the *tap tap tap* of a giant spider. There was a scrambling sound, and then she didn't hear Devlin any longer.

"Devlin? *Dev?*" she hurried forward, tumbling down the

ventilation system face first. After a quick moment of free fall, Ivy landed in a pile of rubble. Roaches ran out beneath the pile of rotting drywall and carpeting.

She squealed and got to her feet, dancing around and brushing herself off.

"Gerrr," Devlin said.

"If that's your version of ewww, then I agree."

Devlin pawed at her leg.

Whhhomp!

The sound of the door rocking on its rusty hinges brought Ivy back to the task at hand.

"Your magic won't hold!" cried the Countess from the other side of the door.

Ivy didn't want to say it wasn't her magic—that it was Daddy Dearest's magic—and if the Countess thought *this* was something, then just wait until she saw what spell good old Dad had in mind for his daughter's next act.

Fresh pain and anger rose inside her. After ten years, she thought he'd have something better to say, like how wrong he'd been, and that he loved her dearly. He hadn't even mentioned how she'd grown. Didn't ask how her mother was holding up. Nothing! Not one fatherly thing. Just *hey, here's the counter curse, good luck.*

Then, he'd left her. Again.

No surprise there.

Whhomp!

Devlin growled and bared his teeth at the bulging door. The doorframe had busted away, and the frail door began to splinter under the Countess's assault on the other side. With each shove, Ivy could see Báthory's maniacal grin and her wild eyes. Her nose had quit bleeding, and a line of dried blood remained caked above her lip.

A muffled noise came from behind another pile of trash. Ivy walked around it to find Shayde bound and gagged. Shayde couldn't change. At least, not the way she'd been tied up. Her arms were duct taped behind her. Her ankles were also bound in duct tape and rope had been looped through the tape at her feet and wrists. The result meant Shayde was bent backward, in an arc. If she tried to change, she'd not only dislocate her shoulder blades, but probably break her legs and her back as well.

Ivy fell to her knees beside her friend, ignoring the sound of the door coming off its hinges. With both hands, Ivy grabbed a section of the rope tethering Shayde's ankles and wrists. She moved it back and forth a few times, then tapped the rope with one finger. The rope continued to apply friction to the tape.

"Saw," Ivy commanded, and the rope began to cut through the tape binding Shayde.

WHHOMP!

The door burst open and the Countess spilled into the room.

Ivy took aim. She just needed a few more seconds. *"REPEL!"*

The Countess's feet went out from under her, partly thanks to Devlin who'd ran behind the Countess's legs. When the Countess flipped backward over Devlin, his eyes squinted shut as though he thought this might hurt. He whimpered, but shook it off, darting away before the Countess could nab him.

Shayde was now free and peeled back the tape covering her mouth.

This wasn't going fast enough. Ivy yanked a couple hairs from Shayde's head.

"Oww!" Shayde complained.

Ivy ripped out a few strands of her own hair.

"This isn't going to work," Ivy said.

"What isn't going to work?" Shayde asked.

"I need some of Bane's hair," Ivy replied. She'd have to start the spell and hope she could come up with something.

Devlin bounced up and down and barked at the Countess's feet. He dashed in to nip at her heels. She went to kick him and Ivy issued another repelling spell. This time, the Countess stayed upright, although she did stagger back a foot or two.

Every little bit helps, Ivy thought.

Ivy slid the book bag to the floor and removed *The Book of Lost Souls.* The book instantly flew open to the page for the counter curse.

The Countess pushed aside some of the debris on the trash pile and lunged for Ivy. Shayde and Devlin were on her in an instant, giving Ivy time to roll out of the way. Ivy heard the sound of shredding fabric and looked up to see Devlin tear off a large piece of the Countess's dress. He brought the material to Ivy.

The Countess's eyes found Ivy and the book. For a moment, her eyes went blank, then she grinned.

"MINE!" the Countess cried. "You have them! And now they'll be *mine!"*

Shayde hit the Countess in her midsection with a board from the trash pile. She didn't even flinch.

Ivy understood what Devlin had done—the piece of dress material had a tuft of Bane's hair on it. She grabbed them, divided up the hairs, stuffing the extras into her jeans pocket. Then she dropped the rest onto the page. The strands of hair transformed into their plant namesakes. The leaves shriveled, which left just the stems. Each stem swirled into words—the deed she'd have to perform as part of banishing the Countess. The damn book wanted its pound of flesh and she was hardly in a position to refuse.

Shoving the thought from her mind, Ivy concentrated on getting the last ingredient—blood from the Blood Countess herself. She shuddered.

"Muridae," Ivy chanted. "Muridae, epulor inimicus."

The sound of tiny nails scratching at the walls grew almost deafening. Ivy placed her hands over her ears.

The Countess narrowed her eyes at Ivy. "What trickery is this? It will not work!" She stepped forward just as a swarm of rats ran over her shoes. They climbed up her dress thirty, maybe forty of them at a time. The Countess swatted at them and they bit at her hands, drawing blood.

"Ivy, what are you doing?" Shayde asked.

"What I have to," Ivy replied.

Shayde nodded without taking her horrified eyes off the hundreds of rats that now nearly covered Countess Elizabeth Báthory. Rats chewed on her ears, her lips, her nose.

The Countess's screams were a mixture of anger and pain. She tore a few of the rodents from her bodice.

"Retrieve," Ivy said quietly. Reluctant to give up the feast, the rats slid backward across the floor. She picked them up, one by one, wiping their tiny paws and their mouths with her fingers.

As she set each rat free, it ran back to join the others. The Countess was bleeding, but no sooner did the rats bite off a small bit of flesh then the Countess regenerated. Still, it was a horrible sight. The Countess teetered on her feet, the weight of squirming rats too heavy for her.

"Ivy," Shayde began to protest.

"Shhh! Don't say it," Ivy said, her voice quivering. She swiped her bloodied hand onto the pages of the book.

The Countess was screaming now, flailing her hands against the army of rats. Her skin had stopped regenerating, and worse, it was decaying before Ivy's eyes.

"Ivy," Shayde called out behind her.

Ivy didn't answer. She wanted to tell Shayde to be quiet. She could hear the rats better if Shayde didn't interrupt. She had to take another look. It repulsed her, but she was unable to stop herself. The Countess fell to the floor, moans erupting from her as the rats continued feeding on her disintegrating flesh.

A large black rat shoved a smaller rat out of its way, perching itself on the Countess's right cheek. The rat's whiskers twitched in tune with its nose a few times before the rat settled in, biting deeply into the Countess's blankly staring eye.

Shayde grabbed the strap of Ivy's book bag, breaking Ivy's trance. Ivy whirled around, furious. "Don't touch it! No one touches them except for *ME!*"

Ivy stopped herself from adding, *they're mine.* Thankfully, whatever hold the books had a moment ago began to fade and Ivy did her best to hold on to the person she still believed she was.

Shayde stepped back. "I get what you did, Ivy. I really do. And thanks. But, *both* books? Where did you find it, anyway?"

"Let's go," Ivy said, gathering *The Book of Lost Souls* and stuffing it back into the book bag.

Shayde nodded and ran for the door with Devlin right behind her.

Yelling, crashing, and small explosions caught their attention, saving Ivy from explaining about her father.

"I should have known you weren't alone," Shayde said, setting off in the direction of the noise. "My brother's here, isn't he?"

Ivy and Devlin raced after Shayde. "And Nick, Raven, and Spike," Ivy added.

They found their way through the dank and dimly lit hallways. Ivy was thankful for Shayde's perfect sense of smell and hunting ability. Shayde made it to the factory floor first. In Ivy's absence, a full-on battle had ensued. Nick was busy hurling anything and everything at Vlad. Nick dodged a spear Vlad threw at him. The wooden spears were all gone, probably no more than ash at Vlad's feet, thanks to Nick's spells. Now, Vlad held an iron one instead.

"Retrieve!" Nick called out, aiming at the spear. Vlad's hand wavered, but the spear still firmly remained in his grasp.

Raven was back in action, although not with her former speed. She had squared off with the newcomer to the scene. Somehow, Mr. Evans had gotten free. Ivy had little doubt that the Countess had something to do with it.

She may not have been as quick, but Raven was holding her own at avoiding the spells Mr. Evans cast at her. With cat-like grace, Raven performed an airborne flip and twist, not only dodging a spell, but managing to make contact to Mr. Evan's chest with her boot heel and knock him to the ground.

Bane had grabbed hold of Vlad, sinking his teeth deep into Vlad's leg. Vlad snarled, then caught sight of Ivy and his sister. Vlad struck Bane across his head. Bane yelped, then attacked Vlad again.

Shayde searched for a weapon of some sort, settling on a splintered piece of lumber. She went to join her brother in his fight.

Ivy walked onto the factory floor. This was it. All she had to do was repeat the counter curse.

And then we can be with you forever! Said the whispering voices from within the books.

She sat the book bag on the floor, knelt next to it and removed *The Book of Lost Souls*. Then, she hesitated. She would not be with it forever. She'd resist it if was the last thing she ever did. The book's smooth, cool surface beckoned her.

I won't give in!

"The book! She has the book!" Mr. Evans shouted from across the room. He shot a bolt of lightning at her just as Nick's own spell knocked Mr. Evans off his feet. The bolt missed her and blasted the pole behind her, weakening the metal walkway above. It shifted and groaned and a small mountain of rusted metal and dirt floated down upon them like bloodstained ash.

Vlad, who had his arm raised, spear in hand, stopped and turned away from Nick. In fact, everyone's attention seemed to fall on her. Ivy flipped the book open. Tendrils of black smoke escaped from the pages. Inside, spiders spun webs around letters and hideously disfigured people stared back at her. Other, even more inhuman things bubbled beneath the page's surface. Trembling, Ivy reached out to touch the page. At the last minute, she withdrew her hand.

"IVY!" Spike shouted.

Spike slid toward her like he was skidding into home plate. He snatched up the book bag and used it as a shield against one of Mr. Evan's spells. The result ripped apart her book bag and sent Spike sprawling to the ground, unconscious.

Leave him! the voices inside the book demanded.

She was aware of the fight continuing around her, and that Devlin had come to sit next to her. Not too close, which was good. She didn't want anyone near her, near the books. It was for their own good, she reasoned. Nothing more.

Ivy stared at Spike for a moment. He was breathing, so he'd live.

He's expendable, inconsequential, echoed a voice in her head.

Yes! Yes! Expendable! The books whispered.

Without another thought, Ivy returned her attention to the book.

Chapter 35

Ivy cared about Spike, and the more she thought about how she'd come to think of him as a friend, the more she realized how the beings inside Skinner's books had reacted—hatred, anger, jealousy. The books wanted her for themselves. How much longer before she stopped caring for anything or anyone except them?

No. I won't join them. I won't give in.

She had to get rid of Vlad. Then, she'd—

"*Retrieve!*" Mr. Evans shouted, and *The Book of Lost Souls* launched itself toward him.

Just as his outstretched fingers touched the book, Shayde slammed into Mr. Evans, knocking him down. The book tumbled from his hands—and into Vlad's.

"*No!*" Mr. Evans screamed. He cursed repeatedly as he struggled against Shayde.

Raven had joined Shayde and together, they held Mr. Evan's hands down on the ground and away from either one of them.

"Ivy, I could use those jumper cables we brought!" Raven shouted.

To Ivy, the book was more important. They'd have to manage without her. Bane and Devlin were snarling and snapping at Vlad's feet. Vlad kicked at them, sending Devlin sprawling backward with a yelp. She wanted to cry out for Devlin. He scrambled back to his feet and rejoined Bane.

He was okay.

For now. But how much longer? Was she willing to risk him to get the book back?

"RETRIEVE!" Ivy yelled in unison with Nick and Mr. Evans.

Shayde grabbed the jumper cables and ran toward Raven who hadn't managed to completely stop Mr. Evans, although Ivy could see she'd most likely broken all the fingers on his left hand.

The combined effort of the Retrieve command was enough to whirl Vlad around.

"The book is MINE!" Mr. Evans shouted. "Let me go!" He struggled beneath Raven and Shayde's grasp.

"Give me the book, Nick," Ivy said. "Let me have the book. NOW!"

He shook his head. "Can't do that. If you can perform the banishing spell, then so can I."

Vlad tugged at the book, tried to break it free of the three-way spell that held it in place. The book nearly flipped from his hands, the giant red gem in the middle brightening like a demonic eye, watching to see who would be worthy of it.

Who is willing to give up everything for us? The book whispered.

"Me!" Mr. Evans yelled. Shayde and Raven had managed to bind his broken hands together at the wrists with the jumper cables, breaking his spell. He didn't seem to care.

"I command you," Mr. Evans said to Vlad. "Bring it to me."

Vlad sneered, but obediently moved toward Mr. Evans. Bane and Devlin tugged on the back of his cloak, trying to stop his progress. Devlin hiccuped, catching Vlad's cloak on fire. Vlad whirled about, sending Devlin flying a few feet. The flames forced Bane to let go.

She had to get rid of Mr. Evans at all costs. Then, she'd deal with Nick. Hand poised, Ivy faced Mr. Evans, ready to hit him with a near-death curse. "Lucis—"

Nick's hand caught hers. "No, stop."

She shoved an elbow into his side. "Get away from me!"

Vlad, who had easily extinguished the flames, paused, as though driven by the book's will. He turned toward Ivy.

"NOOO!" Mr. Evans cried.

Nick took a step closer "Ivy, let me—"

"*Repel!*" Ivy's spell slammed into Nick, knocking him backward. She didn't have time to explain—she didn't want to hurt him.

Everyone stood in horrified silence, Even Devlin. She walked closer to Vlad. "Who do you serve? Him, or me?"

Vlad's expression was unmistakably one of contempt. He raised his chin defiantly. "Neither!"

"ADURO, ALL!" Bound, hands broken, Mr. Evans wasn't done yet. His spell managed to ignite a heap of trash. Every upholstered chair and every pile of garbage burst into flames. Within seconds, the flames raced up walls and doorways.

"We've got to get out of here," Shayde said. "Ivy, let's go."

"Not yet. Get Spike out of here. In fact, all of you, get out."

There wasn't a lot of time to argue. In a few minutes, they'd all be trapped. Nick put out a fire, only to have it self-ignite a moment later.

Vlad laughed darkly. "Stay, why don't you? You and the others will burn. All I have to do is wait. After your glorious shrieks of agony, you'll be gone. Then, the books are mine."

"Ivy, please," Nick urged.

"REPEL!" Ivy shouted, slamming Nick backward again. She raised her hand at him. "Don't make me use something darker, Nick. Get Devlin. Take Shayde and Bane with you."

"And Mr. Evans?" Shayde asked.

"Let him stay for all I care," Ivy said, still staring down

Nick. Truth was, she did care. She hoped they'd take him, too. Banishing evil souls that were already dead were one thing. Leaving Mr. Evans to burn alive was something else. None of her friends could be of help anymore. They had to believe the books had won her.

Ivy had to believe they hadn't.

Nick walked past her. "Come on, guys."

They huddled close for a second, then Shayde gathered Devlin in her arms. He barked in protest, trying to free himself from Shayde's protective hold. Bane walked with his sister, his head and tail low.

Raven gave Ivy a pained look, then she grabbed Spike and began dragging him across the floor toward the closest exit.

Nick bent to do the same with Mr. Evans. Mr. Evans lashed out with a violent kick.

Nick aimed at the tire iron next to Ivy's book bag. "Retrieve!" The tire iron slid effortlessly to him. Nick smacked Mr. Evans with it, rendering him unconscious once more.

With all the hits to the head, Ivy wondered if Mr. Evans wouldn't have a serious concussion.

Nick grabbed hold of Mr. Evans and followed the others.

"So, you're willing to die for your friends?" Vlad asked.

Fighting back tears, Ivy turned to face him. They'd left her. She wanted them to, but it still hurt to know how this was going to end. Even if she were strong enough to resist the books, she'd never get rid of Vlad in time to get out of the building alive.

She aimed for the *The Book of Lost Souls*. "Retrieve!"

The book lurched forward, pulling Vlad with it.

Ivy curled her fingers inward, willing the Retrieving spell to work with all her might. Vlad slid forward just a little more.

Above them, the weakened metal walkway groaned and

rattled. One of the stair railings gave way and clattered to the floor. Around her, a few of the flames were snuffed out before igniting again. She glanced around. "Nick?"

No answer. Of course not. She'd used magic against him, wanting to send a message to the others she'd do the same to them. It was the only way she could ensure they would leave her. But now, she wished she weren't alone.

Choose! Choose us! The voices in the books screamed. *Choose us and we'll force him to surrender the book to you! You'll be safe! You'll rejoin your friends.*

"Unless you want to go hand to hand with me, you lose," Vlad taunted.

Ivy raised her hand again, this time, aiming for the discarded stair railing. She had an idea. "Retrieve!"

The rail flew to her hand. "Okay, she said. Have it your way."

She raised the pole, intent on running Vlad through—or at least die trying. The only other option was to surrender to the books. Part of her wanted to believe them, that the books would allow her safe passage out of the building. In her heart, she knew better.

An echo came from somewhere above. Maybe it was behind her, she couldn't tell.

"Nick?" she called softly.

"There's no one here," Vlad said, sardonically. He extended his hand. The metal spear he'd almost used on Devlin rolled across the floor and then leapt into his hand.

Another echo. Then she definitely heard a faint voice.

The metal pole jerked free from her hand and soared through the air. Vlad raised his own spear when Ivy's struck him in the chest. Vlad surveyed the jutting metal with shocked curiosity.

"You *impaled* me," he said incredulously. Blood spilled onto his cloak. *Blood. His* blood.

"Retrieve!" Ivy yelled. Vlad winced as the metal was wrenched from his body. Ivy caught the pole, then readied herself to fetch the book before the surprise left Vlad's face.

Another whisper. Someone *was* here.

The metal walkway above collapsed. A blast of air—a spell—knocked Ivy backward in time to dodge a large piece of grating. Vlad wasn't as lucky. Much of the walkway collapsed on top of him. She heard him grunting beneath the weight.

When Ivy collected herself, she saw that the book had been thrown clear. It lay on the floor, gently breathing. Watching. Waiting. "Retrieve!"

The book slid forward. Wiping sweat from her forehead, Ivy opened the book. Again, the papery wisps of words drifted up to her.

Ours. You'll soon be ours.

No. She wouldn't believe it. She wouldn't. Never. She'd burn before she surrendered to whatever lurked inside the book.

Too late! She thought. She'd already taken the Countess. Enjoyed it, actually. Without a doubt she'd enjoy Vlad's demise just as much. No one could perform such cruel things, such cruel magic without having it leave a mark.

Little one sees, she understands about the dark stain upon her soul! She sees!

She flipped toward the back of the book. The spell was here, somewhere. On its own accord, the pages turned, slowly at first, then picked up speed.

Ivy took the remaining combination of hair from her pocket. She glanced at the strands—a few black wolf hairs, one red human hair, one brown. What would the book have her do to banish Vlad?

Vlad shifted under the metal grating. He shoved one piece of grating aside, then another. He'd be free in a moment or two.

Inside the book, people leered and pointed at her and bugs scuttled from one page to the next. Grotesque beasties rushed forward as if to leap off the yellowing paper at her, the page turning just in time.

Then the pages came to rest on the spell for the counter curse. Hundreds of screaming faces, skeleton heads, and countless hands pushed against the other side of the yellowing, waxy-like page. Ivy held her hand over the book and let go. As the strands of hair fell, they morphed into their plant counterparts again: ivy, Wolfsbane, and Nightshade. *Luck, strength, sever life.*

As soon as the hair touched the page, the leaves melted away once more. Again, the stems writhed like snakes, twisting, forming into written words. Horrified, Ivy read them.

Please, no. Don't make me do this.

She held the bloody tip of the metal pole over the book, then rammed it into the page. A horrible, orange-red light filtered up to her, making the pages translucent. Strange creatures waddled beneath. An elongated face swam into view, its chin as pointed as its nose. Its lips parted.

A wave of greasy nausea washed over Ivy and she fought the urge to be sick. The room spun. A drop of blood dripped down into the man's mouth.

Vlad shoved the last piece of grating away and rose to his feet.

It was now or never.

Ivy took a steadying breath. "Cursus catomidio per!"

Three metal poles of varying sizes rose into the air. She stood, letting them sail past, some close enough to graze her hair. Each found their mark on Vlad's torso. He shrieked, and staggered backward, eyes wide, hands clutching one of the metal poles.

Ivy tried to turn away, tried not watch, but it was impossible. The last spear, the one Vlad had almost used on Devlin, rolled from the debris. It rose into the air, hovering just so Vlad could see it. Already, he'd started to wither, his skin aging years within seconds.

"And this one's for my dog," Ivy said. The spear jettisoned forward, impaling Vlad dead center of his chest, flinging him backward twenty feet into the wall behind him.

Vlad struggled for a moment, blood spilling from his lips. Then, he disintegrated into dusty black soot.

The flames were nearly all around her now.

The books chimed in, trilling their usual chorus. *Choose us and you'll live with us! Choose, and you'll see your friends.*

Ivy started to reach down to pick up the book. Maybe it was her only way out. Then, she thought of Nick and Devlin. She would miss them so much. How must they feel about her right now? They thought she'd already chosen the books over them, had already turned into a dark Kindred. Her heart ached to the core.

She'd be the only one who would ever know the truth. Ivy stood straight and stepped over the books, ignoring the screams of defeat from within them. The heat from the fire grew. All she could do now was wait and hope her death would be quick.

She wondered where her father was, then remembered that she'd heard voices. He was here, or had been. Maybe he'd helped the walkway to collapse.

But why hadn't he saved *her?*

This wasn't the way she thought she'd die. Witches had been burned at the stake for centuries—burned to death for being evil and treacherous. It was ironic, really. In order to do good, she had to turn to dark magic—sever the soul, the lifeline, of the dead and the damned. Ivy put her forearm across her mouth and coughed. She didn't want to die. Frantically, her mind raced for a spell that'd give her oxygen, douse the flames, anything. Her eyes scanned the wall of fire, desperately searching for any means of escape.

There was nowhere to go. Nothing left to do.

Some of the flames died down, and Ivy made out a figure walking toward her. Nick walked through the fire as though it wasn't there, wasn't lapping at every part of him.

His jacket and shirt had been torn, and there was a bleeding cut next to his ear, but the fire itself hadn't touched him. Of course, demons didn't burn. Only witches.

"I'm sorry. I wanted you to think—"

"We know," Nick said. "If the books really had you, you wouldn't have used a Repelling spell. You wouldn't have told me to take Devlin."

"But, maybe the effects the books had on me will resurface. Maybe I'm destined to be a…" Ivy hung her head.

Nick took hold of her shoulders and she reluctantly met his gaze.

"Dark witch? *You*? This isn't still about the Curse of the Tea Cozy thing, is it?"

"Nick—"

"We're walking out of this together," he said, taking her hand and scanning the flames. "In *theory* I should be able to emit enough power to prevent you from being burned." He didn't sound convinced, and worse, he didn't *look* convinced. His eyes were full of worry.

"Just keep me close," Ivy said with another cough. "I'll try to come up with a charm." She hoped he couldn't detect the lie.

"You've done a pretty good job so far. I wouldn't have been able to find you if you hadn't used the overhead sprinkler systems to emit a Misting charm."

She hadn't done any such thing. *He'd* done it, she realized. Her father. Was he still here? She didn't think so. He had a way of disappearing.

The fire inched closer. Ivy heard it advancing into the space behind her. Why wasn't she sweating? Another couple of feet and the fire would reach them. One final time, she scanned the area for a means of escape.

"We're going to make it, Ivy. We will. Just stay with me, keep moving."

In front of them was a wall of flames.

Nick hugged her tightly against him. "I think there's enough fire in your soul. What do you say we try? Fight fire with fire?"

She offered a thin smile, but her breath caught in her throat. Despite what Nick thought or whatever powers she'd acquired, Ivy suspected the flames would still claim her life. She'd turned her back on the books. Maybe they'd cursed her as she stepped over them.

At least she'd die holding Nick's hand. He'd come back for her. She wouldn't die alone.

If only things had been different. If only it hadn't come to this before they worked everything out. Before *she* worked everything out.

Ivy thought of Raven and Gareth and wondered if they'd visit her headstone. She thought of how Shayde had stolen the book in order to help save her from its clutches. She recalled the way Devlin barked desperately for Shayde to release him so he could be by her side, even though that act of devotion would have cost him his life.

Be brave, she tried to tell herself. With a demon at her side, maybe death by fire would hurt less.

Ivy closed her eyes as Nick pulled her into the flames.

Chapter 36

The sound of the flames roared in her ears, and Ivy couldn't breathe. Still, death by incineration wasn't as bad as she'd expected. Instead of unbearable heat, she felt only mildly uncomfortable. When the din of the inferno stopped, a rush of fresh air hit her face like cold rain. Maybe she'd been allowed to go to heaven after all. Then she felt Nick's hand still in hers and opened her eyes.

How had she been able to walk through fire? Her father had been inside, too. And, although she couldn't prove it, Ivy was pretty sure he'd found a way out—that he'd pulled another disappearing act or had walked through the flames as well.

Bane, Spike, Devlin, and Raven caught sight of them at the same time. Raven beamed, then she ran to them with Bane right behind her. Spike was a bit slower, conscious again, although still unsteady on his feet.

After a quick embrace, Ivy pulled away and looked at them all. "Is everyone okay?"

Shayde hooked a thumb toward Spike. "Your hero here will have a headache, but he'll be okay. And you know us werewolves—Bane will be fine probably before we walk in the front door. Raven—"

Raven finished for her. "I'm pissed my favorite jacket and sweater has a bloody hole in it, but I'm back to my perfect vamp self."

"Devlin?" Ivy called.

A bark echoed from around Bane's truck. Devlin raced toward Ivy and she dropped to the ground to greet him. He washed her face in warm, wet Beezlepup kisses and she hugged him fiercely. "I love you, Devlin. I'm so glad you're okay." She kissed him repeatedly on his head and snout.

"Now that we're all back together, Ivy, how'd you do it? Witches can't walk through fire," Raven said.

Nick glanced over at Ivy, and she thought that same question flickered in his eyes. Then he winked. "True," he said to Raven. "Witches burn, but Demons don't." He gave Ivy a grin. "Call it a little protective mojo."

Ivy returned the grin. Nick wasn't going to tell anyone it probably wasn't him that had allowed her to walk through fire. Nick didn't know how she'd done it, but he seemed content to let it be for now.

"You did it," Nick said. "And you were amazing in there. A bit tense at times, but amazing."

Ivy refrained from breaking into an all-out grin. She scanned the area for two more people—her father and Mr. Evans. Neither were in sight.

"It's weird how Mr. Evans just disappeared," Raven said. "We dragged him outside, then tossed him in the back of the pickup truck. Somehow, while we were making sure Spike was okay, he took off."

Bane shook his head and shrugged. "Damnedest thing ever. He was lights out when we dumped in the truck bed, and we never heard or saw him get out. We were parked only a few spots away."

Yep. It had been her father. The others could believe what they wanted. They didn't know anyone else was here. How he managed to take Mr. Evans without being seen, she'd probably never know, especially since he was long gone. Again.

The fire continued to engulf the building and part of the sagging roofline caved in.

"Come on, we'd better go," Bane said.

That feeling, that odd sensation of someone watching, crept over Ivy. She wasn't sure if it made her feel much better that she knew who it was or not. Now, the only *mystery* about their mystery man was why he'd come back. She caught a glimpse of his dark overcoat, standing by a dilapidated sign just inside a line of shadows. He nodded, then stepped back into the darkness.

She still wasn't able to call him her father. So, what *did* she call him? As much as she disliked admitting it, he had been the one to save them today. Without him handing over *The Book of Lost Souls*, odds were that none of them would be alive right now.

Ivy followed the others toward the cars.

Raven gave Ivy a playful nudge. "You and Devlin go with Nick. I'll handle this crew."

Ivy nodded. "We've got one more stop to make—Forever View. It's time Spike went home. What do you say, Spike?"

Spike nodded and a tear spilled down his cheek.

"Does your head hurt that much?" Shayde asked.

"No," he said. "Sorry. It's been a whole day without any bugs. I tend to get a little emotional."

Shayde patted Spike's shoulders as they got into Bane's Suburban.

Ivy joined Nick and Devlin in the pickup. As they sped away, she looked back at the textile mill. Huge billowing smoke rose above the burning hulk of building while sirens wailed far off in the distance. She had to agree with Spike—she was a bit emotional right now. They could have died back there.

And then, there was her father. She didn't know what to think about that.

"Are you okay?" Nick asked.

Ivy nodded and turned back around to stare out the windshield.

"Ready, Spike?" Ivy asked.

Spike's smile had a hint of nervousness to it, but Ivy also didn't think she'd ever seen him so happy.

"You look great," Shayde said. "You're the best-dressed lizard I know."

"Thanks," Spike said as he brushed a bit of lint off the purple velvet costume he wore.

"The perfect Romeo once again," Raven added.

The four friends, plus Devlin, walked out of the parlor and back to the living quarters. Everyone else had piled into Gareth's room, eagerly waiting. When Spike entered the bedroom, Nick, Gareth, and Bane stepped to the side, revealing Gareth's daybed and the black and copper lizard on top of it.

"*Grrr*uff!" Devlin said, executing a proud sit. His tail wagged furiously behind him.

"Welcome home, Spike. I think you've met Guinevere," Gareth said. "A.k.a., Gwen."

Shayde and Ivy had dressed Gwen in a tiny green Juliet costume, right down to the cream-colored headdress.

Gareth leaned next to Spike and whispered, "Are you sure? You could've dated the whole cheerleading squad."

Spike looked lovingly at Gwen. "Yeah, I'm sure."

"Okay," Gareth said, smiling and clearly happy that Spike hadn't decided to stay human any longer. "Just sayin'."

"Gwen the Gecko," Nick said with a nod. "Nice name."

Spike embraced Ivy. "Thanks, Ivy," he said, still hugging her tightly. "For everything. Check Dev's collar later, okay? And just so you know," he said, releasing her. "The note never was in my underwear. I don't wear any."

"Uh, well... thanks for the visual Spike." Ivy grinned, although the information was enough to make Ivy wish for eye bleach. "Yeah, sure. I'll check. Take care, Spike. As far as pets go, other than Devlin, I love you the most. And as for everything else? Anytime, Spike. Anytime."

She stepped back and Spike nodded, ready. With a swish of a finger, she reversed the changing spell she'd first tried just seven days ago.

How far everything had come since then. The spell worked better this time. Instead of the grotesque transformation he'd gone through before, a vortex of silvery mist swirled around Spike, and all Ivy could see was his outline shimmering behind it.

When the mist disappeared, Spike the human was gone. In his place was Spike the Horned Toad Lizard.

"I'll miss you, Spike," Ivy said, feeling a bit choked up. "I hope you were right. I hope you'll remember your time as a human."

Spike gave Ivy a wink and Ivy smiled. Maybe the Spike she'd come to know and love would always remember—just like he'd thought he might. She considered his lizard's wisdom. Yeah, he *was* right—at least, it felt that way. Once touched by anything that changed your life, how could it not be part of you forever?

Gareth knelt and gently picked up Spike and set him on the bed next to Gwen. Raven raised her small pocket camera and took a picture of the two costumed lizards.

"I now pronounce you toad and gecko," Raven announced.

Gareth placed his two pets into their terrarium and he and Raven tossed in a sprinkling of mealworms on the lizards.

Raven laughed. "You may now eat the bugs."

"I think we'd better go," Shayde said. "Besides, the newlyweds need their privacy."

Raven closed the bedroom door behind them, and they all made their way to the parking lot.

"I'd say we're all dead once our parents find out, but hey! I'm sort of already there, being the *un*dead among us," Raven said with a shrug. "Still, we're all probably grounded for life once this gets out. Think our parents will go easy since we found the person behind all this?"

Ivy grimaced. "I'm not counting on it."

Nick held the truck's passenger door open and Ivy and Devlin got in.

Shayde waved as she hopped into the Suburban. "Well, if nothing else, see you guys at school."

Ivy waved good-bye as Nick put the truck in reverse.

They passed a few vehicles on their way, even a patrol car that luckily kept going in the opposite direction. They were sure that the Northwick local thirteen fire station had responded to the fire by now. She wondered where Mr. Evans was, and if he was still under the influence of the books. She wondered what he'd tell the Council about tonight's events once they caught up with him. Maybe he wouldn't be so eager to explain things either.

The occasional trick-or-treater still wandered the street when they arrived at Ivy's house just after seven. It was already dark outside and her mother had left the porch light on. The living room lights were also on and she wondered if her mother knew yet, but decided she didn't. If her mother had known, she'd been on the front porch, arms folded. Weed control at Forever view would have been the least of her worries.

Nick helped her out of the car and Devlin scurried up the porch to wait.

They walked reluctantly after him, hand in hand, stopping halfway up the walk.

"Thanks for coming after me." Ivy stared into his eyes, not knowing what to say next. All she knew was that words or not, she wanted to stand here with him all night.

"Still scared?" Nick wanted to know. "Still scared of letting anyone in?"

"No. *Yes*. But you're too close to let go, Nick. I'm not sure I could stop it if I tried." She took his other hand into hers, entwining her fingers through his. "And I really don't *want* to try."

Nick sighed and looked away for a beat. "In the woods that day, you were going to ask what I was thinking. Back then, I wasn't sure. Kinda like the words got all jumbled up." He laughed. "And it's not any easier to put my thoughts into words now. See, you took my heart and I never saw it coming. You're pure magic, Ivy, and it has nothing to do with the spell you cast from here." He pulled a hand free and touched her forehead. "You cast the spell from here." Ever so lightly, he slid his hand down her face and throat, coming to rest on the spot above her heart. "There isn't a thing you do to me that isn't magic."

Ivy grinned. He was such a liar. He'd *always* been good with words. But right now, they sounded pretty good. "Did anyone ever tell you that for a demon, you're really cool?"

Nick smiled slyly and shrugged almost confidently.

They stood there, staring at each other again.

"Are you going to force your girlfriend to make the first move?" Ivy finally asked.

"About that," Nick said. "Think you can *handle* a demon boyfriend?" He grinned mischievously.

Ivy narrowed her eyes playfully. "Try me."

He pulled her to him and kissed her lightly, then again, longer this time and she eagerly and readily kissed him back, wrapping her arms around his neck.

He was right—this was magic. *This* felt right. Everything except Nick ceased to exist, not the breeze around them, not the stars just making their appearance high above. It was like that afternoon in the woods, only better. This time, the dancing fireflies were in her heart.

"I'll call you tomorrow," he said, smiling at her. She let her hands slide around his waist, and he kissed her again.

When they broke apart, neither said another word. Other than *wow*, what could she say? She watched, breathless, warm, and unwilling to move as Nick slid behind the wheel of his Uncle's truck and drove away.

"*Yes!*" she said as the truck's taillights drove out of sight.

Ivy raced up the front porch steps, taking two at a time. This is what it meant when people said love could make you leap over mountains.

Devlin hiccuped once and tendrils of smoke drifted out of his nostrils. He wagged his tail and looked up at her, black little Beezlepup eyes shining happily. She knelt down to hug him and remembered to check his collar.

Spike. She'd almost forgotten. At some point, he'd attached a tiny note to Dev's collar. Ivy removed it, watching as the piece of paper unfolded and expanded until it was just longer than her hand. Handwritten words appeared across the page as she read it.

Dearest Daughter,

I can't begin to explain. Just know that I've never been more proud, and that I never stopped loving you and your mother. I left to protect you both. It appears that I didn't do such a good job. You and your mother are still in danger.

I'll do what I can, but I can't be seen, so I'll need your help. No one must know I've returned.

You have questions, and in time, you'll have answers. Unfortunately, more than is probably best for you.

I'm glad that Devlin is safe. He's a great dog.

You'll need a new book bag, but I've returned the gardening book. It's on the chair on the side porch. I've taken The Rise of the Dark Curse and The Book of Lost Souls. As you've guessed, they don't burn. They need to be in a safer place.

With a little help, Mr. Evans seems to have developed memory problems and has a misguided sense of what went on tonight. You won't have to explain, the Council will never know, and your mother won't have to have heart failure—at least until she discovers I've returned.

Maybe that's a secret we should keep for now.

Unfortunately, I believe your mother is a bit upset that you were late for dinner and didn't call. That, I'm afraid, you're still on the hook for.

All my love,

Dad

The noted unfolded once more, words appearing before her eyes.

P.S. Nick is a real nice boy, but be careful dating demons, Ivy. Relationships with them can be rather intense. For the record, my money is on you. Enjoy this time in your life. Right now, the world is yours.

Ivy had no idea what her mother would learn about tonight's events, and she was glad she wouldn't have to explain. Regulars had their memories wiped all the time. She supposed that it wouldn't be any more unusual to wipe the mind of a Kindred, although very few Kindreds even knew how to do it. Kindred minds were harder to alter.

Why her father had changed Mr. Evans's memory was an entirely different matter, and doing it without Council approval was outlaw. Had he done it to protect himself, or his daughter? On the other hand, he could just as easily killed Mr. Evans if he truly *was* an outlaw.

A thought crept into her mind. Could her father be telling the truth? Did he still care? Did he still love her? Ivy looked at the note, unsure of what to do with it. Crumple it up, or stuff it in her pocket? She glanced down at Devlin and decided to tuck the note into her pocket—for now, anyway.

Out of everything that had happened to her in the past week the biggest of them all had occurred just a minute ago. No matter what new powers she had or where she'd gotten them, Nick had said it best—love was the one true magic above all others. Regardless of the chaos it presented.

Chaos.

Ivy smiled. What better way to get to know love than with a demon who knew *all* about mischief and mayhem? "See you tomorrow, Nick," she whispered.

Everything hadn't worked as planned, but turned out fine just the same. Better than fine. Better than *better*, even.

Ivy laughed and spun around on the porch, careful not to knock over the Jack O' lanterns. Dating a demon might be pretty intense, but it was something she looked forward to. Adventure had grown on her as well, and it'd be a nice break from sticking her nose in a book *all* the time. In fact, she might take a reprieve from books for a while.

After tonight, what could *possibly* happen? Change was good. Danger? What was that old saying? If it doesn't kill you, it'll only make you stronger? So, danger or not, with friends like hers, and a boyfriend like Nick, Ivy felt that she could take on all the danger and chaos in the world.

Acknowledgments

Everyone who has ever written a novel has had moments when they've questioned why they ever set out on such a journey. I'm not sure of his exact words, but Stephen King once said some wise words about writing that still resonate with me: that writers don't write just for the money—they write for the love of writing. I've always been a storyteller. To me, that has been the easy part. The writing, the laying down of words? Well, that proved to be a bit more time consuming.

No writer ever goes it alone and stays totally sane, and there are people who have kept me off the Ledge of Crazy on more than one occasion.

First and foremost is my husband, Ray Rogers, who tirelessly read and reread without a single complaint—even the romantic parts. Not once did he object to the amount of time I spent in front of the computer. I don't think I tell him how amazing he is often enough. Of course, he'll tell anyone who'll listen that I live on the Ledge of Crazy and that's where we met.

And although they can't read, special thanks to my dogs who stayed patiently at my feet. When no one else in this world believes in you, your dog always will. They also provide comic relief. Thanks to my dog Ronan for inspiring the character Devlin. Ronan really is the original Beezlepup.

Every writer determined to see their book published depends on critique partners who are honest enough to tell it like it is. I'm honored to call D.B. Reynolds, Leslie Tentler, and Steve McHugh not just critique partners, but friends. Really, guys—your input, corrections, and thoughts have been invaluable. I couldn't have done it without you.

Thanks to my sister, Sherry Nusbaum, who suffered though countless phone calls whenever I had a new idea. I still remember the early days when we first worked on characters and names and so many other details you've read in this book. I swear, it's a wonder that she doesn't have call block because of me.

I'd also like to thank my fellow group members over at Kelly Armstrong's On-line Writing Group (the OWG) who read and critiqued the first half of this book. You guys rock.

Thanks to Danielle La Paglia, proofreader and OWG bud extraordinare.

Special thanks also go to gifted book designer and fellow author Sam Torode who gave me a hand with the cover art. Thanks, Sam! Your version ended up looking so much better than mine.

And, thank *you*, Dear Reader. Because ultimately, every author with a story to tell writes with you in mind.

About the Author

Michelle Muto lives in northeast Georgia with her husband and two dogs. She loves changes of season, dogs, and all things geeky. Currently, she's hard at work on her next book.

Visit Michelle at:
www.michellemuto.wordpress.com

The Paranormal Plumes Society

- A group of independent Young Adult authors who are dedicated to their craft -

Tiffany King, author of *The Saving Angels Trilogy*

Abbi Glines, author of *Breathe* and *Existence*

M. Leighton, author of the *Blood Like Poison Series*

Michelle Muto, author of *The Book of Lost Souls and Don't Fear the Reaper*

Fisher Amelie, author of *The Leaving Series*

Nichole Chase, author of *The Dark Betrayal Trilogy*

Laura A. H. Elliott, author of *13 on Halloween*

Amy Maurer Jones, author of the *Soul Quest Trilogy*

Wren Emerson, author of *I Wish*

Shelly Crane, author of the *Significance Series*

Courtney Cole, author of *The Bloodstone Saga*

C.A. Kunz, mother and son author duo of *The Childe Series*